The Shadows at My Door

Kristen Grafton

Cottage House Publishing

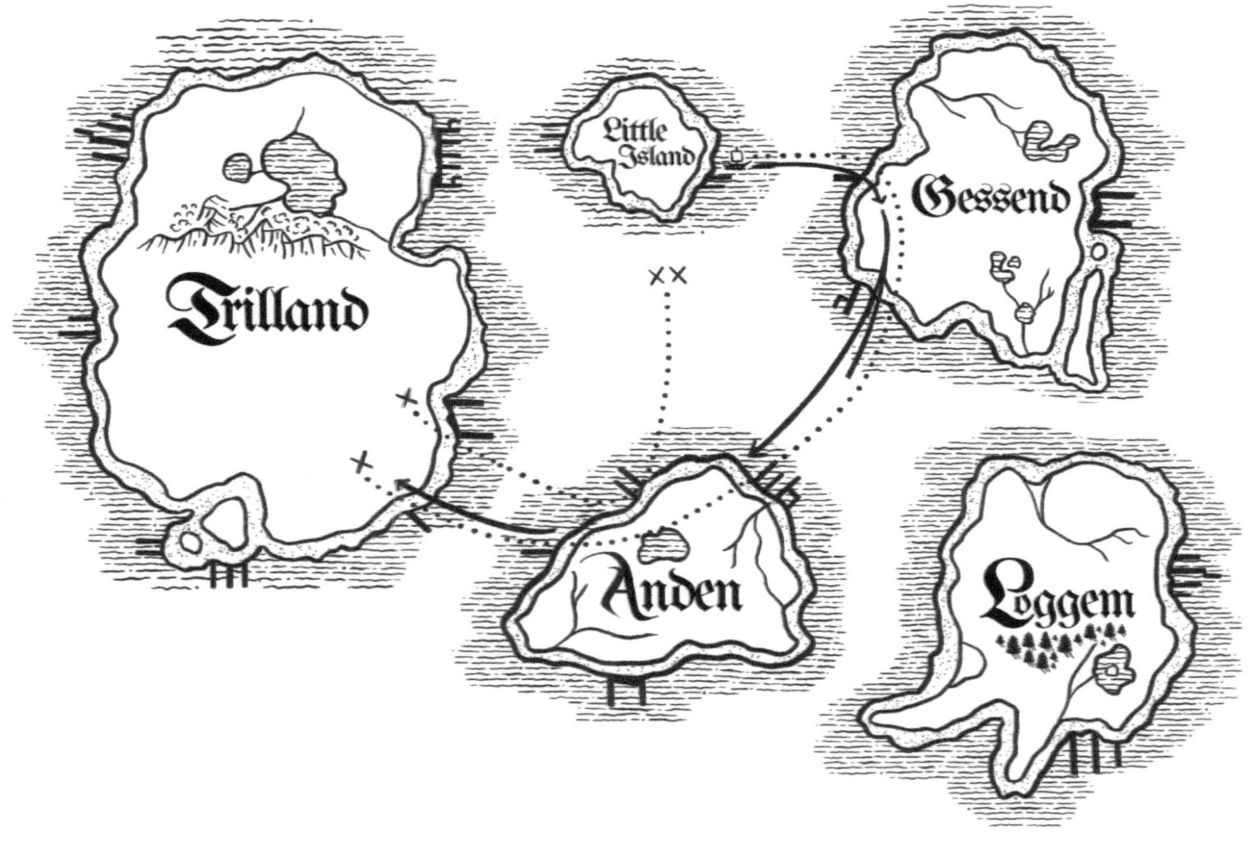

Trilland
Little Island
Gessend
Anden
Leggem

For the readers who have asked for a sequel...

Chapter 1

"There's no reason why we can't have both," I say, trying to test the waters of the room. Parliament has been pretty severely divided on this budget for months. One side wants to cut back spending on the navy, and the other side wants to cut back spending on the oceanography research. They've been at each other's throats and pressuring me to pick a side, but frankly, I don't want to cut spending on either.

"I just don't see how the navy needs more money," says Senator Greene. "All they're doing is floating around out there."

"Floating around?" Uncle Lawrence snaps. "The navy is protecting our country. Do you want to leave our coastlines vulnerable to our enemies?"

"The Department of Oceanography is conducting important research," Senator Greene says. "The threats to our country are rumors at best. No need to overreact."

"How is poking a bunch of starfish considered 'research'?" Senator Emerson groans.

Senator Greene rolls her eyes. "They're examining the reflexes and natural responses of the starfish to make sure that they are healthy. It's a lot more intelligent than just poking them."

"And protecting our borders is pretty intelligent, too, don't you think, Senator?" Senator Emerson shoots daggers out of his eyes at

Senator Greene, and she rolls her eyes so far back into her head that her blue eyeshadow thankfully disappears for a few moments.

"Countries have been threatening us for a decade, and they never act," Secretary Johnson pipes up. "But ever since Princess Lorraine got back, Riagala has been especially hostile. I don't think they're happy about her return."

"Well, sure, they never liked the Everhart family," says Uncle Lawrence. "Which is why it's more important than ever to protect our land and our waters. If we had the money for both, then that would be great, but we don't."

"Scientific research always gets pushed to the back burner," Senator Weston says, pushing up his glasses as he speaks and making it painfully obvious that his opinion is biased since he's on the board of the Department of Oceanography. Then again, Uncle Lawrence is a captain for the navy, so I guess he's biased, too. "Just once can't we prioritize the health of our oceans ahead of war?"

"And how do you plan to conduct your research when there are enemy ships in our waters?" says Secretary Johnson.

"Excuse me, but I wanted to—"

"Do you see any enemy ships in our waters?" Senator Greene cuts me off.

"Well, you might as well send them an engraved invitation when they catch wind of us cutting our navy."

"I think this is getting out of hand—"

"No one's trying to cut the navy all together, Emerson, especially considering Riagala's attitude, which is only going to get worse," says Senator Greene. "They're simply not happy about Princess Lorraine's return."

"Wait a minute, I—"

"Exactly my point," says Senator Emerson. "We have to protect our leader at all costs. Poking starfish isn't going to protect Princess Lorraine."

"Now hang on a second," I say, more harshly than I intended, and suddenly every eye in the room is staring at me. "I think as the person being discussed, I should have some say."

"The Princess is right," Uncle Lawrence says with a reassuring smile. "I'm afraid we haven't let her talk."

"Go ahead, Princess," Secretary Johnson says.

"I don't think we need to make a decision right now. Let me look over the budget again and see if something can't be done. Maybe there's somewhere else where the budget can be adjusted. Both of these areas are important to me."

"With all due respect, Princess, we've looked the budget over a hundred times," Secretary Johnson says. "There's simply nowhere else we can afford to cut. The only way to bring in more money is to raise taxes."

"I'm not raising taxes," I say. "These people are strapped for money as it is."

"There's just nothing else we can do."

"Just let me look it over. Maybe fresh eyes will see something that might be workable." There's a palpable lack of trust in the room that's evident by all the sideways glances the senators exchange with one another. No one seems to think there's anything I could possibly do. They smile at me, but the expressions are empty, and I know I've lost the room—that is, if I ever had it. "Let's call it for the day. I think we're all exhausted. I'll see you all on Monday."

Everyone stands and starts shuffling their papers together, and I just can't wait to get out of the room. Things have been so tense lately. Everything was so great when I first got back, and things were even greater when Cassandra was convicted and exiled. But now, everyone seems ready to fight all the time. How could a few months change everything so much?

As soon as I leave the room, I spot Zane leaning against the wall, and I instantly feel better. He smiles wide and pushes himself off the wall with his foot, and I can't believe how much I've missed seeing him waiting for me outside of the Parliament building. I walk down the hallway, making sure I look dignified to anyone who might be watching, but as soon as I reach Zane, I throw my arms around his neck, and he picks me up and spins.

"I'm so glad you're back," I say.

"So am I," Zane says. "You look beautiful."

"I feel stuffy. I hate suits."

"These suits were specially made for you."

"Doesn't make me hate them any less."

"Well, anyway, I think you look gorgeous." Zane kisses me on the cheek.

"You were gone too long."

Zane laughs. "It wasn't even two weeks."

"And that's too long."

"I agree." Zane laughs again and kisses my hand delicately. "But my mom really needed the help."

"I know, I know. How is she? I miss her."

"She's doing great. She's really excited to see you at the coronation."

"I can't wait to see her either," I say. "And everyone. I miss them all so much."

"They miss you."

Zane and I step outside the Parliament building and start the short walk down to my palace. I can't wait to get out of these clothes into something comfortable and just sit on the couch, wrapped in Zane's arms.

"I'm glad some people still like me."

Zane turns abruptly and stares at me. "What do you mean?"

"It's just this whole budget thing. Everyone keeps bickering. It's navy vs. Oceanography, and they can't make a deal about which to cut back on."

"Is there a way to save both?" Zane asks.

"That's what I suggested, but everyone just looked at me like a naive kid. I don't think anyone is happy to have me there."

"What are you talking about? These people waited for you for a year. Of course they're happy to have you back."

"The Princess Lorraine Everhart that left was an seventeen-year-old kid with no real power. Now that I'm the nineteen-year-old with no political experience who makes the final decision, I'm not the most popular person in the room."

"They'll get over it," Zane says. "People are happy you're back. It's just an adjustment period. Everything will be fine."

"I hope you're right," I say, as we stop on the steps of the palace.

"I am, and you know it."

"How do I know it?"

"Because I'm always right," Zane says with a mischievous smirk. "You didn't forget that, did you?"

"Well, I don't have the best track record with memory," I tease.

"Oh, don't even," Zane tickles me briefly before pulling me in and finally kissing me. Part of me wonders if I should be worried about making out with Zane on the steps of the palace so publicly, but another part of me, the much bigger part, has waited to kiss him for two weeks, so I push appearances to the side. I can't believe how lucky

I am to have Zane by my side during all of this. I don't know what I would do without him.

"Come on," Zane says. "Let's go inside, and you can tell me more about the budget."

"You hate talking about the budget."

"But I love talking to you."

I smile and take Zane's hand, and we start up the rest of the steps. When we reach the door, Timothy gives us a wink. Considering he worked for my father, too, he's older now, but I'm so glad he agreed to stay on as a guard at the palace. I know he'll retire soon, but he said he wanted to finish out his career working for me and not Cassandra. After the way he helped Brent and I escape Cassandra's arrest, I wanted nothing more.

Timothy open the doors for us, and Zane walks almost automatically toward the staircase, but I'm stopped in my tracks. His blonde curly hair cut just above his perfectly tailored navy blue suit looks exactly the same as it always has.

Zane doesn't notice my sudden stop and practically falls over when I don't keep walking. "What?" Zane says. "What is it?"

He turns and smiles when he sees me.

"Alex."

Chapter 2

"Alex?" Zane says, irritation creeping into his voice.

"Hey, beautiful," Alex says, taking my free hand and kissing it. "Wow, I can't believe it's really you. I heard you made it back, and I immediately set sail to come see you."

"Immediately?" Zane says. "She's been back for nearly a year."

Alex shoots a contemptuous glare at Zane, which Zane hardly acknowledges, before jutting out his hand for a handshake. "I am His Highness Prince Alexander Cartwright of Eterand, one of Trilland's oldest allies. And you must be a new guard. I don't remember you from years ago."

"Guard?" Zane scoffs.

"Alex, this is Zane," I say, hoping that if I interrupt, Zane might not punch Alex out. "He's from the island where I was stranded. He's my boyfriend."

"Boyfriend?" Alex asks.

"Yes, boyfriend," Zane snaps, putting his arm around my waist.

"Ah yes, the island. What's the name of that island again? Mara? Mira?"

"Maris," Zane snaps again.

"Yes, Maris, how could I forget. Interesting name. However did you come up with that, Lorraine?"

"Actually it was Zane's idea."

"Really? Well, it's a very pretty name for an island. My hat's off to you."

Through gritted teeth, Zane says, "Thanks, Your Highness."

"Oh no, please call me Alex. Anyway, Lorraine, I'm dying to catch up. Couldn't we talk for a few moments? I'd love to hear all about what happened. Such a fascinating story."

"Alex, I—I would be happy to fill you in, but I actually have plans with Zane right now. How long are you in town?"

"As long as you'd like," Alex says, and Zane scoffs.

"How about dinner tonight?" I suggest.

"Sounds great. I'll see you around seven."

"See you then."

As I watch Alex walk away, I find myself feeling conflicting emotions. On the one hand, Alex is probably the oldest friend I have with the notable exception of Jane. On the other hand, I haven't seen him in years, since before the mutiny, and I can't ignore the reality of how much my life has changed since then. Has he changed, too?

~~~

"Who does that guy think he is?" Zane says as soon as he closes the door to my suite.

"He's an old friend. Eterand is a long-time ally of Trilland's. Our fathers were best friends."

"Some friend. Can't be bothered to show up for a year." Zane is pacing around the room so fast that I wonder if he's going to wear a path into the carpet through sheer friction and anger.

"He's busy," I say, shaking my hair out of its bun, fishing out the millions of bobby pins it took to get my hair to stay up. "He's training to be king right now."

"That guy as king. That's a scary thought."
~~~

"Zane."

"Why didn't you ever mention him before?"

"Well, I didn't remember him until recently."

"Maris, you know what I mean. After you remembered, why didn't you say anything?"

"Believe it or not, Alex Cartwright was not the first thought on my mind. I was kind of busy thinking about my parents and Cassandra and Brent and Uncle Lawrence and Trilland and—and you. Some guy I knew as a kid wasn't priority."

And that's true. Really, it is. But I'd be lying if I said he hadn't crossed my mind at all in the last year. The Cartwrights sent me several letters, and both King Norman and Queen Florence had called. Alex hadn't. It had struck me as odd that he didn't reach out sooner, but Alex had a way of being unpredictable—it was just part of who he was. Honestly, I used to like that about him. After all, everything in my life has always been so predictable. But after two years of nothing but unprecedented events, I would have liked some warning that he was coming. At the very least, I could have warned Zane who is practically seething now.

"And what did you mean by saying the island where you were 'stranded'? Was it so terrible being stuck with us?"

"Zane, you know I don't feel that way." I take Zane's hands in mine and force him to look into my eyes. "Maris Island is as much my home as Trilland. It's just the easiest way to explain that part of my life to people who weren't there. Alex would never understand all that. Besides, how else do I explain my absence without getting into the amnesia?"

"And that's another thing," Zane says, dropping my hands and pacing around the room. I guess his rant wasn't over. "The first and only major thing you've done since you got back, and he can't even remember the name of the island?"

"Zane—"

"Or deduce that maybe the guy holding your hand isn't just a guard?"

"Zane—"

"Not that it matters. It's not like being your boyfriend gets me any kind of status to make me worthy of being spoken to by a prince as if I'm someone important."

"What does that mean?"

"I mean, he probably didn't want to recognize that. He obviously has a thing for you."

"What?"

"Oh, don't tell me you don't see it. And why did it take you so long to call me your boyfriend? Are you embarrassed to introduce me to Prince Smolder?"

"Prince Smolder?" I snicker.

"You get the point."

"Zane, come here." I hold Zane by the arms and look up into his eyes. "You do not need to worry about Alex. He's just an old friend who wants to catch up. He's always been a little egotistical. Come to dinner with us. You'll see that it's nothing. He can't even begin to compare with you."

"Well, I should hope not."

I kiss Zane gently, and he sighs, puts his hand to my cheek, and kisses me back, a little stronger. I slide my hand up to the back of his neck and finger the edge of his hair and feel his smile on my lips.

"That's not fair," he says. "You know how much I love that."

"I do know. Now relax, okay? We still have a few more hours until dinner. Tell me about your trip."

~~~

I grab two dresses out of my closet and hold them up in front of me, one after the other, trying to decide on one for dinner. I step out from behind the dressing screen and hold both of them up for Jane to see.

"Which one should I wear?"

"The blue one," Jane says definitively. "You look too good in the pink one."

"What does that mean?" I step into the blue one anyway and slide it up over my hips, pulling the one-sided strap over my left shoulder.

"Do you really want to look incredible for a dinner with your ex-boyfriend and your current boyfriend?"

"Come zip me up, it's sticking," I say, and Jane starts wiggling the zipper. "Alex is not my ex-boyfriend. We never dated."

"But you came pretty close. And Prince Alex isn't exactly shy with his flirting."

She isn't wrong. Alex has always been a little bit of a walking stereotype of an attractive prince. He certainly flirted with me a lot over the years. I never really felt like it meant anything—it's just part of who Alex has always been.

"You're just as bad as Zane. Nothing happened between us."

"Wasn't he your first kiss?"

"Sure, if you count two twelve year old kids kissing just to find out what it's like and then being grossed out by it." I sit down at my vanity and start on my makeup, and Jane picks up a straightening iron and starts on my hair.

"I think Zane would count it, don't you?"

"Zane is just a jealous guy. He freaked out over Brent, too. We'll have one dinner with him, and it'll be over."

"If you say so."
~~~

"I do say so." I hold up two different lipsticks. "Strawberry or crimson?"

"Strawberry," Jane says. "The crimson will look severe with this dress. And hey, cut Zane a little slack. He's been on quite a roller coaster ride with you."

"What does that mean?"

"I mean he met an amnesiac girl, fell in love with her, waited for her, watched her run around with some other guy, watched her regain her memory, feared losing her, then finally got her and moved away from his family. And now he's watching some guy from your past creep into the picture, and he's scared. He's been through a lot with you and for you. Don't give him a reason to be scared."

My gut reaction to Jane's words is annoyance. None of that is my fault, so I don't really see how it should be my responsibility to manage Alex or Brent or even Zane. I didn't choose the mutiny or my amnesia or Brent's deception. I certainly didn't invite Alex to come to Trilland, but he's here, and Eterand is not only a close ally but the Cartwrights are family friends. I shouldn't have to defend my past or my relationships.

Still, Zane has kind of been a bystander during all my chaos. I didn't consider the active life he was living in the middle of it. I guess I can try to be sensitive of his feelings. Maybe over time, he'll see there's nothing to worry about. "Okay, I won't."

"Good." Jane flips my hair over my shoulder. "There. Just pretty enough to make Zane swoon but not pretty enough to give Prince Alex any ideas."

I roll my eyes. "If you say so. I'll tell you how dinner was tomorrow."

Jane heads toward the door. "Deal. Have fun." Jane opens the door and Zane is standing there, poised to knock. "Perfect timing, Zane. I just finished Lorraine's hair. Have fun at dinner."

"Thanks, Jane." Zane closes the door behind him and smiles. "You look absolutely stunning. Come here." Zane takes my hand and pulls me close to him, kissing me gently, careful not to smudge my lipstick. He smudged it once, and Daisy made endless fun of him for wearing lipstick. "Are you ready?"

"Are you?"

Zane rolls his eyes. "I'll be nice, I promise."

~~~

The dining room looks spectacular, and it's obvious that Annette has gone all out for Alex's arrival. The room hasn't looked anywhere near this good since my welcome home banquet that Annette and Jane threw. The table is adorned with sage green silk table cloths and white and gold place settings, echoing the beautiful summery weather we're having. Even though it's September, it's been unseasonably warm.

I notice that the candles haven't been lit yet, so I grab a match from the hutch on the wall and strike it on the wall and light the candles. Zane strikes another match and lights the other candle.

"Lighting your own candles?" Alex says, throwing the doors to the dining room open. "Have your servants gotten that bad in your absence?"

"If she's capable of running a country, she's capable of lighting candles," Zane says.

"Alex, take a seat," I say, giving Zane a pleading look, and he rolls his eyes and nods. "I hope you still like James's coq au vin."

"Oh, Chef James's coq au vin! Am I so lucky?" Alex says, and Zane scoffs a little but covers it well. Alex doesn't even notice as he sits down across from me. "So how's the palace? Did they change anything in your absence?"

"Not really," I say. "They didn't even touch my suite. I guess every-one was just kind of at a loss as to what to do."
~~~

"They were waiting for you to return," Zane says with a smile.

"Oh no doubt," Alex agrees with Zane, which based on Zane's gritted teeth, makes him bristle. "Trilland would be nothing without you."

"So, how is your father?" I ask. "It's been so long since I've seen him. What were we, thirteen?"

"Fourteen, I believe. I think it was when we came to help out Trilland in your parents' absence."

My heart sinks a little. Of course. I do remember that. Alex and his father came right after my mother died. Trilland was in chaos, I was too young to take over, and after a panicked phone call to Alex's father from Uncle Lawrence, they came. They stabilized the government, got Parliament on track, and reassured the people that Trilland was not alone.

"You're right," I say, clearing my throat a little. "I don't think I ever properly thanked your father for that. He saved Trilland."

"Oh, please, it was his pleasure. He'd do anything for you."

"When you go back to Eterand, you must give him my regards and tell him to visit."

"Speaking of," Zane jumps in, "when are you going back to Eterand?"

I clear my throat. "How long are you in town?"

"Oh, not as long as I'd like to be," Alex says, flipping his hair back dramatically. "I'm actually here on business. My dad wanted me to check in on Trilland since he heard you got back. He also wanted to hash out the details of our alliance since it's been a while since it was formally discussed."

"He didn't want to come himself?" Zane asks with just the slightest snap in his voice, but Alex is completely oblivious.

"He wanted to, of course, but we're in the middle of redoing our budget, and he just couldn't get away. He hoped you and I could come to some sort of agreement, and then he's planning on making a trip to sign the papers, shake hands, that sort of thing. But let's not discuss that now. There's plenty of time in the future for that. Let's just celebrate. So Zane, I'm afraid we've ignored you. Tell me about your little island. Remind me of the name again?"

"Maris Island." Even though Zane is angry with Alex for being so patronizing, there is still a sweetness about him when he says the name he gave the island, the name he gave me. "It's small, but it's completely independent. The fishing there is excellent. I haven't been able to catch a thing since I got here."

"Really?" Alex says, sitting back with surprise. "I'm surprised by that. Fishing is a big industry in Trilland."

"We don't fish out in the ocean on boats on the island. We just do simple spearfishing, night fishing, and small nets on the coast. But we haul in a ton."

"Zane is the best fisher on the island," I say.

Zane laughs. "Hardly. I just help out any way I can."

"He's being modest."

"Well, good for you, Zane," Alex says, and even though I know him well enough to know that he really was just trying to be nice, he sounds very condescending, and I know I'm going to hear about it from Zane later. "It must be peaceful out on that little island. Sometimes I envy that. I never get any peace."

"It is peaceful," Zane says.

"Tell me, has the island changed at all since Trilland annexed it? I'm curious how that all played out."

"I've only been back twice since I came here, but it's pretty much exactly the same."

Alex leans in. "It didn't change at all? Not even a little?"

"No. We didn't exactly want to change. And since we had someone we trusted annexing us, we didn't mind. Mar-Lorraine let us change things or not change things as we wanted." That's not the first time that Zane has slipped and almost called me Maris in front of someone who doesn't know, but somehow, this one panics me more than usual. I know Alex well. He knows me well. What if he notices that something is off? Can I really trust him with that kind of information?

"That must be nice, knowing that you can trust your queen." Guess he didn't notice.

"I'm not queen yet," I say.

Zane takes my hand in his and gives it a gentle squeeze. "You might as well be." He turns back to Alex. "And honestly, we probably wouldn't have let Trilland annex us if she hadn't been running the whole thing. We like things the way they are, and she has fought hard to protect our way of life."

"Well, that's great," Alex says. "I'm glad to hear it. Unfortunately, however, I must be going."

"You're not staying for dessert?" I ask.

"I wish I could, but I need to get some rest. I've got a scheduled phone call with my dad in the morning."

"Are you staying in the guest quarters?"

"Yes, the first building. Same one we always get." Alex stands and takes one last sip of his sparkling cider. "Send me a message when you're ready to meet. I'm ready to discuss my father's offers whenever you are."

"I will do that. Goodnight, Alex. Tell your father that I say hello."

"Goodnight, Lorraine." Alex kisses my right hand, and Zane's grip on my left tightens. "And goodbye, Zane. I'm sure our paths will cross again before I leave."

"I'm sure."

Alex takes a short bow and walks out of the room, though Alex's walk has always looked a little more like a saunter. Even when we were kids, he sauntered. The second he leaves, it's like the room feels lighter yet heavier at the same time. It's been so many years since I've seen Alex. In so many ways, he's exactly the same. In other ways, he's completely different. It's so weird to see someone after so long. Is it weird to see him again because it's been so many years, or is it because I've practically lived an entire lifetime in my year outside of Trilland?

"Well," Zane says after a long pause, "he's, um, interesting."

"He's always been that way."

"Self-absorbed?"

"Well, he's a prince."

"And you're a princess, but you're nothing like him."

"We're not as different as you think," I say. "It just seems that way."

"Well, at least that dinner is over." Zane sighs dramatically.

"Was it really that bad?"

"Nothing can ever be bad when I'm with you." Zane takes my hand in both of his and kisses it. "And *that's* how you kiss someone's hand."

Chapter 3

After I got my memory back and got over the shock of everything and settled into a comfortable rhythm here in Trilland, I had this picture in my mind of how everything was going to be. I pictured myself going to Parliament and holding elegant but productive conversations in a stylish white suit. I pictured slightly boring town hall meetings where I would smile, shake hands, hold babies. I saw myself giving speeches, meeting with foreign dignitaries, planning charity functions, writing budgets, and signing laws.

In short, I pictured my mother. She used to do all of these tasks with more grace than I'll ever be able to fake in my lifetime. Everyone loved her. She was the perfect queen to complement my father as king. She was beautiful, kind, smart, compassionate, and determined. No one could ever question her motives when she spoke because everyone trusted her unconditionally.

And while I've tried to model my life after hers, and I've done just about all of those things I pictured, the transition hasn't been anything like I thought it would be. I don't know if I saw things differently as a child or my memory is playing tricks on me again, but I don't remember things being this hard for my parents. They made everything they did seem so easy, so natural. My father always knew just the right political move to make, my mother the right thing to say to the people. And though I'm sure it happened, I can't remember a single time when either one of them did the wrong thing. They just always seemed to get it right.

I also overlooked so many of the little details with which my mother kept up. She ran the house with ease and poise. I used to think Lady Vivian did most of that, but what I've learned now is that my mother was really operating everything behind the scenes. Lady Vivian was my mother's valued partner, and she always said she couldn't have done it without her, but Lady Vivian always insisted it was my mother, and now I see that she was right. She is constantly asking me for my opinion on things on which I have no opinion whatsoever. I couldn't care less whether the table cloths are cream or eggshell, whether the votive holders are gold or silver. I feel like I don't have time to decide what I, along with Zane, Uncle Lawrence, and whatever foreign dignitary might be joining us would like for dinner two weeks from now. And yet, these are decisions that have to be made. How the palace is perceived is so important, and as stupid as I thought it was at first, the table cloth color really matters. Thank goodness for Lady Vivian who makes some of the decisions for me when she can see that I'm overwhelmed. I've even caught her subtly guiding me to the right answer by saying things like, "the cream is perfect, don't you think?" or "I've never been a fan of rose petals on the dinner table, but that's just me." I'm not sure what I would do without her. A few weeks ago, she mentioned something about retirement, and I nearly had a panic attack. I'm not sure this house would function without her. I'm not even sure *I* could function without her. The day she retires, I'm doomed.

Every day, it seems as though another little detail of something I'm supposed to be doing pops up, and I feel a little more like a failure. Today, for instance, I have to choose which flowers to plant outside all of the government buildings, which seems like a simple decision, but the flowers all come from different provinces. It's a tradition for the Trilland mainland to choose flowers from a province as an act of political good will, so choosing the wrong one could end up offending the other provinces. Everything is political.

Lady Vivian has the servants lay out several floral arrangement options on the wood table in the garden and starts fluffing them and positioning them just the way she wants them. There are four options: pink and red roses from Gessend, yellow and white daisies from Anden, green and purple orchids from Loggem, and pink and yellow lilies from my own Maris Island. Each arrangement has beautiful, hardy greenery with it, complementing the colors.

I stroke the petal of one of the lilies and smile a little. I know Harper picked these for me. When I was staying with her in the beginning, she used to put fresh lilies on the windowsill of Zane's room every couple of days because she says I smiled for the first time since I'd been there when I saw them. I don't know if that's true or not, but she's always brought me lilies for special occasions.

"So what do you think?" Lady Vivian asks.

"I don't know," I say. "They're all beautiful."

"Well, why don't you start with a color scheme. Any colors you don't like?"

"I'm not sure."

Lady Vivian lets out a small sigh. "Flowers really aren't your thing, are they?"

"Not when I have to pick them for an entire island."

Lady Vivian starts waving to someone inside. "Oh good, Brent, come here."

I turn and see a very startled Brent hesitantly coming out to the garden with a face that seems to say that he's never been asked for his opinion on flowers before.

"You're asking me about flowers?" Brent says.

"Yes." Lady Vivian grabs him by the arm and drags him over to the table and explains what each arrangement is and where they came from.

Brent glances over at me briefly before Lady Vivian practically turns his body so that he'll pay attention to her floral crisis. We haven't spoken much since I got back—not socially anyway. He asked to stay in Trilland because he wanted to pursue a career in politics, so I made him my press secretary since the former press secretary was loyal to Cassandra, though he's weirdly become kind of a personal assistant. We talk quite frequently, but it's always about professional matters and always very cordial, so cordial it feels stifling. I wonder if we'll ever be friendly again.

"So, what do you think?" Lady Vivian asks Brent.

"Well, I think the orchids are too expensive, and you'll have a hard time getting them to take in our sandy soil."

"Okay, so Loggem is out."

"And I would avoid the lilies."

"Why is that?" I ask.

"They're from Maris Island."

"So?"

"Look, I'm not saying people are angry you annexed the island, but everything has kind of been all about them since you got back. I think people are feeling a little left out."

"That's a little unfair, don't you think?"

Brent winces. "I'm just looking out for you and your image. It's my job, remember?"

I open my mouth to fire back that he has no right to tell me how to maintain my image or how to feel about Maris Island or anything like that, but I catch myself. Arguing in front of Lady Vivian won't do any good. He's right—it is his job to think of these things so I don't have to. I hate that it's a reality of this job, but my public image does matter.

I twist my mouth and stare at the lilies. I don't want to admit it, but there has been a little hostility about the annexation. I think people are a little concerned about adding new territory when the current territory is already struggling. Best not to irritate the situation with something as silly as flowers.

I look at the daisies and the roses side by side. They're both beautiful, and either one will look great, but my eyes keep going back to the daisies. I like the lighter colors, and they remind me of Zane's sister. I miss her. I wish she were here.

"Where did you say the daisies were from?" I ask.

"Anden."

I think back to the last time I was in Anden. It was before I got my memory back. The people there were angry and hostile toward me. They felt abandoned, and if I were in their shoes, I probably would have felt the same way. After I got back, I looked into their situation and found that of all the provinces, their economy was struggling the most. They're big on seafood, and I guess Cassandra hated seafood because she completely left them without any income. They could use the gesture, and I could use some good will where they're concerned.

"Go with the daisies and pay the gardeners well for them."

"Excellent choice, dear," Lady Vivian says with a smile, and somehow, I feel like I passed the flower test.

"And buy a couple of lilies and put them here in the garden. Tell Harper I said thank you."

Lady Vivian winks and starts writing up the orders while Brent and I slip away, grateful to be unnoticed for the moment.

"I think you made the right choice," Brent says once we're inside. "I think Anden will appreciate the gesture."

I exhale. "Thank you. Stuff like that is so hard."

"Could I hassle you with one more hard decision for the day?"

"Of course."

Brent pulls out his portfolio and flips quickly to the right page. Brent really is so good at his job, and he's managed all of the details of my daily life so well. Still, it's hard for me to ignore the tension that is always simmering just beneath the surface of our forced conversation. "We still haven't picked a time for the next Parliament meeting, and the senators are starting to ask."

"Great," I groaned. "What about Monday?"

"That's already scheduled. They want to know about after that. How's next week? Thursday?"

"Make it Friday. I've got a walk through at the school on Thursday, and I don't want to cut it close."

"Right, I forgot about that. Okay, Friday. Same time as always?"

"Yes."

"Perfect." Brent jots down the time in his calendar. "Speaking of, the press will be at the school."

I shrug. "I figured. How many?"

"Not many. One or two journalists, two cameras tops."

"Fine. Schedule a post-walk interview with the more favorable of the two. I want to talk through some of my plans for education."

"Got it." Brent scribbles furiously again. "Anything else?"

"That's it for me. Thank you, Brent."

"Anytime. See you later," he says as he walks off with a wave.

Cordial, as always. I wonder if we'll ever get past this.

<div style="text-align:center">~~~</div>

On Saturday nights, the fishermen like to go night-fishing for fun. They're off the clock, and they get to keep whatever they haul in. That was something Zane and I came up with together. We thought it would boost morale for the fishers in Trilland, and it seems to have worked. Of course, it probably doesn't hurt that Zane usually goes with them, especially since he started officially working with them. It's hard not to get along with Zane. Plus, he's been able to show them some of his fishing tricks. These guys are used to fishing with all of their technology, machinery, and large boats. Zane knows how to catch fish at night with spears, small nets, or just by hand, and they love trying out his new techniques. It's been really good for me to see something I had a role in starting becoming so popular. Maybe I'm not all bad after all.

The only downside to it is that I end up spending almost every Saturday night alone. Zane looks forward to every Saturday night, and he hates to miss them, and here he's missed two in a row since he's been helping his mother with some repairs around the house. I won't deny him his fun night out even if I really missed him.

I walk down the hall, all the way to the other wing of the palace, and tap on Jane's door. She cracks the door and pops her head through almost immediately.

"Mint chocolate chip or Neapolitan?"

Jane breaks into a huge grin. "As if that's even a choice."

Jane and I run downstairs, giggling like little girls all the way, and head straight for the freezer, the little one in the very back of the kitchen. This is the private ice cream freezer of the royal family—always has been. I grab a pint of mint chocolate chip and toss it to Jane and grab the pint of Neapolitan for myself. Jane responds by grabbing two spoons and tossing me one.

This is an old tradition. Every so often, we would sneak out of bed at night, run downstairs, and devour as much ice cream as we could before we either got sick or got caught. We've always eaten the same flavors. We deviated once and tried the white chocolate macadamia nut one my dad used to eat, but we both hated it and swore we'd never eat it again, questioning why on earth my dad would eat such a terrible flavor. The whole situation was made even funnier when my dad accused my mom of eating his ice cream, and Jane's and my giggles gave us away as the culprits. Now that we're older, we've learned a little self-control and we don't always eat until we get sick. Since the weather's been really nice lately, we've been going on walks in the garden with our contraband ice cream. I guess it's not really contraband anymore since technically I'm the leader of the house, but it's more fun to pretend that it is. It tastes better when you think you're not allowed to have it.

Jane and I walk in silence for a couple of minutes, me inducing a brain freeze from scarfing ice cream a little too quickly in the warm, slightly humid weather. It's not until I look down that I notice something a little unusual.

"Are you wearing bunny slippers?"

"Jealous?" Jane says, holding her spoon in her mouth with mock seductiveness.

I laugh. "Definitely not. Why on earth are you wearing bunny slippers?"

"I was chilling in my room, and you came and asked about ice cream."

"You didn't want to change?"

"There was no time. Ice cream waits for no man."

"Where did you even get those?"

"Brent gave them to me as a joke. He came to my room one night to tell me something, but I was already dressed for bed. I opened the door in all my no-make-up-pajama-wearing glory and scolded him for catching me in curlers and bunny slippers. He pointed out that I had neither of those things, so he bought them for me to be funny."

"Didn't want to go for the curlers?"

She laughs. "No, I think that would have been too much for him."

"How is that going?"

"The curlers? I don't use them. My hair is too thin."

I roll my eyes. "You know what I mean."

Brent and Jane started dating a few months ago, once Brent really got settled into his role as press secretary. Jane was practically head over heels for him the moment she saw him, but Brent took a while to get his feet under him. I'd be lying if I said I didn't feel really weird about it at first—not because I have feelings for him but because of everything that happened. But they really connected, and when I see them together, it's so obvious how happy they make each other.

"It's good," she says with a big smile, and I know that things are actually really good with Brent but she's trying to be cool. "He's really sweet. And so funny. And, miracle of miracles, my mom loves him."

"Wow, the Annette stamp of approval. That's big."

Jane nods. "Yeah, they really get along. He bought her flowers for her birthday the other day."

"Flowers for the gardener? And she liked them?"

"She picked them."

"What?" I ask around a mouthful of ice cream.

"He came with us to the florist when we went to pick out that corsage you wore to the charity event to rebuild the southside dock. The whole time we were there, she was obsessing over these beautiful dahlias. So later he went back and bought them for her."

"Wow, very smooth."

"Right? He's so thoughtful."

"Mhmm."

"Are you sure this isn't weird for you?"

"How many times are you going to ask me that?"

"Until I'm sure that you really are okay with it."

"Jane, I do not have any feelings for Brent. And I'm really happy for you guys. You two make a great couple."

"But you barely talk to him."

"What are you talking about? I talk to him all the time. Daily, practically."

"You know what I mean."

I sigh and sit down on a bench in front of the newly planted lilies, and Jane joins me.

"I know. I'm working on it, but it's just going to take time. It doesn't mean that I'm not really grateful for all of his help or that I don't think he's a really great guy."

"But you'll tell me if it does bother you?"

"I won't have to."

"You won't have to what?" Alex says, suddenly turning the corner of the garden.

"Alex," I say, jumping up, and Jane follows me. "What are you doing here?"

"Just taking a walk through the gardens. They're so lovely at night, and I haven't seen them in a while." Alex looks at each of our outfits and laughs. "Are you in pajamas?"

"It's the middle of the night, and we didn't think anyone was out here."

"Especially not the prince of Eterand," Jane says.

"Good to see you again, Jane," Alex says with a smile. "Sorry to have disturbed you. Lorraine, I'm actually glad I ran into you. I've been wanting to speak to you since I rudely cut our dinner short."

"And that's my cue," Jane says. "It was good to see you again, Prince Alex." Jane holds out her hand to me, and I hand her my pint of ice cream. "See you later?"

"Thanks, Jane." After Jane walks inside, I turn to Alex. "What did you not have the chance to say?"

Alex shrugs and turns just a little red, and I can tell he's a little nervous, maybe even embarrassed. This is the Alex few people really see. Alex puts up an arrogant front, but he actually has a very soft side. He just doesn't let it show very often. I think I'm one of very few people who have actually seen it.

"I don't think I fully expressed how happy I am to see you and know that you're safe. My family—we were very worried about you in the months leading up to your disappearance. We knew Cassandra was after your throne, and she seemed willing to do anything."

"I know. I saw it coming, too. Plus, your dad warned me in a letter just before I left on that trip to the provinces. I just didn't think she could try anything without being physically on the mainland. Honestly, when I left on that trip, I thought she would try to take the throne in my absence, so I made preparations for that. I guess I should have considered all possibilities."

"No one could have anticipated what she did. I'm just glad you're okay."

"Me, too."

Alex sits on the bench I was sitting on before and stares at his thumb for a moment, casually picking at a small hangnail. It's always been a nervous habit of his. Drives his dad crazy.

"Lorraine, what happened?"

"What do you mean?"

"I know you better than most people. Other than Jane, her mother, and the Captain, I think I've known you the longest. I know you would have found a way back. Why didn't you?"

"It's complicated," I say before realizing that a response like that totally makes it sound like I'm hiding something. "There were a lot of factors at play. Uncle Lawrence was stranded, and I didn't know where he was or how to reach him."

"What about me? You could have contacted me or my father, and we would have dropped everything to come get you."

"It wasn't that simple." I fidget with the hem of my shirt and studiously avoid eye contact with Alex. How do I explain what happened without explaining *what happened*?

"Did you think we wouldn't come? Or that Cassandra was too dangerous?"

"No, no, no, that's not it at all. I knew I could best Cassandra when it really came down to it. And I certainly never doubted you or your family. I just—"

"What?" Alex's voice sounds a little irritated, but his softly furrowed eyebrows and watery eyes betray concern. When I came back to Trilland, I made the decision to tell my closest friends and family about my amnesia. Doesn't Alex fall into that category of people?

"It's really difficult to explain."

"Please try." Alex holds one of my hands in both of his and looks directly into my eyes. I've known Alex long enough to know when he's being earnest and when he's putting on a front, and this is undoubtedly genuine.

But as I open my mouth to explain, to actually tell Alex all about the concussion and the amnesia and the struggle to remember, I hear the patio doors swing open abruptly. Alex drops my hand, we both turn to meet Brent's startled gaze, and there are several awkward throat clearings from all parties involved.

"Sorry," Brent says, "I didn't mean to disturb you. I just had to grab something from the garden shed."

"That's okay." I grab Alex's hand and bring him over to Brent. "Alex, have you met Brent? This is Brent Grayson. He's my press secretary. He also helped me get back to Trilland. Brent, this is Prince Alex Cartwright of Eterand."

Brent shakes his hand and bows slightly. "I think we spoke over the phone before your arrival. It's nice to finally meet you, Your Highness."

"Please, call me Alex. We did speak, but I didn't know what an important person you were. I'm sure all of Trilland is indebted to you for saving Lorraine."

Brent shrugs a little awkwardly. "I'd hardly call it saving. Captain Wilson should really get the credit. He's the one who organized everything and told where to go and what to do."

"Still, it's quite impressive what you did."

"Well, thank you. Anyway, I didn't mean to interrupt, so I'll just get going. It was nice to meet you, Sir. I'll see you tomorrow, Lorraine."

"Bye, Brent." As soon as Brent starts walking away, I force a yawn and take this opportunity because it's as good as any. "Well Alex, I'm afraid I have to be the one to cut things short this time. I need to get some sleep."

"By all means. I'm sorry to have held you up."

"Oh no, it's fine. I'm very glad we got to talk. I'll see you later?"

"Definitely. Good night, Lorraine."

Alex waves, so I do, too, and walk as quickly as I can to the patio door without it being obvious how quickly I'm walking. I close the door behind me and let myself exhale before sneaking a peek to see Alex walking toward the guest house.

Maybe trying to tell Alex is a bad idea. What would he think? Would he even believe it? Would he lose all faith in me, too? So many others already have, although, oddly enough, the ones who are losing faith have no idea about my memory loss. And maybe it would be a good thing to tell Alex and maybe his parents. Eterand is an old ally, and the Cartwrights are old friends. Maybe they could help me. They've always helped in the past, and I know they would be willing to help again. They've already offered. They know what it takes to run a country. It might be worth the risk.

"Psst."

I look around and finally spot Jane at the end of the hall.

"What did he say?"

"I'll tell you tomorrow. I'm exhausted."

"Deal." And with that, Jane runs off to her room, and I go to mine, collapsing on the bed. At least that much is true: I *am* exhausted. I'll tell Jane everything tomorrow.

But will I tell Alex everything tomorrow?

Chapter 4

I know that saying you hate Mondays is such an overused cliche, but I really do *hate* Mondays. I have no problem with any other day of the week, but Mondays are just awful. Every Monday, I have a Parliament meeting, the obligatory Parliament meeting, and those are the worst ones. When we schedule an extra Parliament meeting, like the one scheduled for this Friday, it always goes better than the Monday meetings. I don't know if people are more prepared or if they like the productivity of meeting multiple times in a week or what, but the Monday meetings are always the worst. Maybe everyone else just hates Mondays as much as I do. That's why it's a cliche, right?

So just like every Monday, here I sit in front of my vanity trying to do my make-up while I'm half-asleep and yet somehow still hold still enough for Jane to do my hair.

"Up or down today?" Jane asks.

"Down, I guess."

"Got it. So how did he react when you dodged the subject?"

"He seemed weirdly hurt by it. Like he expected me to tell him everything."

"Well, do you want to tell him everything?"

I plunk my elbow onto the counter and slump into my hand, and Jane sighs after losing grip on a strand of my hair. "I don't know. I thought I did. But what if it's a bad idea?"

"Prince Alex isn't some creepy villain." Jane says, and I laugh. "I think you can trust him."

"I think I can trust him, too. But, I mean, Brent and Uncle Lawrence didn't even want me to tell all of you. They thought if too many people knew, it would get out. And now I'm going to involve a whole other country?"

"You just said you can trust him. He's not going to go home and blab to all of Eterand. At most, he would tell his parents. Would that be the worst thing?"

"I just don't want to make the wrong decision."

"I know you don't." Jane delicately places a few pins in my hair to hold the side-swept look she's created. She's much more delicate with pins than Elise is. Whenever Elise did my hair, it would look fantastic, but I always felt like I had pins sticking straight into my brain. "But you have to do what's right for you."

"I guess." I fold my arms on the counter and let my head fall onto them. Jane seizes the opportunity to douse my head in hair spray.

"Did you get any sleep last night?"

"Not really," I mumble into my arms. "The whole Alex thing had me all riled up. Plus, the waves were really bad last night from that storm."

"Yeah. I can never hear them from my room, but it was ferocious. Kept you up?"

I nod.

"All right, I'll finish your make-up just this once, but don't get used to this."

"Jane, you don't have to—"

"Nonsense. Everyone needs a lot of concealer and eyeliner when they haven't had enough sleep."

Jane skillfully dabs some liquid liner on my top lid and smudges a little bit on the outer bottom corner. It looks good, but I can't help but think that it looks better when I do it myself. That's the way it's always been: she's the hair pro, and I'm the make-up pro. For how tired I am though, it may be better than what I'm capable of right now.

I grab the jacket that matches my cobalt suit skirt, thank Jane for her help, slip into the most comfortable pair of heels I own—the ones I bought immediately after my return and have worn into the ground ever since—and head downstairs. Some days I can handle the nicer, prettier, wildly uncomfortable heels that I have copious pairs of, but Mondays are just not that day.

Zane is waiting for me at the bottom of the stairs like he does every Monday, and hand-in-hand, we start the walk toward the Parliament building. For how stormy it was last night, it's a beautiful day today with just a little bit of a breeze. We sidestep a few downed palm fronds as we walk.

"Waves were pretty insane last night," Zane says. "I'm thinking the fishing will be really good today. Usually is after the ocean gets all churned up."

"I hope it goes well for you," I say, but my mind drifts to the oceanography department. I wonder how storms interfere with their research. For the fishing industry, it can be temporarily positive, but I wonder if it has the opposite effect on scientific research.

"I want to try something new today. Usually, we all go to the same spot, but maybe if we spread out like we Tito and the other guys do on Maris Island, we'd have better luck."

"Do you have enough guys to spread out that much?" Fishing is a big industry in Trilland, but the kind of hand fishing Zane has introduced is not common here. It's mostly commercial ships out on the waters.

Zane shrugs. "Probably not, but we could at least cover more ground. If it works, maybe we can recruit more guys. Although, sometimes more guys does the opposite because the fish get scared."

Zane continues on describing his fishing ideas, but this time, my mind drifts to the navy. Is that what we're doing with the navy—playing scared? Or are we the ones doing the scaring by increasing naval forces?

The problem with whenever I try to figure these things out is that I really don't know as much about the navy or oceanography or even fishing as I probably should. I don't know how much other monarchs know about their countries' industries, and I don't even know how much my parents knew, but I do know that I feel like my knowledge or lack thereof is wildly inadequate.

And maybe that's the problem. Maybe I need to take a more hands-on approach. I've thought that for a while now, but I haven't been sure exactly how to go about getting more involved. Perhaps I'm just over thinking it. It seems like these industries need help, and I need to be more involved. Two birds, one stone?

I think I've got an idea that I'm probably going to pitch to Parliament, but I don't really want to risk saying the wrong thing—again. I need to make sure it's a good idea, and Zane seems like a good practice target.

"I have an idea," I blurt out kind of suddenly since our last bit of conversation consisted of Zane's fishing successes the other night.

"I should wear those cheesy headband flashlights to fish like everyone else does? Because I'm sorry, but I just can't do that. They scare off the fish. Besides, that's not how ancient people used to—"

"Not a fishing idea."

"Oh." Zane turns a little red. "So what's your idea about?"

"I want to propose something to Parliament, and I want you to tell me if you think it's crazy. I might propose it anyway, but I want your feedback."

"That's my girl." Zane laughs. "Shoot."

"I'm going to suggest an observation."

"Of what?"

"Of the navy and the Department of Oceanography. I think each party is so afraid of getting a budget cut that they're afraid of admitting to weaknesses within. Maybe an outsider would have a different perspective. I certainly don't want to cut either program entirely, but maybe there's a way to cut down on unnecessary expenditures. What do you think?"

"I love it. I think it's a great idea."

"Yeah?"

"Absolutely," Zane says. "So, who's going to do the actual observing?"

"Me."

"You?"

"Why not? I'm simultaneously partial and impartial all at the same time. I'll be able to judge things objectively while also focusing on helping their programs. Plus, it'll get me more involved which might help some of the awkwardness."

"Well, I say go for it. I think it's got merit."

"Thank you." I kiss Zane on the cheek. "See you for lunch?"

"Can't wait."

Zane waves and starts walking back to the palace as I walk up the steps to the Parliament building. Senator Flint walks up at the same time and smiles.

"You two are almost nauseatingly cute," she says. Senator Flint is the youngest senator and definitely my favorite. She's about thirty and is one of very few senators who isn't completely convinced that I'm totally unqualified for the job that's rightfully mine. I really appreciate having her around. Everyone else is so much older, and I feel like they're all judging me all the time. I feel so out of place around them. Senator Flint is the only one I feel truly comfortable around.

"I keep telling him we shouldn't be so blatantly affectionate in public, but he doesn't seem to agree," I say.

"Eh, you're young and beautiful. If you can't kiss your handsome boyfriend out on the street, who can?"

Senator Flint and I end up laughing all the way to the meeting room. Once inside, the levity enjoyed in the company of Flint quickly dissipates into tension. A typical Monday morning. I take my seat at the head next to Uncle Lawrence, and I really wish Flint sat closer to me than she does. I wonder how these seats were chosen. I wonder if, as princess, I can change them. But is that really the hill I want to die on?

"All right," Uncle Lawrence says. "Everyone's here, so we may as well get started. Lorraine?"

"I've been thinking quite a bit about our budget problems this weekend, and I think I have an idea that will be a step in the direction of figuring out what our next steps can be."

Everyone stares at me, and it's so awkward that I start to wonder if they can even hear me. No one reacts at all. Finally, Senator Flint says, "Go on."

"I think we can all agree that the two departments under the most scrutiny are the navy and the Department of Oceanography. I propose that both departments be observed to see if there is any excess spending that could be cut back. Sometimes it's difficult to see things clearly from within, so I think an outsider would have a more objective view of things. Both of these departments are doing crucial work, so by no means is this a suggestion of cutting either department. I think we can find areas to cut back to make both departments more productive."

More silence. A few blinks. Senator Greene looks around the room, her powder blue eyeshadow on full display. Everyone dutifully avoids eye contact with her.

"Who will be the observer?" says Senator Greene.

"I will," I say cheerily, but the reactions I get are far from cheery. Several people express their disapproval audibly, groaning or sighing, while others start looking around nervously. Not really the reaction I thought I was going to get.

"Are you sure that's the best idea?" Senator Emerson asks.

"Yes, I am," I say, even though I'm not really sure. "Look, I care deeply about both programs. I don't want to harm either one or the people associated. I just want to improve how we do things and maybe streamline things a little."

"With all due respect, you don't really know much about either department," Senator Greene says.

"I know that. I'm hoping I can learn from my observation. The people in each department know it far better than I do. I think I can learn from them, and maybe by talking through things together, we can come up with a solution that makes everyone happy."

"I think it's worth a try," Uncle Lawrence says, and many people look at him surprised. "It can't hurt."

"Exactly," I say. "If we find nothing to cut back, then we're back where we started. No harm done."

"Sounds like something your father would say," Uncle Lawrence says.

"The king never interfered with our business," Senator Greene mutters.

Senator Flint whips around. "What was that, Senator?"

"Nothing."

Senator Flint turns back to me. "So when do you start?"

"How about Wednesday? I have the meeting with the school on Thursday. I can report back to you all on Friday."

"Sounds perfect," says Uncle Lawrence.

"With which department will you start?" asks Senator Emerson.

"You can start with the navy," Uncle Lawrence says. "I'll meet you in the morning."

"Sounds like a fantastic idea," I say, trying to sound optimistic even though almost everyone else in the room is grimacing. I knew they'd have a reaction to me getting involved, but I didn't think it would be so severe. It's starting to feel like I can't do anything right in their eyes. But I'm glad to hear that it sounds like something my dad would do. That gives me at least a little bit of confidence that I might be doing the right thing.

<div align="center">~~~</div>

Today's meeting runs longer than I had hoped. Talking Parliament into letting me do my job took much longer than I thought it would, and then Senator Emerson and Senator Greene spent several hours arguing, much like they always do, but this time it was about the schools since I have my walk-through on Thursday. It was a classic argument: science and technology versus creative writing, sports versus the arts. Miracle of miracles, there's actually enough education funding to adequately service all fields, but both senators want to reallocate funds to enhance whichever program they prefer.

Education is actually one field I don't worry about and one field I actually enjoy discussing. It's got enough funding, and I like meeting with all of the students. Students have such bright ideas that it really does give you glimpses into what the future will be like. Sometimes students even hold the answers to a problem you haven't been able to solve simply because they're young, innovative, and have fresh eyes. At least that's one meeting I'm not dreading.

By the time we finally end, it's well past my scheduled lunch with Zane, and frankly, I feel a little too exhausted even to go out. We could probably go back to the palace to have a late lunch there. That might be the best option.

But when I walk down the steps, all my hopes of a quiet, laid back lunch are dashed. At the bottom of the steps, I see Zane and Alex standing together talking about who knows what. Great.

"Hey," Zane says, kissing me on the cheek. At least he seems relatively chill right now. "Ran late today, huh?"

"Yes. There were some disagreements between a few senators."

"What else is new?"

I laugh. "Exactly. Alex, what are you doing here?"

"I thought I'd come and see if you wanted to have lunch and talk politics a little, but it looks like Zane beat me to it."

"If it makes you feel better, I wasn't going to talk politics with her," Zane says, and it sounds cheerful and lighthearted. I'd like to believe it means that Zane and Alex are getting friendlier, but I have a feeling it's not that simple.

"Well, I'd hate to interrupt your lunch."

"Why don't you join us?" Alex and I both look at Zane with the same shocked expression on our faces. Is that Zane actually being friendly, or is he jealous and trying to keep an eye on me and Alex?

"If that's all right with you," Alex says.

"Of course," I say. "Zane, did you pick a place to go?"

"Yeah, I thought we'd go to Ally's. What do you think?"

"Sounds great."

"Ally's?" Alex raises one eyebrow. "What is that?"

"Oh, it's the best," Zane says. "They make the best shrimp you'll ever eat."

I add, "I promise it's really good. You'll love the crab there."

"Well, if there's crab, I'm in."

The walk to Ally's is short, and Zane and Alex make polite conversation the whole way. I'm not sure what has gotten into Zane, but I like it. At least I don't have to worry about Zane biting his head off anymore. Maybe he finally realized that Alex isn't a threat at all. Seems unlikely that Zane would ever willingly choose not to be jealous, but hey, anything can happen.

Ally's might be my favorite restaurant in Trilland. It's not exactly upscale, but that's what I like about it. It reminds me of Maris Island. I think that's why Zane likes it so much, too. It's definitely his favorite restaurant by far. The owner Ally Fallon uses all local seafood and produce to make her food, which boosts Trilland's economy tremendously. Plus, it's good for me to be seen there every once in a while; it reminds the people that I still care. I never want to give the impression that I think I'm above them.

Ally always reserves a table for me as the princess of Trilland, which is kind of weird, but today, it serves me well because it's really crowded. I guess everyone decided to have a late lunch today. The host takes the three of us back to my usual table, which I have to say, is the best table in the place. Ally's is pretty big, but the tables are all pretty much crammed together. The only tables that have any breathing room are the ones along the big window in the back. It's a beautiful feature of the restaurant because it looks out on the water, and my table is on the corner which means there are windows on two sides. I like looking out on the waves and watching people swimming and sailing and fishing. They look small from this high up the cliff, but you can see siblings splashing each other, couples embracing each other on sailboats, fishermen casting their nets, and teenagers anxiously rushing to the beach now that school is over.

The host hands us menus, but Zane and I don't even look—we always order the same thing: the shrimp platter. It's technically an appetizer, but it's more than enough food for the two of us. We usually just devour a shrimp platter and then either split a dessert or we each take one home, depending on how much we either can't agree on a dessert or don't want to share at the moment. Alex, of course, is completely out of his element, so he reads the menu carefully, his eyebrows slightly furrowed.

"You said the crab was good here, did you not?" Alex asks.

"Yes, it's fantastic," I say.

Alex flips the page of the menu, and his eyes widen. "My goodness, there's a whole page of crab dishes."

"Ally doesn't like to leave people without choices."

"Clearly. What are you both ordering?"

"We always order the shrimp platter and split it."

Alex smiles, but the corner of his mouth twitches. "How adorable."

Our waiter comes by and takes our order rather quickly. Alex settles on the crab bisque, which is a great choice for him. Alex has absolutely no tolerance for spicy food whatsoever, and Zane nearly sold him on some curry dish which would have given him heartburn for sure.

"So, Alex," Zane says, and I wonder when Zane ended up on a first name basis with Alex, "you were telling me earlier about Eterand's scientific work."

"Yes, so I was. We've been working on some ideas for energy effi-ciency. Eterand utilizes solar power, but it's not quite enough for our current needs. We're looking to expand in a cost-effective way."

"I'm surprised solar power isn't enough."

"Well, it used to be, but it's too individualized. The problem is that solar panels are expensive, and while the government may be willing to incur the costs, individuals are not necessarily so willing."

"Is money an issue in Eterand?" I ask.

"Not overall, no. But we can't demand that small businesses shell out the money needed for solar panels. It's unrealistic for them. What we'd like to do is find a new source of energy efficiency that would be cheaper for the government so that individuals can pay less in taxes and afford to apply the same."

I say, "That makes sense. I've always wished that Trilland could adopt more solar energy, but my father was never really on board."

"Why is that?" Zane says.

I shrug. "I don't know, really. He always said it was fine for Eterand, but he never wanted it for Trilland. The only thing he ever really said about it was that Eterand was a bigger country, and so maybe they were better equipped for it."

"Well, that's not really the case anymore," says Alex. "Trilland is just as big now, if not bigger with the incorporation of all the provinces."

"Oh, I don't think it's bigger. The mainland is quite a bit smaller, and the provinces individually are pretty small."

"Either way, maybe solar is an option now," Zane says.

"Maybe," I say. "I'm not sure how I would go about adding it to Trilland though. If Alex can't convince Eterand businesses to adopt it, I certainly won't be able to in this economy."

"Once you fix the economy, you could do it."

"Oh, Zane, I wish it were that simple."

"You're definitely a dreamer, pal," Alex says, giving Zane a friendly slap on the shoulder.

Zane points at me. "It's dreamers that believed she was still alive. Maybe we just need a few dreamers."

"If I could get Trilland back to half of what it was under my father, I'd consider that a dream come true," I say.

"Oh, Lorraine, do you remember what a joy it was when our fathers were so close?" Alex says. "Those were some of the best years in Eterand."

"In Trilland, too," I say. "Our fathers really knew how to run each of their countries."

"I think a major strength was their close alliance. They always called on each other whenever they needed help. I can remember a time when your father came to Eterand and talked my father out of a terrible decision."

"When was that?"

"We must have been about ten. My father wanted to disband the navy completely because no one had threatened Eterand in more than a decade. When your father heard, he immediately set sail for Eterand and talked my dad out of it. He warned him that doing that was basically sending an engraved invitation to your enemies. Who knows what would have happened if your dad hadn't stopped him."

"I don't remember that," I say. Whenever I'm told a childhood story like that and I don't remember it, it's very difficult for me to process. It always makes me very paranoid. Do I not remember because I was a kid, or do I not remember because there are still spots in my memory? Ten years old is pretty young, but that's also a time when my father had really started to involve me in major decisions so that I could learn. I feel like he would've told me about that. What if this is a gap?

Oddly enough though, Alex's story is timely. Cutting the navy completely is a bad idea, and I've known that this whole time, but I like knowing that somehow my dad has confirmed my decisions.

Alex doesn't know it, but he's given me the gift of just a little bit of reassurance.

"My dad didn't tell many people," Alex says. "He was pretty embarrassed about it after he came to his senses. Maybe your father never told you." It's possible, but highly improbable, that my dad didn't tell me. I feel a little weird about that, but I can't worry about it now. "I just know that as king, one day I want to have an ally like your father. Eterand and Trilland were never better than when they were together. Maybe you and I can reignite that closeness one day."

The waiter brings our food, and thankfully, Zane changes subjects. I don't really want to think about the navy or Trilland's failing budget or my possible memory gaps right now. But even though I don't remember Alex's story, I do remember that friendship. It really was like no other. They really understood each other. I don't know what I would have done without Alex's father after my parents died. He helped me through a really difficult time. Trilland may not have survived Cassandra's takeover if he hadn't done the repairs he did back then. Reconnecting Trilland and Eterand may not be the worse idea.

By the end of the meal, Zane and I decide we don't feel like sharing a dessert today, so I order a slice of the coconut cake, and Zane orders a slice of the key lime pie. After much negotiating, Zane finally talks Alex into ordering the pineapple cake. We get them to-go, and after a brief fight over the bill with Alex, I pay, and we start walking toward the palace.

"It was lovely having lunch with you all," Alex says. "Thank you for letting me crash your lunch."

"You didn't crash, Alex, we were happy to have you," I say.

Zane adds, "Well, you had to try to best seafood in Trilland. It's a requirement."

"When did that place open? I don't remember it being there."

"It opened when I was sixteen or seventeen, just before I left," I say. "Ally started the place with her grandparents."

"I bet you missed a place like that while you were gone."

"Uh, yes." I glance over at Zane, who has the best poker face right now. "Luckily for me, my roommate on Maris Island was a fantastic chef, so I didn't miss out much food-wise."

"Roommate?" Alex scoffs. "You had a roommate? How odd."

"I really preferred it that way, actually. She reminds me of Jane."

"Well, that's good then," Alex says, but his face still betrays his skepticism.

"Are you coming back to the palace?" Zane asks.

"No, I'm going to take a walk down by the beach. It's such a beautiful day. I look forward to seeing you both later."

"Bye, Alex," I say.

"See you later," Zane says.

After Alex gets a ways away from us, I take Zane's hand and squeeze it. "All right, spill. What happened?"

"What do you mean?"

"Why are you suddenly so friendly with Alex? You hated him."

Zane rolls his eyes. "I never hated him."

"You practically bite his head off all the time, and then today, nothing. Just polite chatter and conversation."

"Look, I may not like him, but I can't change the fact that he is a part of your life. It's not going to help things for he and I to be going at each other. I figured I'd try on my end and maybe he would on his end. And he did, mostly."

"Mostly?"

"He scoffed quite a bit at the idea of you living with Elise."

"He doesn't get it. That's not exactly the royal lifestyle."

"And don't tell me you didn't notice his face when we shared lunch."

"He said it was adorable," I say, but Zane just stares at me. "Okay fine, he was a little ticked. But it's not a big deal."

"No it's not." Zane gives me a quick hug, and as we approach the palace, Brent comes out to meet us. "I'll get over it, I promise. Brent."

"Zane," Brent says. They haven't really spoken much since Zane and I came back from the island, and they're still a little tense with each other. I suppose things haven't exactly been comfortable between Brent and me either, but both Brent and Zane stiffen whenever they see each other. I'm not sure that they ever really talked over everything that happened. "Get over what?"

"It's nothing. Zane is just clashing with Alex."

"I am not."

"You are."

"I didn't mean to get in the middle of something," Brent says.

"You're not," Zane says. "Alex is."

"What?"

"Oh come on, Maris," Zane says a little too loudly even though we're inside the palace now. I always get a little nervous when he uses my "other" name, even though everyone in the palace knows the whole story. "He was practically pushing co-dependent countries."

"What do you mean?"

"He kept bringing up your father and how he helped out his father and how he wants that when he's king."

"What would be wrong with that?"

"I don't think he really wants just a close friendship like your dad had. It sounded more like compromising Trilland's independence and maybe Eterand's, too. Plus, he asks too many questions about your time away. He's getting too nosy."

"I agree," Brent says. I never thought I'd see the day that Brent would ever agree with Zane or vice versa. "He seemed a little invasive the other night."

"What other night?" Zane says. *Thanks for that one, Brent.*

I say, "Saturday night. Jane and I ran into him in the garden, and he really wanted to know why I didn't contact him after the mutiny. Luckily, Brent interrupted, so I didn't have to explain."

"Would you have explained?" Zane asks nervously. "If Brent hadn't interrupted, I mean."

"I don't know. I thought about it."

"I think that's a really bad idea, Lorraine," Brent says and Zane "mmhmm"s in agreement. "That's inviting another country into a very private story. I wasn't even comfortable with you telling the palace household."

"I had to do that. They're basically family."

"But Alex isn't."

"The Cartwrights might as well be."

"Look," Zane says, "I wouldn't even tell his father, and I would trust him more than Alex."

"You don't even know his father."

"I know enough about him to know he would be more likely to treat the subject with sensitivity than Alex would."

"King Norman is a well-respected man," Brent says. "Alex is not. At least not yet."

"You make him sound like a villain," I say. "I've known him my whole life. He wouldn't do anything that would hurt me or Trilland."

"I'm not saying he would do it on purpose," Zane says. "But it seems like he's picked up on a secret he doesn't know, and he's determined to find it out."

"Just be careful," Brent says. "That's all we're saying."

"Chill out, both of you," I say. "I haven't decided to tell him anything. Besides, he's only in town for a little while. He'll be gone soon."

Brent asks me to sign something authorizing a purchase of candles for the charity ball later this month, and then he and Zane both leave with no more than a nod at each other. They're back to not talking, I guess.

More than once, I've wondered if I should try to broker some peace between the two now that Brent works for me, but it feels wrong to interfere in their relationship, whatever it is. If they're going to get past this, they're going to have to figure it out for themselves.

But what does it mean for Zane and Brent—who have rarely agreed on anything—agree that Alex needs to be kept at arm's length? My initial thought is that they are both just too protective all the time, but I can't ignore the nagging feeling that if they both think something, they might be on to something. And if they are on to something, where does that leave me in terms of Alex?

Chapter 5

Probably the worst part about this job is having to care about things that are important but simply not interesting. Ask me to care about education, fishing, the budget, or international relations, and I'm there, but ask me to study the military's strategy patterns or pick out tablecloths for a ball, and I'm out. Although I can avoid caring about tablecloths and balls because Brent and Lady Vivian take care of all that for me, with our threats from Riagala and its allies, unfortunately, I can't afford not to be interested in the military.

The one positive aspect of spending the morning with the navy is that Uncle Lawrence is the one showing me around. He seems so excited to present his work to me. Even with his limp, he's the fastest moving sailor here. He's far outpacing the sailors who are my age, and I have to admit that it's really fun watching them pant, trying to keep up with him. Even Brent, who is in pretty good shape, is having trouble keeping up, but he insisted on coming with us because he wanted to make sure the press coverage was appropriate, so he did this to himself.

"This right here shows a real-time map of where all of our ships are," Uncle Lawrence says, pointing at a screen that makes absolutely no sense to me. It's a black screen with blue graphics which I assume are the ships, but there are no land masses on the screen, so I don't really understand how that helps.

"So we're here?" I say, pointing to the bottom left blue blob.

Uncle Lawrence points to the bottom right blue blob. "No, actually we're here. Trilland is on the eastern end of the sea."

"Oh, of course." I can feel my cheeks turning red. I should know better than to say anything about this. The last thing I need is for more people to think I'm completely incompetent.

"As you can see, we're expanding our forces to defend our borders and our seas, particularly in the northwest sector."

"Why? What's special about the northwest sector?" Brent asks.

Several soldiers stiffen, and Brent definitely looks aware of the blunder he's made. Most of them look to Uncle Lawrence for an answer, but this is something I actually know well, so I hold up my hand to stop Uncle Lawrence.

"The northwest sector is where Riagala is."

"Isn't our ally Lithilea up there as well?"

"Yes," Uncle Lawrence says, "but we can't assume they are monitoring Riagala as closely as we are."

When Brent raises an eyebrow, I add, "They don't have nearly as much conflict with Riagala as we do, and Lithilea is dealing with its own domestic affairs right now. They've also seen some transfer of power, and there's been some conflict with their provinces that they've had to sort out. We have excellent allies, but we always have to keep an eye on Riagala ourselves since they are so antagonistic toward us."

"But they haven't formally threatened us, have they?"

"No," I say, "but we have a history of conflict with them. My father actually ended a decade-long war with them, but their hostilities toward us never subsided."

"Forgive my poor education regarding Trilland's history, but what is the source of the conflict?"

"Territory disputes," I say. "They claim that we stole land and sea territory from them. Some of our outer provinces out there previously traded with Riagala, so they think they have claim. But honestly, at this point I think it's just a power struggle. They want to prove they can beat us, but their military is disorganized, and a revolt might be brewing."

"But that doesn't minimize the severity of their antagonism toward us," Uncle Lawrence adds. "We can't afford not to take the threat seriously. They've made it clear they aren't happy about Lorraine's return."

"Why?"

"Cassandra was easier to push around," I say, though that isn't the entire story. I don't mind telling Brent about the alliance documents I found in her—my—desk a few weeks ago, but I don't need the entire navy knowing about that. An alliance with Riagala not only would have been detrimental, but it would have effectively ended our alliance with Eterand, a much better and longstanding alliance. I wonder if Alex and his father know Cassandra almost joined together with Riagala. Maybe that's really why Alex is here.

"What's this here?" I point to a blue blob to the north. "Isn't this near Eterand?"

Uncle Lawrence says, "It is."

"Why are we building up defenses there? Eterand is certainly no threat to us."

"I'm building up defenses everywhere. Of course Eterand is no danger, but I don't want to leave anything to chance. We might as well protect all our borders. Besides, if we leave any gaps, Riagala or another force might try to sneak in that way."

"But Eterand would respond," I say. "Or at least warn us."

"I trust King Norman, but I trust our own forces more. I feel better knowing that we have ships everywhere."

Now I know why Senator Greene is so upset about the navy's spending. It's costing a fortune to fund our entire navy indefinitely. Riagala's hostility is important, but fleets at Eterand? Over by Gessend? There's no reason to man those areas so heavily. I wonder why he's doing that. Our navy should really be at half capacity since we're currently not in wartimes. But maybe Uncle Lawrence knows something I don't. After all, he's the captain. Shouldn't I trust his judgment? It just seems excessive to me. The one thing I know for sure is that it will not be easy to get Uncle Lawrence to pull back the navy.

Uncle Lawrence walks me through a few other naval operations, but they make even less sense to me than the blue blobs, and I end up zoning out way more than I probably should. Brent notices a few times and elbows me, but I just can't focus. I'm so out of my element here. I wonder if my father ever felt like this when he toured the operations of Trilland. Was there ever a department where he felt hopelessly out of place and incapable? I wonder if I would still feel this way if he hadn't died and I hadn't gotten lost and I'd had the amount of time to learn under him as I should have.

Occasionally, I have a fleeting thought that maybe I *did* learn how to do this, but that the knowledge is lost somewhere in my corrupted memory. When I saw Dr. Offen shortly after my return, he assured me that my memory was without gaps, but I just can't shake the feeling that something must be missing. Sometimes I even wonder if the reason I have trouble understanding this stuff is because my brain's ability to retain information is permanently damaged. Maybe my memory will always be faulty. I wonder if I'll always feel this way.

"That way, if Riagala or anyone else makes a move, we'll know about it within a few hours," Uncle Lawrence says, ending a speech of which I understood maybe thirty percent.

"I wish there was a faster way," I say.

"Faster options mean more money, something that we already don't have enough of. Anyway, that's basically the gist of it. Shall we go back up the docks?"

The sailors get back to work, and Brent, Uncle Lawrence, and I walk back to the decks alone. Uncle Lawrence takes this opportunity to try to get some intel about what I thought of the navy.

"Impressive, right?" he says.

"Very."

"So what are your first thoughts? Any ideas for improvements?"

"I do have a question I didn't want to ask in front of everyone. Why are we utilizing our entire navy when we're not at war? It seems like we could reduce our fleets quite a bit."

"Like I said, Riagala is unstable right now. They could implode into a civil war or attack us at any given moment. I can't take a risk when it comes to them."

"I agree, but do we really need fleets around our provinces and near Eterand? I hardly think King Norman and Alex are any more of a threat than Gessend and Maris Island are."

"Threats are unpredictable," he says. "Look, we all knew Cassandra was power hungry, but we never thought she would come after you like she did. Danger can come from anywhere. It is my job to protect Trilland and you, and that's what I'm going to do."

"It just seems like an easy place to cut spending."

He shakes his head firmly. "Too much damage was caused to Trilland and to you because I overlooked a threat. I'm not going to make that mistake again. I have to keep you safe, and I'll do whatever I have to do. Now, if you'll excuse me, I have to get back to work for now. Can we talk more later?"

"Of course," I say, and he smiles, waves, and runs back on to the ship.

"Seems like somebody's a little paranoid," Brent says.

He's right. Uncle Lawrence is artificially inflating the navy because he's got some kind of guilt over losing me before. But he's burning through money for no reason. Eterand would never attack us or allow anyone to. Plus, not only is it unnecessary to station fleets around our provinces, but it might even make them even angrier than they already are. How can I possibly communicate that I'm trying to help them when I'm sending war ships to sit in their waters for no reason? I have to talk Uncle Lawrence down on the navy, but how can I possibly tell him not to worry about me without upsetting him?

Chapter 6

Anyone who knows me knows that I am not a fan of public speaking. It's really quite a gift in life to be born a public figure who must appear in front of crowds frequently and also have extreme stage fright. Who decided I should get dealt both of those cards?

But speeches are manageable. Speeches can be written, edited, proofread, approved, rehearsed, and performed very carefully. A lot of planning can go into them to make them not absolutely petrifying. Press conferences and town hall meetings are not that way. These can't be planned because you can only anticipate the questions of others so much. I have people around me whose job it is to figure out what the atmosphere of the room will be and what questions will be asked so that I can prepare, but it isn't a perfect system. Often times, somebody will surprise you, and really, it's a toss up of whether a journalist or a citizen is worse.

For this reason, Brent thought it would be a good idea to combine the town hall with the press conference to get them both out of the way at the same time. When he first suggested it, it seemed like a good idea to combine two or three hours of pain into one and a half, but now I'm dreading it. There's so much room for unpredictability that I'm not sure what to expect. Brent's intel tells me that the media will mostly ask about new policies and what their effects will be, but the citizens are really the wild card here. I haven't had many formal town halls since I returned. The first one mostly consisted of people asking about my lost year and me dodging questions that came to close to my memory. Then there was one where I asked everyone to tell me what they needed and what damage Cassandra had done. That was a hard meeting just listening to all of the destruction and chaos Cassandra caused. I had trouble not crumbling and bursting into tears as I listened to all of the heartache, but it was helpful because I got to know exactly what I needed to do most urgently. Then there was a very small one with significant members of the business community, and that was much more of a conversation than an interrogation.

This one will be an interrogation, I suspect. The rumors from Brent are that everyone is feeling a little uneasy with the lack of progress in almost a year's time. The truth is that a lot has been accomplished, but it hasn't quite trickled down yet, and some battles are still being fought in Parliament, but that's not something I can disclose to all of Trilland without looking like a jerk. Sometimes I just have to take the hits, but that knowledge doesn't make it any more fun.

"Are you ready to go?" Brent says, poking his head around the corner.

I nod. "I guess as ready as I'll ever be."

I stand up and smooth the lines in the skirt suit I chose to wear. At the time, I was hoping it would communicate some kind of business-minded attitude, like I was hard at work trying to find solutions, and maybe the people—and Parliament, for that matter—would view me as a serious leader and politician, not just a princess who looks pretty in a glittery dress. Now, I'm uncomfortable and wishing I'd chosen something more forgiving for my nerves.

Brent's eyes flit momentarily down to my hands which are smoothing non-existent wrinkles in a frenzy. "It'll be fine. Try not to worry about it."

Zane walks in behind him and smiles sweetly. "Brent's right." Not sure I'll ever get used to hearing Zane say that. "And you look beautiful."

I put my hands on my hips and huff. "It'll be fine, right? I mean, it's not going to be great, but it won't be terrible, right?"

"It will be fine," Zane says. "This town hall is a good idea. Giving people a chance to vent will show that you care, and you will get a chance to tell them what you're working on. I'll be watching from back here, and I'll be here when you finish."

I nod, but I'm not totally sure I believe him. It doesn't really matter though because I can't put it off any longer. Zane kisses me on the cheek and heads out, and Brent and I head down the hallway. At the end of the hall, Secretary Johnson joins us with an easy smile. Secretary Johnson has always been kind of like a grandfather. He's much older than everyone in Parliament, and he's been involved in government since before I was born. I always liked him. Sometimes the senators would get annoyed when my father would bring me to meetings, especially when I was very young, but Johnson never did. He was always so sweet but never condescending in that way that some older people are when they talk to kids. He never talked down to me, and he always made me feel welcome. Other than Flint, he's my favorite person in government.

"Ready to go, Lorraine?" he says with a bit of levity in his gravelly voice. I'm not sure if he's actually optimistic, or if he's faking it for my sake, but honestly, if he is doing it just for me, then I'm grateful. He's reassuring; he always has been.

"Ready when you are," I say.

"I'll go out and let everyone know we're ready to go," Brent says, and I thank him.

"He's an excellent press secretary," Johnson says. "He's quite an impressive find."

"Yes, he's been great. He's perfect for the job."

"He is, but it's more than that. Do you remember Shane Tisdale?"

"I do." Shane was my father's favorite press secretary. Unfortunately, he got sick and died pretty young, but my father adored him. He managed everything so well, and my parents never had to worry. My father also trusted his advice, which is unusual for a press secretary. Shane wasn't shy about contributing his opinion, but my father always welcomed it because he knew Shane cared about the Everhart family and about Trilland.

"He reminds me of Shane," Johnson says. "Different personality, of course, but I like him the same way I liked Shane. I think your father would have liked him, too. He would have been glad that you chose him to be your press secretary."

Secretary Johnson's comment makes me more uncomfortable than I'm sure he realizes. I'm trying really hard to put everything behind us, but it's hard not to think of how angry I was at Brent for so long. He long ago apologized, and I wouldn't have given him the press secretary job if I didn't trust him, but feelings like that die hard, I guess. Still, it's nice to know that someone who knew my father so well thinks he would have respected my choices. He really has become such an asset, however unexpected that might be.

We hear the announcement from Brent that the town hall is beginning, so we head out onto the stage. I take my seat in the middle, Secretary Johnson to my right, Brent to my left, and face the giant crowds. At first, I have trouble really seeing the crowds because of all the camera flashes, but when my vision stabilizes, I wish it hadn't because I feel suddenly nauseated seeing how many people showed up. Town halls are always pretty popular on the Trilland mainland, but that never makes it any easier to stare at the masses, and knowing that most of them are unhappy or at the very least concerned, I'm even more uncomfortable sitting up here.

Brent runs through a few policy issues, like how I'll begin with a short statement, then the press will be allowed to ask questions, then the mics will be opened up to the public, but every word he says puts us closer to the actual event, and I wish he would just keep talking.

"With that, I'll turn it over to Princess Lorraine."

There's a pretty decent round of applause, so I guess that's something. I take a deep breath, smooth the lines of my dress, clear my throat away from the mic, and somehow start talking. I explain how important it is to me to be transparent and to hear what people want. I reference the specifics from that first town hall when people said they wanted lower production costs, better materials, more involvement in government, and obviously, more income. I had promised to deliver all of those things as quickly as I could, but I naively thought it would be easier to do than it has been. I don't know how to make materials cheaper or how to involve people more in government. I don't know how to raise their incomes. I want to do it, desperately, but I don't know how.

But I don't say that, of course. I explain that we're working every day to find a solution, which we are. I explain some of the basics that we're working on, but I don't have to hear from them that it isn't enough. Nothing tangible has really happened yet. Sure, a lot of sanctions from other countries have been dropped that were put up because of Cassandra since I returned, and that has made a huge difference for our manufacturers and tradesmen, but internally not much change has occurred.

When I finish, there's more applause, weaker than before, and Brent opens up the floor for questions from the press. One of the things I hate most about press conferences is not necessarily the ques-tions themselves but the way everyone talks at once while simulta-neously taking pictures of me, which results in me being blinded by flashes and unable to single out one of the many voices. It's nearly impossible to distinguish who's who even though I know all of the journalists individually since there aren't really that many. I remember Zane thought it was funny when he first saw them. He pictured a mob of like twenty or thirty people, and when he saw that there were only like eight, he could not stop laughing.

Luckily, the first voice is easy to distinguish, and I call on Tony.

"Has there been any change in the status of Riagala?"

"We're continuing to monitor them," I say. "Nothing has changed at this point. No active threats have been made, but we remain cau-tious and diligent in our efforts to keep Trilland and its provinces safe." Yeah, that seemed good, right? That sounded professional and regal. Nobody seems angry, so I think it was an acceptable answer.

The second voice is not as easy to pick out other than that I can tell it's coming from the left, so I just kind of vaguely point and hope I'll be able to recognize the voice when it's by itself.

"Can Trilland's national budget sustain a continued watch over Riagala?"

No. "Yes, because we are prioritizing the missions of our fleets in a way that best suits our purposes, but we're always looking for ways to scale down without compromising our safety."

"Would it be in Trilland's best interest to temporarily suspend our scientific research until our budget stabilizes? Many are concerned that it takes up more money than we can currently afford."

It is too much money. Maybe we should suspend it? That would just make me so popular with Senator Greene, I'm sure. "We get a pretty significant amount of money from our research, so it does benefit us to continue it."

Secretary Johnson adds, "Of course, we're always looking for ways to cut costs and make that research cheaper to perform, but it does not make sense to suspend it completely at this time."

I point to Erin in the center. She says, "If we're not cutting military or scientific spending, then how are we reducing costs? It sounds like the budget is still suffering."

It is. "We definitely do not want to cut prematurely and suffer more economic loss than we already have. It's important that we do the research first."

"But isn't that what you've been doing for nearly a year? Where is the change?" Erin has always been one of the biggest critics of the Everhart family. In general, she thinks Trilland should no longer be a monarchy. I was hoping she wouldn't be here today since she's been talking about retiring, but alas, I'm not that lucky.

"Fixing the economy as quickly as possible is my number one goal, but these things can't be rushed as much as we'd like to rush them," I say. "This is why we've been conducting extra Parliament meetings."

"Princess Lorraine also had a wonderful idea that we will be implementing over the next week or two," Secretary Johnson says. "She will be visiting all of our major operations to learn more about how they function. She has already visited the navy. Not only will she gain invaluable knowledge about how the most critical parts of our country work but she will be an objective observer who will be able to identify areas of excess spending that could be cut down. This should make a big difference."

I knew that somehow we were going to mention this plan today, but I thought I would be the one to do it, and now that Johnson has said it, I'm wondering if it should have been said at all. The people start murmuring quite a bit, and I'm concerned that they aren't reacting well to this news. Maybe it would have been received better if I had said it myself, but I guess we'll never know now.

"Isn't that rather Big Brotherish?" Erin says, continuing her efforts to get me dethroned. Sometimes, I wonder what she was like when Cassandra was in power. Cassandra didn't do many press conferences because everyone hated her and she knew it, but sometimes I can't help but wonder if she is a Cassandra sympathizer.

"My goal is not to get in the way of anything our operations are doing but to help them do it better. I would never interfere with something that's working, but sometimes it's difficult to see what needs to change when you're so close to it. Hopefully, I'll be able to see the possible areas of improvement as an objective observer with fresh eyes."

Brent glances in my direction, and when I return a wide-eyed look, he leans forward quickly before I can take another question. "At this time, I'd like to open the floor to the citizens of Trilland who so graciously took time out of their day to be here. We'd really like to hear from all of you, and we're so thankful that you chose to attend today to make your feelings known to us. Your concerns are Princess Lorraine's chief interest."

Man, he's good. Thank goodness Brent shifted focus away from the press to the citizens. Maybe Secretary Johnson is right about him. He really is so good at his job. I'm not sure how I would have been able to handle all of these public appearances without him.

An older gentleman steps up to the mic, and though he's got quite a severe limp, he seems to demand a great amount of power to the point that several people who got to the mic before him step aside to defer to him.

"Your Highness, I was unable to attend the previous town halls, so I want to begin by expressing my sincere happiness that you returned safely."

"Thank you so much."

"I'm no spring chicken anymore, and I was hoping to retire soon. When Cassandra took over, I knew I'd have to try to wait her out, and luckily, you returned. I thought I'd be able to retire pretty much as soon as you returned, but my family wouldn't be able to get by if I did that right now. I'm a fisherman, and the physical strain of my job is too much for me these days, but I need to support my wife. When can I expect improvement to the point that my pension is stable again?"

The pensions aren't stable? Why didn't anyone tell me that? "May I ask your name, sir?"

"Eddie Poulos, Your Highness."

"Mr. Poulos, thank you for letting me know what's going on in your life. One of my main goals is streamlining our fishing industry so that the physical wear and tear is not so severe. However, that is not your primary concern. Once our national budget is stabilized, the pensions will be the first priority, so you can expect to see some change almost immediately at that point."

"But when will that be?" Erin says. I look over at Brent for some kind of confirmation of whether or not the press should be speaking at this point, but he shrugs in a way that communicates, *She already said it, so just roll with it.*

"Cassandra Wellington's spending was out of control. That's why we're trying to reign it in first and foremost by doing these observations."

"But is that going to be enough?" says a younger man at the mic next to Eddie Poulos. "I mean, I'm not looking to retire, but my wife is pregnant. I don't have enough money to provide for a family right now. I can't just sit around and wait for things to get better."

Secretary Johnson says, "We're working tirelessly to fix this quickly. Many people don't see this, but Princess Lorraine has been working overtime to catch up on everything she's missed and figure out a solution. I haven't seen anyone work this hard in a very long time."

"I mean no disrespect to Her Highness, but that doesn't mean very much to us until something actually changes for us," the young man says.

"If I may," a woman at the other mic says, "I think we're all just feeling a lot of anxiety over the fact that not much has changed. We were all so ecstatic to find that Princess Lorraine was alive, and we still are, but we all hoped that that would mean things would get better, and they're not. We've just been struggling for so long, and we need things to get better or at least see the evidence that things are improving."

"I can promise you that we are working on it," I say, but even I know that a statement like that is wildly inadequate. "I really do wish we could deliver faster."

"These are very complex processes," Secretary Johnson says, and I know a comment like that won't go over well. "It is certainly not the policy of the Everhart family to steamroll any operation or department because it would violate the independence of those organizations. It is important to us to respect those operations and work together to find a solution."

"If Princess Lorraine, as acting queen, can't do anything quickly because it would be an overstep of power, then why do we even have a queen?" Erin says. "It seems like maybe something about this system isn't working."

"I'm doing everything I can," I say. It isn't a particularly warm day, and still, I can feel the sweat beading on my forehead.

"We need money, Princess," says a young woman with several children clinging to her clothes. "We respect you, but we're barely getting by."

"Is Eterand going to get involved somehow?" Mr. Poulos says. "We've all see Prince Alex around town. Is he here to help?"

"He is here to help," I say, but I actually still don't really know why he's here.

"But only within the appropriate bounds of our alliance," Johnson says. "He is restricted by our sovereignty as a nation."

"Somebody has to do something," says a journalist that I can't quite identify. "I think we're past the point of rejecting help based on alliance documents."

"Our sovereignty has to be most important," I say.

Several people complain audibly, but one voice comes above the others. "Our well-being has to be most important."

Erin says, "Does our sovereignty really matter after we removed a dictator and a foreign dignitary is snooping around?"

Another citizen shouts, "Nothing has changed. This is just as bad as it was under Cassandra Wellington." Several murmur agreement.

My eyes are stinging, and I'm afraid that if I try to say anything that I'll babble incoherently or say something that will make everything worse. It doesn't feel like there's a right thing to say right now. I look over to Brent and silently plead for help. He nods but urges me to speak again.

"Please know that I hear your concerns," I say. "Nothing is more important to me than all of you. But if I'm going to help, I must get back to work and focus on new work in light of the concerns expressed today. Are there any final questions I can answer?"

"Please fix our country, Princess," says Eddie Poulos. "We desperately need it."

"I will," I say. "I promise. I will do everything I can."

"Thank you all for coming today," Johnson says as he stands and urges me to stand as well. "We greatly appreciate it. When we have more news, we will schedule another town hall, and we hope you will all attend again."

Johnson and I walk off stage and back into the building while Brent says some concluding remarks, but my hearing feels muffled like I'm underwater. That felt like everyone was a lot angrier than they even let on, and they let on quite a bit.

We turn down the hallway, and when we reach Johnson's office, he smiles sadly.

"Try not to stress out about it," he says. "You and I know how much work we're doing. Things will get better even if they don't see it yet."

I nod and try to convince him that I believe what he says, but I don't, and I suspect that he knows anyway. He pats me on the shoulder, smiles again, and says, "I'll see you at the next Parliament meeting."

I nod again and walk straight down the hallway.

"Lorraine," Brent says behind me. Lorraine, wait."

"No, Brent," I say, not slowing down or turning around.

"It'll be fine, I promise."

I spin on my heel. "Don't make promises you can't keep."

Brent looks taken aback, and I know I've said too much, that I've gone too far, but the panic is rising in my throat. I turn back and keep walking. I hear Brent still calling out behind me, but I wave him off without turning around to look at him this time and keep walking.

Hopefully, I don't lose it before I reach the office. Once I get there, I throw the door open, causing a very startled Zane to jump off the desk where he was sitting, turn off the TV, and smile.

I walk straight into Zane's arms and press my face into his chest, hoping that if all I can see is a red blur from his shirt and all I can smell is the ocean salt on his skin, then maybe I can pretend to forget what just happened. I intertwine my fingers together behind his waist and hope that he doesn't let go too soon.

"It wasn't as bad as you think," he says.

"You're just saying that," I mumble into his shirt buttons. "It was bad. They hate me."

"They don't hate you. They're just worried. It's natural."

"I just feel like I'm doing so much work all the time to try to fix this, and none of it is having any impact for people, which is all I want. It's just—"

"Just what?"

"Nothing."

Zane sits us both down on the chaise and holds my hands in his so gently and yet so firmly. I wonder if there will ever be a time that that doesn't feel so healing.

"Tell me." When I don't say anything right away, he adds, "Who am I gonna tell if you totally trash somebody? It's not like anybody listens to me."

I can't help but laugh a little bit, but what does he mean by that? Nobody listens to him? His words from the other day about Alex come back to me, about how Alex didn't think he was important. Nothing could be further from the truth—Zane is the most important person in the world to me.

"Sometimes I feel like Parliament just gets in my way, which sounds absolutely terrible."

"Why does it sound terrible?"

I huff. "You didn't really know her, but that sounds exactly like Cassandra. That's the kind of garbage she used to say because they always wanted to stop her from being a tyrant. I just sound like an overbearing monarch."

He kisses me on the cheek. "You don't. You could never sound like that. But based on what you've told me, Parliament is willing to work with you. They're just cautious. Wouldn't you be?"

"Of course. I don't want to make a mistake and make everything worse for Trillandites, but I have to do something, and they don't trust me."

"So what if they don't trust you?"

"What?"

Zane sighs and grits his teeth. "Does it really matter if they don't trust you? You're the soon-to-be queen. Do you need their approval to do something?"

"Well, yes, because the structure of Trilland's government prevents too much power resting anywhere, which is why Cassandra couldn't do more damage than she already did while I was gone. But even if I didn't, is that really the kind of queen I want to be? Just running over Parliament because I want to?"

"But what you want to do is help people, so it's not the same as Cassandra."

I shift a little and bite the inside of my mouth. "It's a dangerous precedent to set. I can't take advantage of my power."

Zane jumps up and starts pacing around the room. "It's not taking advantage when it's your power. You could do so much good with your position. I can't even begin to fathom the stuff that I would do in your position. I wish I had the kind of power that you have. Can you imagine what I could've done for Maris Island if it had a government like Trilland's and I was involved? It's a huge opportunity that you have been given and worked for, and I can't believe that you consider it a negative."

"I don't consider it a negative, but it's a responsibility that comes with a lot of trouble. I just don't know how to avoid the problems that come with it."

"It's worth it though. I wish I had those kinds of problems."

"Having power isn't that simple. Is that what you think this is for me? Just one big opportunity with no downsides?"

Zane sighs. "Of course not. I'm just trying to help you see the positives. You have the power to enact real change. I wish I had that sometimes."

Is this how Zane has felt about me being queen this whole time? Is he right, or does he not understand the dangers of a government like this? And does questioning his potential understanding or lack thereof make me a terrible person?

"The pressure is just unbelievable," I say, standing to mimic Zane. "The expectations of these people are so high because of my father and Cassandra and my return, and I can't possibly live up to them."

"You don't have to live up to them. You just have to show that you care and fix the problem."

"How can I possibly fix the problem? And you're wrong, I do have to live up to that. I'm some kind of superhero to them, and that's not what I signed up for by being born royal and then getting hit in the head. I'm not equipped to follow through on their high hopes."

Zane runs his hands through his hair and sighs in frustration. "Maris, you're not a superhero because these people think you're going to make everything perfect as soon as you become queen. You're a hero to them because you came back and because you care. They know that you aren't totally prepared for this position and that you're doing your best. They're just anxious to see progress, and they don't necessarily understand why it's not happening sooner."

"It's because of my stupid amnesia."

"It's not."

I throw my arms in the air and let them fall to my side with a thud. "It is. That's why I lost so much time and didn't come back sooner, and that's why Cassandra caused all the damage she did."

He takes the sides of my arms in his hands and squeezes them warmly. "You are not the reason Cassandra did what she did. She did what she did because she was a selfish, angry, vindictive, power hungry person who didn't care who she hurt getting what she wanted. You're here to pick up the pieces, and that's what you're going to do."

"But my amnesia is the venue she used."

"She caused the amnesia."

"But how can I possibly expect Trilland to understand that?" The words I've been suppressing for months rise in my throat, and briefly, I wonder if I will say them or vomit them. I haven't said these words to anyone, much less Zane because I know how he'll react, but they seem impossible to prevent now. "How can I expect them to trust me if I don't tell them?"

"Tell them what?" Zane says, though I suspect he knows the answer.

"I have to tell them about my amnesia."

"Oh Maris, no," he says quieter than I expected. "You purposely made the decision not to tell them because it would protect them and prevent panic or attacks."

"And it was the right decision at the time, but maybe now it's not. Maybe if they knew, they wouldn't be so hostile toward me about the lost time. Maybe they would understand that I really am trying my best."

"They do understand that."

"It doesn't feel like it."

He sighs, but it isn't an angry or frustrated one this time. "You have to give them time."

"It's been nearly a year."

"I mean time to see what you're doing to help. Town halls like this do make a difference. They show you care. It's going to make a difference to them one day. Think about when you pitched the annexation to the island. I didn't think anyone would go for that, but you convinced them because they believed in you. They may not have totally trusted it, but they trusted you. That's what you can have with Trilland. That's what I always wished I had on the island."

"You do have that on the island."

He smiles, but the vacancy in the smile and the sadness in his eyes tell me that he doesn't believe me.

<h1 style="text-align:center">Chapter 7</h1>

I had hoped that the town hall would give me the reassurance that I'm doing the right thing, that I'm making the right decisions, that Trilland supports me.

I hadn't really believed I would get that, but deep down, I had hoped.

The navy visit didn't go exactly as I planned, and now that the town hall was a complete catastrophe, I feel panicky at the thought of even walking into the oceanography labs right now, but Brent doesn't stop walking, and since he's behind me, I can't stop either.

As a child, I liked visiting the labs. They're right on the water, and they don't feel as sterile and rigid as labs usually do. They were always busy with activity, excitement, and life. The passion practically oozed out of the walls.

When I was little, the scientists were like heroes to Trilland. They were an opportunity for Trilland to be something more than just a fishing town. They were ahead of the curve, something reminiscent of what Eterand already was, what Trilland could be someday. It was always a hit to the budget, but it was a hit Trilland could endure at the time. Fishing was successful enough, and our foreign relations were stable enough that other areas of the budget could sustain the research.

Now, it's hemorrhaging money, and all the scientists think I have it out for the department. The last thing I want to do is cut this program. I love it, and I really think it benefits the country overall. I just don't know how to fix all the problems Cassandra created. How is it even possible that she caused this much damage in such a short amount of time?

Brent holds the door for me, and when I walk in, the lab still looks the same and even smells the same—that smell of disinfectant mingled with ocean spray—but it doesn't feel the same. There's a tension in here that's palpable and new. If I'm honest with myself, I hadn't been here for a couple years before the mutiny, so I don't really know if Cassandra is the cause for that, but somehow, I feel like I know that she is.

Dr. Angelos and Dr. Galanis meet me in the lobby. Dr. Angelos is a younger man who just recently became one of the lab heads, but the stress of the job is already weighing into lines on his face. He still exudes a certain energy, but the worry in his eyes is undeniable. Dr. Galanis has been here since I was a child. When I would visit with my father, she always had a special project for me to do while my father worked. The tasks were really simple when I was really young, like counting the starfish in the tank or counting how many times the scientists said "where's the lab report?" When I got older, she would let me do more, like cleaning lab equipment, transferring coral from one tank to another, or shadowing a lab tech to learn about their job. In hindsight, I realize she was probably just trying to keep me busy, but I always felt so special that she prepared something for me to do, no matter how trivial. She's a big part of the reason I enjoyed visits to the lab. I wish it were still that way. I wish I would hear her tell me now to count the starfish or clean the beakers, but everything is so much more complicated.

"Good morning, Princess," Dr. Galanis says, giving me a warm handshake and smile. I've never had a sense of how old she is because she's kind of always looked the same. She has that warm, grandmotherly appearance. I wonder if she has grandchildren, or children for that matter. I'm disappointed with myself that I've never thought to ask.

"Good morning," I say.

Dr. Angelos greets me as well before directing his attention to Brent. He's clearly the new worker bee that has taken my spot. Dr. Galanis must have tasked him with managing the press communications with Brent.

"I'm very glad you're here," Dr. Galanis says as we start walking the halls. "It's been a very long time since I've seen you here."

"It has," I say, and it's true. I think I only visited once or twice after my parents died. Secretary Johnson and Uncle Lawrence kind of handled things for a while. "I hope to visit more often now. The lab was always one of my favorite places to visit."

Maybe it's my imagination, but I get the sense that several of the scientists stiffened at my mention of visiting more often. I just want to scream, *I'm not here to shut you down, I promise,* but that wouldn't look good on camera.

"I'm certainly hopeful of what will come of your visit. I know you're trying to help." Did she see the stiffening, too?

"Absolutely," I say, attempting to exude as much positivity as possible. Maybe it just comes across as really fake. Is there a difference right now? "So, what is your biggest concern right now?"

Dr. Galanis sighs and beckons me into one of the smaller labs. "Cost of equipment. We're using extremely outdated equipment. Science is always evolving, and things become outdated so quickly, but we haven't updated anything since your father's time, and it wasn't exactly state-of-the-art then. I'm afraid we're spending more time repairing broken equipment than conducting actual research."

"What would the cost be of getting new equipment?" I ask. "Even just replacing some of it?"

She hands me an order quote. "Too much, unfortunately." When I look at the numbers, I have to make a conscious effort not to let my eyes pop open on camera. It's a lot. It's nearly as much as we spend on our entire military combined to replace everything. Even replacing some of it is beyond Trilland's budget right now. If I could cut cost somewhere else, maybe I could replace some, and that research would bring in revenue, and we could replace more.

"Is there anyway to increase productivity without new technology just yet? Maybe with new funds coming in, we could cover the cost of this equipment over time."

She points to the docks. "Follow me. I'd like to show you something."

Her evasive answers make me not want to follow her, but of course I have to. Docked outside is one of the research boats the department uses to go out for on-site research. Sometimes removing the wildlife harms the ecosystems, so research has to be done remotely.

When we get on board, she walks me over to a couple of scientists who are preparing to head out. She says, "May I interrupt for a moment? I'd like to show Princess Lorraine the equipment before you head out."

They nod and walk away, but they eye me nervously. Again, I have the urge to scream and don't.

Dr. Galanis picks up one of the underwater cameras. It's rusty, and the plastic coating creaks when she picks it up. "This is our best underwater camera right now. It still works well, but it doesn't hold a charge for very long. The crew has about an hour, maybe two on a good day, to capture their material. Sometimes you don't find what you're looking for for a few hours." She picks up a small device. "These are our salinometers."

"What?" Brent says.

"They're used to measure salinity of the water—the saltiness of the ocean," she adds when Brent still looks confused. "We mostly use these in the lab for the tanks, but we have to know the salinity of the sea to make the tanks correctly and to know how weather, fishing, and other factors are affecting the water. Most of them overheat in the sun. We try to keep them in coolers when on the boat, but in the summer, the heat is fierce, and they'll turn off if they overheat."

"This is a Ule scale," she says, holding up what looks like a sound mixer. "We use it to track the changes in the color of the sea water. The color is indicative of the sea's health. These are very old, so they don't have as many features as we'd like. Plus, they are not waterproof. We have the same problems with our fathometers, which measure depth."

"What kind of oceanography tool is not waterproof?" Brent says.

Dr. Galanis points at him and smiles. "Exactly. In addition, it also works with a charge and is experiencing the same issues of holding charge as the cameras."

She leans against the railing of the boat. "I could keep going, but I think you get the idea. Most of this equipment has broken several times, and we've had to repair it. At this point, it's not just not helping, it's slowing us down. I realize the cost of new equipment is high, but this department simply cannot function without it."

"Can anything be done to make this equipment more sustainable?" I say. "I'd hate to spend a lot only for it to break in a short amount of time."

"Nearby countries with more advanced departments are shifting to solar powered devices, but the cost of those is even higher than the quote I gave you. However, they do last for many, many years. Eterand has been using the same solar powered equipment for nearly a decade now."

"But if they're so expensive, are they a viable option?" Brent asks.

"Yes. We wouldn't need many of them. These devices don't require a lot of power, and even just a few would make a big difference. I just don't know where the funding for those would come from."

I lean against the railing opposite Dr. Galanis. "It seems like finding a solution is going to be extremely challenging, then."

Dr. Galanis lowers her voice, but the cameras still pick it up. "You know, Princess, as much as it pains me to say this, temporarily cutting this program might be for the best. I believe in this research, but maybe it's just not possible right now."

"No," I say a little too quickly. When everyone around me jumps, I make a point of locking eyes with the scientists and talking loudly for the cameras. "I'm not cutting this program. That would mean lost jobs and lost revenue, not to mention the importance of protecting our ecosystems. We'll just have to find a way to get you the funding you need."

"I certainly hope you can solve the enigma, Princess," she says with a smile, but it isn't quite as warm as it was before. It seems to say, *There's nothing you can do, but it's sweet that you want to try.*

We walk off the boats back into the labs, and the scientists all follow me, listening to somewhat empty promises I make about not cutting funding. At the end of the day, I'm not sure if I'll have to cut funding. It might be the only option. The only other option is the navy.

"Thank you for your visit, Princess," Dr. Galanis says as she opens the door for me. Dr. Angelos also shakes my hand and offers a heartfelt smile. "I'm very glad you are back."

"Thank you," I say, but a thought I didn't wish for enters my mind: *Am I glad that I'm back?*

~~~

Uncle Lawrence meets us outside with a big smile and a bear hug. One thing that never fails to make me laugh is when he gets Brent with one of those hugs. He always looks startled and just a little afraid to be lifted into the air like that.

"So, how did it go?" he asks.

I shrug half-heartedly. "Dr. Galanis is great, of course, but there's nothing I can do for her or for any of them with the budget the way it is. There's just no money to help them."

"Have you given suspending the research temporarily any more thought?"

I look around to see if the cameras have clicked off, and I'm glad to see they have. "I just can't do that. That research is important."

"I'm not saying it's not, but maybe other things are more important right now."

Yeah, and other things are more important than military on Eterand's border and around the provinces. "It's just not an area I'm willing to sacrifice. It sounds like they're already struggling with the limited funding they have. Funds have to come from elsewhere."

"Like where? I don't think we can cut anywhere else."

I risk a glance at Brent, and he twitches his mouth into the slightest smile and nods, just enough for me to see, just enough for me to know what he's trying to say: *You have to tell him.*

"Uncle Lawrence, I'm concerned about the navy's spending. I've been meaning to talk to you about it."

"What do you mean you're concerned?"

"Look, you know I respect you and how well you run this military, but the amount of forces near Eterand and the outer provinces is
~~~

excessive. Eterand is not our enemy, and the provinces certainly are not our enemy."

"I never said they were." He folds his arms. "But I'm not leaving anything to chance."

"But this is why we have allies. What's the point of an ally if they can't help you out when you need it? I've talked to Alex since he's gotten here, and he's assured me he and his father would step in if needed."

"You know I love the Cartwright family, but they're not Trilland. I'm not putting your safety in someone else's hands."

"And what about the outer provinces? Do you really think Anden is dangerous?" I gesture toward Brent. "And Gessend? Are they really a threat?"

"No, of course not, but—"

"They're angry, Uncle Lawrence. They think we don't trust them. They feel like they're under military occupation out there, and how can I possibly tell them they're wrong when naval fleets are in their waters?"

"My job is to secure our border, and that's what I'm doing."

"But we don't need wartimes-level fleets crawling all over our waters. I don't trust Riagala either, but we don't need this much to protect our country."

"What are you saying?"

I close my eyes and take a deep breath before opening them again. "I'm saying that I think we need to cut back a little. It would save a lot of money, and our waters would still be secure."

"So that's it? You've made your decision? You're cutting the navy?"

I let out a huff. "No, I'm not saying that. I'm just saying what we currently have is too excessive for our current budget."

"Excessive?"

"No I didn't mean it like that—"

He waves a hand at me. "No, that's all right. I think I understand."

I lower my voice. "I didn't want to have this conversation like this in front of the oceanography labs, but it's a conversation we needed to have."

"I got it. Don't worry about it," he says in a way that does make me worry. "I'll pull back by the outer provinces and some in Eterand. I'll have someone get you the budget report."

He turns sharply in the military way and walks away without waiting for an answer. I have the undeniable urge to burst into tears, and even though the cameras are off, the crew is still lurking, and a lot of people are walking by, so I suppress it as best I can. Brent steps a little closer to me, and after a slight hesitation, rests a hand on my shoulder.

"He'll be okay," he says. "He's just a little mad."

"More than a little."

"He'll calm down. It'll be okay."

Sure, he might calm down, but will it be okay?

Chapter 8

One thing I definitely do not remember about childhood—and I'm pretty sure it's not because of my memory issues—is seeing my father sign papers for hours. It seems there is at least one day a week that Brent brings me a pile of papers to sign, and it takes forever. Maybe my father kindly did not make me watch the boring process. Maybe after your nation survives a dictator there's just a lot of paperwork. I can feel my hand cramping.

"Only two more," Brent says, as if he read my mind. He's gotten pretty good at doing that these days.

"Thank goodness," I say with a laugh. "What are these?"

Brent slides a paper in front of me. "This is the press release from the oceanography lab visit."

I glance up at him. "You've read it?" He nods. "Does it sound okay?"

"It wasn't written by Erin," he says, a small smile spreading on his face. "It's flattering."

I sign the paper and hold it up for Brent to take, but when he doesn't, I look up to see him staring at me with a confused expression. "What?"

"You don't want to read it?"

I shrug. "You said it's fine. I trust you."

"Really?"

"It's better if I don't read every press release about me. They make me a little uncomfortable."

"No, I mean—" He sits down in the chair across from me on the other side of the table. "Could we talk for a moment? Not about business."

I sit up a little straighter. There's a number of directions this could potentially go. "Of course."

He seems to struggle for a moment to find what he wants to say, opening and closing his mouth a few times before letting out a small huff. "How do you feel about me? As your press secretary, I mean."

"You've been wonderful. Honestly, you're way more helpful than I think you realize, than I even expected you to be."

"I'm glad to hear that." He fidgets with the papers in his lap. "I want you to think well of me."

"I do."

"I can't help but feel like we never fully got past everything that happened. Lorraine, are you still angry with me for withholding information about your memory loss from Captain Wilson?"

"No," I say so immediately that I surprise even myself. I hadn't really given it any thought, and if I had, I kind of assumed I was still hurting from all of that. But somewhere along the line something changed. When I look at Brent now, the last thing I think is anger.

"Are you sure?"

"Positive. I was angry for a while. You know that. We don't have to relive it. I'm not sure I could even tell you when I stopped being upset with you, but I do know that I don't know how I would have made it through this year without you."

He smiles, but it's cautious. "That means a lot."

"I hope you haven't been thinking I hated you this whole time," I say, managing to elicit a laugh. "The fact is that I never would have made it back to Trilland without you."

"Oh, I don't believe that. Somehow, I think you would have found a way."

"But you were a big part of it. I'll always be indebted to you for that."

He shifts in his seat. "That's my other concern. Am I only your press secretary because you feel bad?"

"Are you only my press secretary because *you* feel bad?"

"No, of course not."

I nod. "Same here. Brent, you're not a pity job. You never have been. You're exceptionally good at this job."

Although it was awkward at the start, now that we're having this conversation, I'm so glad. It feels like we're finally tackling all of the issues we've had this whole time that have just gone unspoken. We've been avoiding reality and the tension between us, and it's only made it worse. Maybe now we'll finally be able to push past the weirdness.

"This might be presumptuous of me to say, but if you'll have me, I'd like to have a career in Trilland. Maybe we could discuss that sometime soon?"

I practically exhale a sigh of relief. "Absolutely. I can't do this without you."

He smiles again, but this time, it seems genuine. I catch a glimpse of the old Brent, the Brent I knew on the island who helped me regain my memory, who refused to let me give up when everything seemed hopeless. I've missed that Brent.

"Okay, he says, "only one more thing to sign."

"Finally."

"It's Prince Alex's statement to be distributed to the citizens of Trilland and the provinces. Policy dictates that it has to be approved by you first."

I start skimming the document. "Nothing weird in here, I assume?"

"No," Brent says, but something in his voice seems unsure, and I look up at him. "I didn't mean to make it sound bad. It's perfectly fine."

"But?"

"I don't really think it's my place to criticize the crown prince of Eterand."

"It's just the two of us. Didn't we just decide to be honest with each other?"

"It's a little self-congratulatory," he says, wincing.

"That's not really surprising. Alex always had that kind of streak in him."

"I'm not sure it's appropriate for an address he's directing at Trilland's citizens, not Eterand's."

It's a valid point. I take a few more moments to read it more thoroughly. It isn't long, and I see why Brent is objecting. Alex does kind of make a show of commending himself for coming to negotiate the alliance renewal himself. It's tradition—my father and his used to take turns visiting each other—but Alex makes it sound like something special he did. I imagine it's just a little bit of insecurity bleeding through. I know he's nervous about transition to being king. It's probably harmless, but I definitely don't need more bad press right now, so I make a few edits to the document and sign at the bottom.

"He's not a bad guy," I say.

"I believe you."

I smirk. "Do you?"

"I trust you. You know him far better than I do."

"At least you're calmer than Zane."

Now he's the one who smirks. "Oh, I imagine he's just thrilled with Alex's presence."

"Ecstatic."

"Zane will be fine," he says, and I wonder why he feels so confident saying so. He picks up Alex's statement. "I'll add these edits and send it off."

"Thank you."

Brent shuts his portfolio. "No problem. That's everything for today."

"No, seriously, thank you. For everything."

Brent smiles, bows his head ever so slightly, and leaves the room. In spite of the chaos of the last few days, I feel a little more confident knowing I have Brent fully in my corner again.

Chapter 9

"We're very proud of our reading program," says Headmistress Vaughn. "Our secondary scores have increased twelve percent since last year, and our elementary scores have increased more than twenty percent."

"That's impressive," I say. Walking around the schools today, I find it funny that they still look exactly the same as when I was a child and toured them with my mother. Sure, the buildings have been maintained, but the overall feel of the school is still the same.

I was always a little jealous that I couldn't go to school here. I wanted to, and I took a few classes here as a child, but mostly, I had to be tutored at home to allow for my training as a royal. I used to beg Jane to tell me absolutely everything about her school day. It seemed like such a happy place. Still does.

"If you still have time, I'd love to show you the high school wing."

"I'd love to see it. I've always got time for our students." I try to smile without it looking too fake for the cameras. I do genuinely care about the schools, but the press from the last two visits hasn't exactly been favorable. Too many citizens feel like I'm meddling. Education is something I actually have a lot of knowledge about and passion for. It'd be nice if this visit went better than the last two.

We walk down a kind of narrow hallway that opens up into a big common area. The walls here are painted a light seafoam green, a contrast to the pale blue hallways in the elementary building, and the whole area feels just a little colder than everywhere else. I think that's how it always is with schools. The elementary buildings are warm and full of nurturing, fun energy; the secondary buildings are strictly functional. I know the schools have enough funding to function, but I can't help but think what they could do with a little more.

I wish I had worn different shoes for this visit. It's been a lot more walking than I anticipated, and the three-inch heels I'm wearing are just not cutting it. Unfortunately, it probably would not look very professional for me to take them off and go barefoot, no matter how beachy Trilland is. Even the students aren't allowed to do that, let alone the future queen.

"This is our high school common area. All the main subject class-rooms are down those two hallways and the electives are down those two. This is actually a fantastic day for you to visit because the science and technology classes are having a fair today where they are present-ing their studies."

I take a look at Brent, and he gives me a wink. His scheduling skills are exceptional.

We walk into the science classroom, which is bigger than the others to accommodate lab tables, and start circulating through the different projects. There are standard ones like simple electricity experiments or erupting volcanoes as well as more complex ones that the older students have created. I hesitate at the project of one young man because it looks fishing related.

"What is your project about?" I ask.

The boy stares at me with wide eyes. "You-you want to hear about *my* project?"

"Absolutely. I'm very interested in fishing."

"Wow."

"Don't keep Her Highness waiting, Dennis," Headmistress Vaughn says with gentle reproach, and Dennis immediately straightens up and grins.

"My dad is a fisherman, and he always tells me about how his nets break too easily. When they haul in big catches, the nets can't support the weight. They lose a lot of fish, and sometimes, the fish die before they can be brought onto the ship. It's a big economic loss and harmful for Trilland's waters."

"That sounds like a big problem, Dennis," I say. "So, what can we do about it?"

"My solution is two-fold," Dennis says, putting his hand on his puffed up chest and smiling with pride. "First, the nets will be made of a three-cord braided rope that won't break as easily as the current one-cord style. Each strand of the rope will be three times stronger. Then, each rope will be tied in a triangle pattern instead of a diamond pattern so that there is more rope surface area and smaller holes for the fish to slip through. These nets will be nearly unbreakable."

"Wonderful idea, Dennis," Headmistress Vaughn says.

"May I ask you a question?" I say, and he nods. "Your net idea sounds like a fantastic solution, but braiding the rope and then tying closely knit nets would utilize more rope on the manufacturing side, making the cost of materials and labor to make the nets go up. Is the cost sustainable for our fishing industry?"

Dennis twists his mouth and bites the inside of his cheek. He looks just a little deflated, and I briefly worry that I've just crushed this poor kid's dreams, but then he perks up again and says, "I think so. If the fishermen lose less fish, then they have more profit. The profit from the nets should more than offset the cost of making them."

I smile brightly. "I agree. What a wonderful idea, Dennis. I'd love for you and your family to join me for dinner one day so we can pitch your idea to the fishing department. I think we should implement your idea as soon as possible."

"Really?" Somehow, Dennis's eyes get even wider than they were before.

"Definitely. Your idea could make a big difference for Trilland. Thank you so much for telling me about it. I'm looking forward to meeting your parents and commending them for raising such a smart young man."

We keep walking through the fair, but I take a quick glance back at Dennis, and I'm happy to see that he looks absolutely ecstatic. Maybe I do know what I'm doing—at least with kids.

"I think you made his day," Headmistress Vaughn says.

I chuckle. "It seems like it. He really does have a very good idea."

"I'm so glad you think so. He has struggled in school quite a bit recently."

"Why is that?"

"His mother passed away almost a year ago."

"Oh no, I'm so sorry to hear that."

"Well, it was more than that. Their family doesn't have a lot of money. She was a teacher here. When she passed, his family lost a significant source of income as well as a family member. His father has been struggling to pay the bills ever since. I think Dennis is so passionate about improving the fishing industry because he knows it will help his father make more money. Unfortunately, under Cassandra's reign, a lot of costs skyrocketed, and he's been struggling to keep up."

I don't say anything right away because I don't know what to say. I become acutely aware that I need to say something, anything, because the cameras are running, but what can I possibly say that will bring this boy's mother back and fix his father's finances?

Headmistress Vaughn starts fidgeting with her hands, tugging at a hangnail on her finger. "I'm sorry to bring up Cassandra, Your Highness, but the sting of her actions is still felt by many, especially in the working class."

"No, don't apologize for that. I want to know where her damage was most severe so I know the places that need help most urgently. I really do think Dennis's project will make a big difference. I want to get that going as soon as possible. Hopefully, it will encourage his father and the other fishermen as well."

"I've no doubt that it will," she says with a smile. "I'd like you to meet one of our juniors, Amelia Yearling. She's one of our brightest students. She's on track to be valedictorian of her class. She's very interested in science, specifically technology, and I think you'll find her idea very promising as well."

We walk to the back of the room and find that one project seems to be attracting a lot of attention, so I can only assume it is Amelia's. When we get a little closer, I see a young woman with more confidence than I currently possess, and I find myself almost envious of this sixteen-year-old who seems to derive so much power from herself. I'm so close in age to her, and the few measly years I have on her feel so inconsequential. Maybe one day, I will be able to command a room the way that she does. I can see that the crowds she's drawing are here for more than her idea: they're here for inspiration and hope, and she seems to be delivering.

"Amelia," Headmistress Vaughn says loudly enough so Amelia will hear past all the people, "Her Highness would like to hear about your idea."

The crowds part a little so that the two of us along with Brent and the camera crew can approach. I take a quick look at her display, but something tells me Amelia's verbal presentation will be far more impressive, so I stop reading to avoid spoiling the impact.

"Certainly," Amelia says with an easy smile. What a difference from the boy who lacked confidence. "Trilland is known for many things, and chief among those are all the different projects we have related to the ocean: fishing, naval defenses, tourism, and of course, oceanography. However, the cost of ocean research continues to skyrocket, and it is difficult for a nation of our size to sustain our research as is with costs climbing." Watching Amelia is truly inspiring. She could hold her own in Parliament. "I believe that solar power is the answer here."

"Why do you say that?" I ask.

"Microscopes, imaging computers, and other tools that our oceanographers use regularly could all be run on solar power."

This is exactly what Dr. Galanis said. If I'm lucky, maybe this girl has an idea. "Solar power is often expensive, especially in the beginning implementation stages. Is this economically possible?"

"Absolutely." Amelia talks me through her research into solar panels, how she interned at the plant that produces them, how she figured out exactly how much solar power each device would need and what size solar panel is needed to produce that energy, and though I don't totally understand all of the science and research behind it, I can tell that she does. She also has references from all of the scientists and manufacturers she worked with affirming that her calculations are sound. If her plan works as intended, this could significantly reduce the costs of our scientific research without cutting any of the actual research. This idea from this high school student could nearly fix Trilland's budget if it works.

Of course, my father was never really into technology, but maybe it's time that changed. Maybe now is the right time for Trilland to start considering technological advances. It's scary to think of stepping outside of my father's clearly defined shadow, but maybe this is the right thing.

"Well, Amelia, this is very impressive," I say. "Your idea shows significant promise. Could you develop a proposal to deliver to Parliament?"

"Are you serious, Your Highness?" Headmistress Vaughn says.

I nod enthusiastically. "Absolutely. This idea could be exactly what Trilland needs. I'm very excited about it, and I think Parliament will be, too."

Amelia grins, and for the first time, she looks like a teenager. "I'd be happy to do that. Thank you so much for this opportunity, Your Highness."

We keep walking through the science fair, and we talk to a few more students with promising ideas. I've been stressing about what to do for weeks if not months, and little did I know that most of the answers were right here. The young people really are the future. Zane's words float back into my mind: they are the dreamers we've needed this whole time.

Brent pulls me aside while the cameraman is making some adjustments and says, "This is perfect, Lorraine. This is going so much better than I even hoped. I think this is going to help your image a lot."

I smile and thank Brent for what he said, and I hope it's true, but looking around at the pure intelligence, inspiration, and hope that these kids have created and are offering to the rest of Trilland, somehow my image doesn't seem to matter as much anymore.

~~~

Despite the burning that is somehow persisting in my numb feet that have since swollen to a size beyond my size 7 pumps, I feel positively elated and carefree walking back to the palace. The visits at the school went well, everyone seems to have regained some faith in me,
~~~

and I actually have some really good ideas to take to Parliament. I was hoping that visiting the schools would be a kind of morale booster for me at the very least, but it turned out to be so much more than that.

"I can't wait to get home and start drafting those proposals," I say to Brent, who keeps with me in pace but not in energy. "I didn't think I'd ever be so excited about drafting proposals, but here we are."

"Didn't you ask the kids to draft their own proposals?" he says.

"Yes, but I don't want them walking into a cold room. I'm going to make a soft proposal first. You know, get Parliament at least semi on board before a couple of kids walk in and get eaten alive."

"I hope this works out the way you want it to."

I stop and turn to face him. "You don't think it will?"

"I didn't say that."

"You implied it."

Brent sighs, but it isn't the sigh of someone who thinks I'm being ridiculous; it's a sigh I can't quite identify. "Lorraine, I really do hope this works out. I haven't seen you this happy since—I don't think I've ever seen you this happy. I just want you to be happy and for Trilland to be safe. If this is the answer, then so be it. I want Trilland to succeed as much as you do."

I smile. It's nice that things with Brent are easy and natural again. "I don't think that's possible."

He allows himself to smirk just a little before forcing a professional expression back on his face. "If you say so."

When we reach the palace, I'm happy to see Zane waiting for us outside. Well, for me. I doubt he was really waiting for Brent.

I sort-of-hop-sort-of-run as much as my aching feet will allow me straight for Zane, and luckily, he meets me halfway with a hug and a kiss. Brent smiles awkwardly and tries to duck past us, but Zane reaches out his hand, and Brent tentatively shakes it.

"How'd it go?" he says to neither of us in particular.

"Really well," Brent says. "Everyone adored Lorraine."

"Obviously," Zane says.

Brent smiles, genuinely this time. "It was a big success. If you'll excuse me, I have to get to putting together the official statement right away. I'll bring you a draft later tonight, okay?"

I nod. "Thanks for everything today. I really appreciate all your work."

"My pleasure." And with that, he's gone again. Every time we speak, it's just the tiniest bit less awkward than the time before, the tiniest bit less forced, more genuine. Hopefully one day I won't notice that subtle gradient in our relationship.

"So, tell me about it," Zane says as we walk straight through the entryway to the garden. Zane's favorite part of the palace is that garden. The whole thing has been a little much for him. It's far more extravagant than he's comfortable with even though I've tried to tell him it's one of the least extravagant palaces in all the neighboring countries. He claims the word "palace" negates that statement, and, I mean, I guess he has a point, but the garden is different. Most of the landscaping out here was done by my mother, so it has that familiar, maternal feel that no landscaper can possibly duplicate. Lady Vivian has been very strict with who maintains it so that it retains that feel. Luckily, Cassandra has never really been an outdoorsy type, so she mostly left the garden alone. She only changed the spots visible from her window, and Lady Vivian quickly put those back the way they were once I returned. I like that, for the most part, this garden still looks the way it did when I was young. Sometimes I feel that I might turn a corner and suddenly see my mother pruning roses, wearing the blue dress from before she was a royal that she always wore to garden for fear of ruining her new, expensive clothing.

"It went perfectly," I say. "Better than I could have hoped for. The schools are actually doing okay considering everything that's happened. Of course, they could always use a little more funding, but they're not hurting right now."

"That's fantastic."

"It gets better. The older students were having a kind of science fair, and I took a tour of their projects, and some of their ideas are truly incredible. One of them reminded me of you. This one boy's father is a fisherman, and he was worried about his father's livelihood, so he designed new fishing nets that won't break as easily."

We sit down on one of the benches deep in the garden, and I show Zane the picture I took with my phone of his net design, and he lights up with excitement.

"This is so cool. The nets we used back on the island were braided like this, but the triangle design is genius. I bet this would work."

"Based on the trials he ran for his project, it does. I asked him to put together a pitch for the fishing and manufacturing departments so that we can implement his design."

Zane grins widely. "You probably made that kid's day." He takes another look at the net design. "I can't wait to use this design. Will you market this to the other provinces as well? Could the island use it, too?"

"Of course. And this other girl, a junior, she has an idea that just might fix some of my budget concerns."

"How so?"

I explain Amelia's idea and how I think it could be implemented, and Zane listens carefully, but something about his expression—the furrowed brows, the twisted mouth—tells me that he isn't sold. I can't tell if he doesn't understand Amelia's idea much the same way I didn't when she first explained it to me or if he doesn't have confidence in the idea and therefore not in me.

"So," I say, "what do you think?"

"It's certainly an interesting idea. I'm not really sure if it work, but I guess it does have potential."

"Why wouldn't it work?"

He shrugs. "I don't know. Solar panels are really expensive to produce. I'm not sure this is really a cost-saving idea. It might do wonders for scientific research, but it sounds like it comes with a hefty price tag."

"What's that I hear about a hefty price tag?" Alex saunters around the corner with that classic smile of his—that smile that feels warm and yet a little too coy all at the same time. Zane quickly suppresses the irritation that flashes across his face. I'm sure he thinks Alex interrupted on purpose, but something about the cup of tea and rather casual beige dress pants and short-sleeve button down pink shirt tell me otherwise. Alex prefers that his clothes speak for him, and this look hardly screams "king."

"Alex," Zane says.

"How nice to see you," I say quickly before Zane's temper comes out in his voice, even if he's hiding it in his face. "What are you up to?"

"Just taking a stroll of the gardens. It's amazing how little they've changed."

"At my request," I say. "I like them this way. They remind me of my mother."

"Yes, it does look like her. I feel like I can still see her in these gardens. It was such a natural place for her."

"Yes, that's exactly how I feel."

For a moment, Alex looks just a little bit embarrassed. "I'm sorry to have interrupted. I didn't think you'd be back so soon today."

"Today was the visit at the schools, so I ended my day right after that."

"I assume it went well?"

"Very."

"She connects so naturally with the students," Zane says, and Alex nods enthusiastically.

"I actually think a few of them have some wonderful ideas that I'd like to implement in Trilland."

Zane squeezes my hand gently but enough to let me know that he doesn't think I should be including Alex in this conversation. Well, too late now.

"Like what?"

"Several students have ideas to improve function and process for a few of our industries. Not major changes, but changes that will make a significant difference in profit. But the one I'm really excited about is a student who has developed solar powered scientific instruments. Her idea is that our oceanographers could use them for their research because the equipment would be more durable and would provide more accurate data faster."

"That sounds fascinating."

"The concern is that solar panels are expensive to produce which is why we haven't been able to do it. It seems like the student might have found a way to make it more cost-effective. If it works, this might actually save Trilland some money, but if it costs too much, it will only cause more damage to the budget."

"We'd have to find a way to produce them affordably or cut costs elsewhere to compensate," Zane adds.

"Oh, I'm sure there's a way," Alex says. "You know, Eterand is quite known for our technology. We could help you find a way to produce these at the price you want, or we could even get the equipment to you in some kind of trade."

Trading with Eterand for their technology has always been an option, but despite our fathers' strong relationship, my father never did that, and even though I don't know why, something about that tells me it's a bad idea. My father never told why mostly because I never asked, but I feel like he would have if he thought it would benefit Trilland. But that was so long ago. Is it different now? Would this benefit Trilland now?

"I mean, I only just heard the idea today," I say. "I'm still weighing all of the options."

"Of course," Alex says. "Well, let me know if I can be of service. I'll get out of your hair now and let you get back to your evening stroll. By the way, are these new?" He points at the lilies planted in the center by the statue of my grandfather. "I don't remember your mother growing lilies."

Zane's head whips around and the cutest smile spreads across his face when he sees his mother's lilies. Not that I don't thoroughly enjoy the lilies myself, but having them planted there was worth that reaction from Zane alone.

"She didn't. She never much cared for them. Those are from Maris Island. Zane's mother grows them, and she sent me some as a gift."

"And you had them planted by your grandfather's statue? That's a place of high honor."

"Yes, it is," I say without adding more, and Zane squeezes my hand again, this time with gratitude.

Chapter 10

One of my favorite things about Maris Island was watching the fishermen work. It gave me a kind of peace that I didn't have on my own at the time. It was my favorite part of Gessend, too. So today, I decided to do something that I haven't done much at all since I got back to Trilland: I decided to watch the fishermen.

I haven't afforded myself this luxury because I feel like I'm skipping out on my responsibilities if I'm not always working, but I've done the three most important visits, and I think I need the break to think through everything. I know what I want to pitch to Parliament, and I've already got notes for what I want to remember to say. What I don't know is exactly how I'm going to do it. I have a feeling that Parliament is not going to react well, but I have to try something. Uncle Lawrence didn't take well to being told to cut back, and even if he does what I want him to do, it isn't going to come anywhere near to fixing everything. Trilland needs this.

But today, I need this. I need this break, this peace. The fishing in Trilland is obviously more commercial, and there's something lost watching them use their fancy equipment and boats instead of just wading in with nets like they do on the island, but it's still relaxing.

The best part about watching the fishermen is watching Zane. He looks at home here. It's kind of funny to see how he's almost taken over. The other fishermen allowed him to join them partially because they were open to hearing about his techniques and mostly because they're not going to turn away the soon-to-be-queen's boyfriend, but it looks like they're more than happy to have him now. As a kid, whenever I saw the fishermen, they were always laughing and joking around. I haven't seen that since I got back. Zane has brought a tiny bit of it back, but it seems like they're also bringing a spark back into Zane's life. I know he misses home, but seeing him like this makes me realize just how much.

They're just about wrapping up, so I head down to the docks and hang a right toward the beach where Zane is working. He spots me and waves, so I decide it's okay if I interrupt.

"Good evening, gentlemen," I say once I'm close enough. "How did it go today?"

"Better than usual," Derek says. After I came back, Derek Ingraham started volunteering extra time with the fishermen when he's not sailing. He seems to like it, and I'm happy to let him do whatever he wants. After all, he was instrumental in proving that Cassandra had lied and tried to murder me. It seems Derek and Zane have struck up a friendship. He grabs Zane by the shoulder and shakes him. "This guy is a gold mine of fishing information."

"Cool it, Derek, he's not all that," says John, one of the head fishermen, with a crooked smile. "Not sure the haul we get with him is worth all the chatter."

"I don't talk that much," Zane says.

"Uh, yeah, you do," I say.

"The princess agrees with us," John says, and the others cheer.

Zane raises his hands in surrender. "Fine, fine. I know better than to fight a losing battle." He turns to me as the others go back to sorting out nets. "What are you doing here?"

"I thought I'd watch for a little bit. I haven't checked in down here in a while."

"We're seeing improvement, especially with Zane's help, but we could be doing better," John says. He's kind of the unofficial leader of this group of fishermen who don't work full-time on the commercial boats. "The nets are still breaking way too often. Zane's teaching us some hand-fishing techniques that we can use on the fish that get away, but it's a big problem."

"Well, I might have a solution for you soon," I say. "I met a young man named Dennis at the high school science fair the other day with a new net design. I showed it to Zane, and he thinks it will work. It might be the answer you're looking for."

"Did you say Dennis?" one of the other fishermen says, and I nod. "That's my son."

"Oh yes, he mentioned his father was a fisherman." I put out my hand for a handshake, but he refuses, citing smelly fish guts smeared on his hands. "I'm so glad I get to meet you. Dennis raved about you."

"He did? I had no idea he entered the science fair. I guess I've been too busy working lately. I wish I had known."

"He designed the nets in your honor. He was hoping it would make your job easier."

He smiles just a little. "He doesn't have to worry about his old man. Thanks for being so kind to him. I'm sure it lifted his spirits."

"If I'm being honest, I wasn't trying to encourage him. I really do believe his idea will work."

He allows his smile to widen. "I'm glad to hear that."

"Well, I have to be going," I say, "but I'm glad I got a chance to see you all today. I hope to make more time for this in the future."

"We're happy to have you," John says. "Tomorrow, Zane?"

He nods. "See you then."

Zane takes my hand, and even though he smells a little fishy, I kind of like it. This is Zane. This is how I always knew him on the island: a little sunburned, soaking wet from the waist down, smelling like fish, and smiling. It may not be the best he's ever looked, but I love it all the same because it's real.

"So, what made you come down to the beach today?" he says as we take the long way back to the palace.

I shrug. "I haven't done it in a while. I miss watching the fishing on the island."

"Me, too. The actual fishing, I mean. I like helping these guys out, but it's not the same as Maris Island."

"Why is that? You miss everyone?"

"I mean, yeah, but it's just different. Tito and I didn't have to talk. We just knew what each other was going to do. I haven't known these guys my whole life, so it's kind of hard to have that sixth sense. But they're cool guys."

I nod. "I always used to watch them from my bedroom window." I point to the palace where my balcony is visible. "I guess that's why I liked watching you and the other guys on the island."

He flexes. "It's not because you just liked watching me?"

A chortle bursts out of my mouth. "Maybe partially."

We walk in silence for a little bit, but something Zane said the other day after the press conference keeps nagging at me. I haven't been able to shake it, but I haven't known how to bring it up. I think I'm afraid of what he'll say. "Do you miss the island?"

"Yeah, of course," he says with so little hesitation that my stomach surges. "But I like Trilland. I'm getting used to it."

"I don't want you just to get used to it. I want you to feel like you're at home."

"Anywhere you are is home."

"But is that enough?"

"What?"

"I'm just worried I made you give up everything by coming to Trilland with me."

Zane stops walking. "Okay, first of all, you didn't *make* me do anything. I decided to come here all on my own. And second, it's not like I gave up everything. I wanted to be with you, and I am."

"But your family and friends—"

"It's not like I never see them. Isn't this why you annexed the island, because you wanted to keep them close, too? It's way faster to get there and back now that I don't have to wait for merchant ships to come around."

"Yeah, but that was your home."

"And now this is."

"I just don't want you to resent me one day because you left for me."

He tilts my chin up so we look into each other's eyes. "Maris, I could never resent you. It was my decision, and I don't regret it. Sure, I miss a lot about the island, but I've found a lot that I like about Trilland, too." I take his hand, and we start walking again. "I guess what's weird about being in Trilland is that it's just so different."

"It's a lot bigger, busier."

"That's not what I mean. The island is just a simpler lifestyle. I knew what I was doing every day out there. Here, I don't know, it's like I'm just winging it every day. Just weird to get used to."

"Why are you winging it?"

"You know, you're busy, and you've got a lot of important things to do, and I'm not mad or anything because I'm so proud of you, but it's weird. We used to just waste away our time on the island. I guess I just haven't figured out what I'm supposed to do here."

I look down at the sand as it squishes under my shoes. "Well, you're getting into fishing now."

He sighs. "It just seems like maybe I should be doing more than that. Like that isn't enough anymore."

"Enough for me?"

"No."

"Enough for you?"

He shrugs. "I don't know, just talking out loud. Maybe it's silly."

I shake my head. "It's not silly."

One of the things I always loved about Zane from the moment I first met him was how he was a take charge kind of guy. He always did what was best for the island, never waiting around for anyone else to do something or tell him what to do. He's done the same here in Trilland, but it's different. He doesn't seem to have any long-term goals. That bothers me, and based on this conversation, it bothers him, too. I can't help but feel like he needs to be really sure that he wants to stay in Trilland.

"Hey," I say, "maybe you should make another visit to the island."

He smirks. "You trying to get rid of me?"

"No, but maybe some time on the island will help you relax and figure out what you want. Maybe even talking to your mom would help."

"Listen, I love my mom, but she's not that helpful with those kinds of conversations."

"She is with me."

"That's different."

"Just think about it. We need someone to take Dennis's nets to the island anyway. Who better than you?"

He scoffs. "Definitely no one."

"Then it's settled. Take the trip, Zane. You deserve it."

Zane agrees, and we keep walking and joking and talking and kissing, but something feels wrong. I can't help but feel like I just talked Zane into walking away from me. It might only be for a few days, but what if the answer he finds on Maris Island means staying there?

Chapter 11

I'm not really sure what I'm doing, but I'm doing it. I'm walking across the gardens to the guest house to ask Alex to come with me to Parliament. This idea has the potential to go spectacularly well. It also has the potential to go spectacularly poorly.

I need somebody else on my side in that room, and since they still don't trust Zane—*he's just a fisherman from the island,* they say—and they barely let Brent in for press and scheduling purposes, Alex is the best option. Honestly, he's a great option. He's the future king of our strongest ally. Parliament should be happy to have him there. They *should* thank me for bringing in another great mind from a country that is prospering to help with our struggling country. They *should.*

But something tells me that they just won't like the idea. I'm not sure if it will be because they don't trust Alex based on his age, they don't want a non-Trillandite in the policy-making room, or they just flat out don't trust me or my decision-making, but I just have this heavy, sinking feeling in my gut that they will be furious that I made this decision, especially without getting prior approval.

But I'm going to be queen soon. I have to be confident in my decisions, right? I have to do what I think is right no matter what they think. I have to insist when they object. I have to be firm that Alex is going to be in that room and that we are going to hear him out at the very least. I can do that, right?

I knock on the door pretty loudly, and I hope I don't disturb anyone, but Alex sleeps like the dead. I wait a moment, and I'm about to knock again when I see the curtain in the window move. The door unlocks, and Alex greets me with a sleepy smile, half-closed eyes, and the wildest bedhead I've ever seen.

"Nice hair," I say.

Alex's eyes pop open, and he immediately tries to smooth his hair, a futile effort. "The-uh-humidity here messes with it."

I smirk. "Eterand isn't *that* far away."

"Whatever," he says, pretending to be annoyed, but the laughter in his eyes betrays him. "Come on inside."

"Thank you." I close the door behind me.

"I mean, it is technically your house."

I walk in without really trying to observe, the house, but I'm surprised to see that it looks exactly the same. Did no one ever visit Cassandra? Not even the Riagala dignitaries? Or did she just not bother to redecorate? My mother decorated the guest houses to all look the same and complement the main palace. Everything is clean white with beige accents

"Wow, it's identical in here," I say. "It's like time has stopped in this room."

He laughs. "You hadn't been in here since you got back?"

I shrug. "Didn't have a reason to come out here."

"So, what can I do for you?" he says as he tightens the tie on his robe and sits on the couch.

I sit next to him. "Alex, I need to ask a favor."

"Anything."

"It might not be something you want to do."

"That's okay."

"Are you sure?"

He takes my hands in his. "Lorraine, any time you need me, I'm here. What do you need?"

I drop Alex's hands because something about the gesture feels weird. "I'd like for you to come with me to Parliament's meeting today."

"Any particular reason?"

"Well—"

"I mean, I'm there. I'm absolutely there. I'm just curious why you're asking."

"I'm doing my soft proposal of some of the ideas from the secondary students, and I'd like some back up. I'm not totally sure that Parliament is going to support it right away, and I need numbers in the room. Senator Flint is already on my side, but maybe if somebody else of significance supports it, they'll be more willing to listen. Eterand is doing really well right now from what I understand, so maybe if they hear that you think it's a good idea, they'll be more willing to bend."

"I'm not sure if I carry that much weight with Parliament just yet, but I'll certainly try. I think we're both facing some youth discrimination."

I snort. "Yeah. And I'm sure it won't be any better for these high school students. So, you'll help?"

He smiles brightly. "Of course. When do I need to be there?"

"Uh, in half an hour?"

"Wow." He chuckles. "Don't want to give me too much primping time?"

I roll my eyes. "Yeah, that's it. I'll meet you in front of the palace. We'll walk in together to present a united front."

"Deal."

~~~
~~~

The tension in the room is palpable when Alex and I walk in. It's practically airless in the small chamber when I ask Alex to take the seat next to me. During Parliament meetings, there is always an empty chair to my left. This is a symbolic gesture that my grandfather instituted. He felt that it was important to remember that we could always ask for help and never to become so egotistical or stubborn as to refuse help when it was needed. He decided the best way to make everyone constantly aware of that policy was to keep a chair by his side regardless of whether or not there was someone to sit in it. Ideally, he hoped it would make Parliament feel empty if they weren't seeking help. It isn't always needed, of course, but it is always there. During my father's reign, the only person that regularly sat in that chair was Alex's father, so it seems fitting now that when I sit in what I still think of as my father's chair that I should ask Alex to sit in his father's chair. There's something synchronous about that evolution in the room.

I assume no one sat in that chair during Cassandra's time, and no one has sat in it since I returned. Alex is the first of this era, and it is clear that the senators are not happy about it. They're too respectful to say anything, and most of them manage not to glare at the future king of Eterand, but they've made their feelings clear. I lock eyes with Senator Flint and silently beg for her help, and thankfully, she always picks up on my cues.

"Prince Alex," she says sweetly, holding out her hand as she curtsies, "so lovely to see you. I haven't seen you since I was an intern for the late King Arthur."

"Yes, that's right. I remember that. You were supposed to get files or budgets or something like that. I'm sorry, I was fourteen at the time. I obviously didn't care too much about paperwork back then. Still don't."

Senator Flint, Alex, and I all laugh, and Uncle Lawrence tries to chuckle along, but no one else in the room seems amused. Typical.

I ask everyone to take their seats, and they do as if there are cacti on the chairs, never taking their eyes off of Alex. I try to make eye contact with Uncle Lawrence, but he either avoids me or doesn't notice, and it feels like the rock in my stomach grows in size. Secretary Johnson calls the meeting to order as he always does and passes it off to me. It's now or never.

"Good morning, everyone. In the spirit of my beloved and respected father, I've asked Prince Alex to join us as I present some of the findings from my observations. Eterand is our dearest ally, and Alex and I both have the utmost respect for the relationship our fathers had, and we feel very strongly that we would like to reinstate something similar. We haven't had anyone advise our Parliamentary meetings since my return, and I think it only fitting that Eterand be the first."

The room doesn't soften at all like I hoped it would, but I can't let that rattle me. Or, at the very least, I can't let it look like it's rattling me even though it is. I look over at Alex, and he smiles that easy smile of his, that smile that he has honed over the years to hide whatever he's really thinking and inspire all the confidence and faith in him. I wish I had that talent.

"As you know, I visited the schools, and I feel that a lot can be gained from what I observed there."

I start with the easy stuff: all the things the school is doing right, the improved test scores since I returned, the just-getting-by-comfortably budget margins, and then I transition into the smaller scale ideas. I tell them about Dennis and his fishing nets prototype, and no one in the room audibly objects, which I take as a win. Alex expresses a desire to buy some of those nets once produced to be used in Eterand's more fishing-centric provinces, and once again, no one lunges across the table—at least, not yet.

I tell them about another student who had developed a new communications system that would enable our navy ships to communicate with each other better, and it may even speed up communications in the event of a threat, something I remember Uncle Lawrence talking about at the naval observation. Uncle Lawrence gives the idea a thumbs up, so that seems promising as well. But before I can get to Amelia's idea, which I consider the real star of the show, I'm interrupted.

"If I may," Senator Greene says in that pedantic way of hers, "I'm not sure I understand why this is a topic of discussion in a Parliament meeting. These sound like perfectly fine ideas but nothing groundbreaking."

"In the current condition of our economy, any improvement is significant," I say. "Fishing is our biggest industry, and hauling in bigger catches means more profit. Plus, if the ships can communicate with each other instantly, then we may not need as many."

"I'm not sure about that," Uncle Lawrence says, shifting in his seat. "I definitely think his invention has use in our navy, but I don't think it can replace ships."

"It's at least a possibility," I say.

"I still don't think we should be cutting our navy down," says Senator Emerson, and Uncle Lawrence agrees.

"I think it's worth considering," says Senator Greene. "If we can make improvements, then let's make them."

"I'm so glad you feel that way, Senator," I say with just a little too much glee. "One of the older students had an incredible idea to improve our scientific research. I asked her to prepare a formal presentation for next week when she'll lay out all of the details and numbers according to her very detailed research, but I wanted to introduce the concept to you first so that everyone is prepared for her proposal."

I relay all of the details of Amelia's invention that I can remember and explain decently, and I keep waiting for the moment when somebody interrupts me, argues, complains, or otherwise expresses disapproval, but it doesn't happen. I don't get approval either, but I just kind of get—nothing. I can't tell what it means. When I finish, I don't say anything for quite some time, hoping for somebody, anybody, to step in, but no one does. Uncle Lawrence looks lost in thought, and Senator Flint is writing down some notes, so I can't even silently ask them for help. I make eye contact with Brent in the back of the room, and he just shrugs his shoulders.

"I, for one, think it's a fascinating idea," Alex blurts out so suddenly that several people in the room jump visibly. "Solar energy seems so obvious once you hear it. In Eterand, we have something similar for our astronomers, but it sounds absolutely perfect for oceanography, provided it's waterproof, of course."

Alex laughs, but no one else does except for Secretary Johnson's pity laugh. What should I make of this silence? Was bringing Alex here the wrong decision?

"I suppose it has potential," Secretary Johnson says, and I almost don't care that his tone is less than enthusiastic because at least somebody said something. "My concern is the cost to produce it."

"Yes, I have the same concern," Uncle Lawrence says.

"I don't have all the numbers, but when Amelia comes, she can show you the specifics. Based on what I saw, it's doable."

"How?"

"The cost of producing is offset by fewer materials needed and fewer instruments breaking and needing replacement."

"Plus, if the research is higher quality and faster to conduct, we can probably get more funding and payback for the work," Uncle Lawrence adds.

"Exactly," I say.

"Hold on just a minute." Senator Greene waves her arms around erratically. "Are you serious? Is this actually a conversation we're having in the middle of a Parliament meeting?"

I say, "What do you mean?"

"I mean, are we actually considering taking scientific and financial advice from a sixteen-year-old?"

"Yes. I don't see the problem with that."

"Look, I'm not questioning this girl's intelligence, but she's just a kid. It's bad enough to incorporate simple ideas like the fishing net, but we're really going to base our naval communications and our oceanographic research on the musings of a bunch of kids?"

I focus really hard on sounding authoritarian and say, "Yes, we are. If we're going to design our schools to be scientifically minded and encourage them to pursue studies that serve their country, then I think we owe it to them to take their ideas seriously."

"Kids are the future," Alex adds, and I'm so grateful. This is exactly what I hoped he'd contribute. "Some of the best ideas come from the younger generations. If we want the next generation to be passionate about being productive members of society, then we certainly can't crush their involvement and excitement now."

"I don't think anyone here is saying to crush these kids' enthusiasm," Senator Emerson adds, "but we have to be realistic. They don't have all of the knowledge, experience, and training that we all gained in preparation for this job. They can't possibly know what is best for Trilland right now."

I shake my head. "Of course not. I'm not saying we hand over the keys to Trilland to them. That's why I took the time to consider their ideas. I do have the knowledge, experience, and training to judge whether or not an idea has merit in practical application."

Secretary Johnson sighs. "Your Highness, with all due respect, we've been doing this for quite a bit longer than you."

I expected a comment like that from Emerson or Greene, but Secretary Johnson has always been kind, grandfatherly. It takes me back to hear him say that. "I've been training for this job my entire life."

"But you were a child," he says. "I'm sure His Majesty, may he rest in peace, was a wonderful tutor, but there's only so much that can be learned that way. Real world experience is what makes the difference."

I don't know what makes them think that years of my life spent training by my father's side and surviving a mutiny is not "real world experience," but I'm getting a little tired of the way they treat me like a kid.

"Besides," Senator Emerson says, "you haven't even been back for a year. We've barely been holding this country together for years now. We understand that you are soon to be queen, but on some things, you have to consider deferring to us because we have more experience than you do."

"I think it's a little unfair to hold Cassandra's mutiny against her," Senator Flint says, and I make a note to get her an extra nice Christmas gift this year. "Not much she could do about that while she was getting clubbed in the head."

"My point is that whatever education she received, which we all know was quality because we all knew His Majesty, simply cannot compensate for the time she's lost," says Senator Emerson.

"With all due respect," Alex says, leaning forward just enough to assert some dominance, "the only two people in this room who could possibly understand the rigor of training to be king or queen are Lorraine and I. Our fathers were meticulous and worked us very hard to be prepared for this position, and part of being prepared is taking action personally and being confident in and sure of the decisions made based on that action. Obviously, I wasn't at that school because it's not my place, but if Lorraine is taking time out of an important Parliament meeting to bring these ideas to your attention, it's because she saw potential in them and thinks that they will benefit Trilland. She has no interest in a vanity project; if she is pitching an idea, it's because it is in Trilland's best interest. I assume you all respected her father as king and respected his decisions, so why not trust that he has adequately prepared his daughter to assume his position, a position that is rightfully hers?"

There's just a moment of silence in the room after Alex speaks, and I'm sure that it isn't because he has suddenly changed their minds, but at this point, I don't really care if he angered them. I agree with every word he said, and I hardly think their attacks on me today were appropriate, so I'm glad that somebody put them in their place that wasn't me.

"We all know that Her Highness will be a great queen," Secretary Johnson says. "We all just hope that you will be thoughtful in your actions and not be too eager to put your faith into something highly risky."

I answer back, "And I ask that you consider suggestions I bring to you before shooting them down in the name of inexperience either on my part or on the part of the students."

"And if we consider it and still deem it a poor decision," Senator Greene says with a sneer, "will you listen then, or will you bring in another foreign dignitary to try to convince us?"

My cheeks burn with rage, and I seriously consider lashing out, but when I see Brent in the back of the room making a slashing motion across his neck, my anger cools just enough to prevent an outburst. Yelling at Senator Greene certainly won't help, and it may only make matters worse. If I want to dispel this stupid image they have of me as a child, then I have to prevent any kind of scene that may be interpreted as a tantrum.

"Before we continue with the rest of our agenda for today, I suggest we take a twenty minute break."

"I agree," Uncle Lawrence says brightly, trying in vain to bring some levity to the room. "I could really use some coffee."

"I'll see you all back here at 10:45."

Brent motions for me to meet him outside, and I'm certainly not leaving Alex alone in here, so I ask him to come with me. In the hallway, Brent urges us to go to another room, and when Senator Flint follows, Brent is concerned, but I insist that she join us. In the smaller meeting room down the hall, we all let out a heavy sigh almost simultaneously.

"Well, that was fun," Flint says, and Alex laughs.

"Your Parliament meetings are a lot more fun than Eterand's," he says.

"Okay," I say, "I knew they weren't going to love Amelia's idea right away, but did that attack seem excessive to anyone else?"

"I think there are just still so many problems to be worked out with your return," Brent says. "They've never had to deal with you as anything other than the under-aged princess, and then they had Cassandra. They don't know how to interact with you as queen."

"Brent is right," Alex says. "I have the same problem back home. Any time I say anything, I always get told some version of, 'Have you asked your father about that?' It isn't fun, but it's a learning process."

"But your father is still king," I say, and when everyone starts to say something like a condolence, I continue: "It's not about my father being gone, but at least Eterand's senators can be excused since Alex isn't king yet. But I am the acting heir and ruler, and they still treat me like a little kid. I just wanted to go off on them."

"Yeah," Brent chuckles, "I practically saw steam coming out of your ears."

"I'm glad you stopped me. Dana, what do you honestly think?"

Flint twists her mouth a few times before answering. I don't often call her by her first name, but when I do, she knows I'm serious. "I think the idea has potential. I'm cautious about it until I see the full research, but I'm willing to hear it out if it means good news for Trilland."

I gesture dramatically toward Flint. "See? Why can't everyone else be like that? It's not that hard to give it a chance and just trust me."

"I think it's less about you and more about not wanting to trust a kid to save Trilland."

"Yeah, but if I vouch for it, that should be enough. Their issue is that they still see me as a kid, too. And Alex."

Flint shrugs. "Maybe they'll feel better once they see the numbers. Emerson is a straight facts kind of guy. If the numbers check out, he might get on board, and Johnson seemed at least a little affected by Prince Alex's speech, so maybe he's amenable, too. They're just worried because you were gone for so long, and everything that happened with Cassandra was so weird. Obviously, you couldn't because you were injured, but maybe if you had come back sooner, it would be different."

"I sure hope so," I say. "I feel like they're never going to trust me until I—" Brent's eyes widen significantly, and he shakes his head just enough for me to see. If I'm going to tell either Alex or Parliament about my memory loss, it can't be like this.

"Until you what?" Alex says.

I sigh. "Until I make them trust me. I'm just going to have to prove it to them."

"Right on!" Flint says, pumping a fist in the air. "Well, Captain Wilson gave me a craving for coffee, so I'm going to grab some before we resume this joyous event. Prince Alex, care to join me?"

"Absolutely," he says. After Flint walks out, he turns to me and says, "Do you want me to come back for the second session or leave? I don't want to overstep."

"I'd like for you to stay if you can." I don't want them to think that yelling at me and taking not-so-subtle digs at Alex means that they get their way and he leaves. Besides, after his performance in there, I want him around. "And thank you for what you said. I really appreciate your help."

He smiles. "My pleasure."

As soon as Alex leaves, Brent closes the door behind him. "I'm not sure bringing him to this meeting was the best idea."

I fold my arms. "Why?"

"I know he's your friend, and obviously Eterand is our ally, but the senators don't have the best opinion of him right now. Many of them feel that he or his father should have come to help Trilland when Cassandra took over."

"How do you know that?"

Brent shrugs slightly. "To the people in that room, I'm nobody. They mostly forget I'm there, so I overhear a lot of things that they probably think no one hears. Ever since Alex got here, they've been complaining. They feel betrayed that Eterand didn't try to remove Cassandra from power."

"That would have been a complete violation of Trilland's sovereignty."

He nods. "I know that, but I wasn't here. I mean, Gessend had some problems, but the mainland was worse. You and I don't really know what it was like here under Cassandra. It's easy for them to say now that Eterand should have intervened."

"And if they had, they probably would be complaining now that Eterand usurped their power."

"Maybe, but those are their feelings. They might have accepted King Norman, but even he would have been a touchy subject. Alex is worse."

"That's ridiculous."

"I'm just telling you what I know. I didn't know you were bringing Alex today or I would've told you sooner."

"It was a spur of the moment decision this morning," I say. "Besides, I probably would have brought him anyway. Thanks for letting me know."

"Anytime. See you back in there," he says before leaving the room. I'm hardly excited to go back to a room full of people that think I'm just a rash kid who doesn't know what she's doing. I always thought the transition would have been so much smoother if my father were still alive, but it sounds like it's no better for Alex in Eterand. Maybe this is just always how it is. I wonder if there's anything I could do that would change that.

Chapter 12

"Ugh!" I exclaim as I throw the stack of papers onto the table.

"That's the spirit," Alex says.

Zane shoots him a glare then says, "What's wrong?"

"Really, Zane? Everything. Everything is wrong."

"I meant right now. What caused you to fling paper across the room?"

I chose to do some work today in one of the conference rooms of the palace, and when Zane, Brent, and Alex said they'd join me, I thought maybe it would be more productive than it has been. All that's happened is that I've gotten more frustrated with the budget.

"This budget is not going to come together without some drastic change, and Parliament already shot down my idea, so I don't know what else to do." Part of me just wants to implement the ideas I had anyway, but that's not going to win me any brownie points with Parliament or with Trillandites. "There's got to be some solution, but I just don't see it."

Zane picks up my hand and rubs it gently with his thumb. "I'm sure you'll come up with something. I know you can do it."

"That makes one of us."

"Zane is right," Brent says. "You'll come up with something eventually. Maybe you've just been staring at it too much for too long.

You're too close. You need some distance. Maybe you need to take a break."

Alex jumps up out of his seat, startling Brent. "I've a wonderful idea. Let's go for a walk. All of us."

"All of us?" Brent says with a raised eyebrow.

"Yes, all of us." When no one says anything, Alex continues, "Oh, come on, it'll be fun. Let's go down to town square. I haven't really had a good walk around town since I've been here. You all can show me around, and it'll get your mind off of the budget."

Zane shrugs, then stands. "I could stand getting outside for a while."

I say, "Zane, you're outside constantly."

"And I've been inside for nearly two hours. I can't go on like this much longer."

Alex pumps a fist. "All right, Zane is in. Brent, how about you?"

"I should really get some work done."

"Don't be silly," I say. "It's nothing that can't wait."

"But—"

"I'm your boss, remember, and I insist. Come with us."

Brent smiles slightly and nods. Alex waits for the rest of us to find our shoes since we almost never have any on. I often wish that I could walk around town barefoot, but it wouldn't be very queenly. That doesn't stop me from being envious of Zane when he does it. Zane wears shoes so rarely that it actually takes him some time to find his, and when he does, they're three rooms over. As Zane puts his shoes on, we talk Brent out of taking work with him and Alex out of bringing an umbrella when there's not a cloud in the sky, and finally, we head out.

I feel better almost instantly once we step outside. It is a beautiful day, and since it's nearly dusk, there aren't many people around. This is the Trilland I've always liked. Sometimes things can get a little hectic, but at its core, Trilland is just a simple, beachy fishing town not too different from Maris Island. It's always been a comfortable place to be. I remember feeling so lucky not only that I got to grow up here but that one day I would have the immense responsibility and privilege of ruling it. I never could have imagined a better place.

"So, Alex," I say after we've walked for a little while, "anything in particular that you wanted to see while you were here?"

"You know, what's funny about Trilland is that it never really changes. It still looks exactly as it did when we were children. Other than a couple of minor changes and new businesses, it's exactly as I remember it. Don't you think?"

I nod. "Trilland isn't a place of change like Eterand is. Everyone here is happy with the way things are—or, the way things once were. When I got back, I was so glad that it hadn't changed. I don't know what I would've done if it had been different."

"Why is that?"

Zane and Brent both glance in my direction, Brent looking concerned and Zane looking angry. "I just would have missed what I had here in Trilland. I would have felt like I lost something if Trilland had changed, especially without me."

Alex nods. "Is the old museum still operational?"

"Yeah, why?"

"I'd love to see it again."

"Why?" Brent says rather brusquely. "It hasn't been updated in a decade. It's not very exciting."

"That's exactly what's exciting about it. It'll be nostalgic."

"Do you remember the way?" I ask, and he nods, so we start following Alex.

"Museum?" Zane says. "You never showed me the museum."

I lower my voice. "Brent's right. It isn't exciting. In fact, it's a little hokey."

"Then why does he want to see it so badly?"

I shrug. "I guess it's what he said. He wants to see it out of nostalgia. Our fathers both really liked it, so they always dragged us there."

"This is an interesting idea of a fun outing he's got," Brent says, and Zane snorts with wild laughter.

When we get to the museum, the ticketmaster looks surprised to see us. He probably doesn't have many, if any, visitors. Of course, we don't have to pay, but I still do because I feel bad about the museum's lack of patronage. Honestly, closing this thing would probably save money on the budget, but nothing substantial, not enough to matter. I doubt anyone would even notice if I did close it.

There is actually a small section of the museum that is shut down currently for renovations. When Cassandra told everyone I was dead, many people memorialized the section about the Everhart family in my honor. There were flowers, letters, photos, newspapers, anything they could think of that at all signaled me and brought it here. It was rather touching to see once, but after that, it kind of creeped me out. I didn't ask them to take it down right away because I didn't want to offend anyone, but I desperately wanted it gone. I didn't like being reminded of the fact that I was dead for a year, physically to Trilland and mentally to myself. Eventually, Parliament made the motion themselves, so I didn't have to feel like the bad guy. I've been told it's nearly cleaned up now, but I don't want to see it until it's back to the way it was with portraits of my relatives and statues in their honor instead of mine. They deserve the honor far more than I do.

"Look at this," Alex says, pointing to a large map that spans the entire wall in the international wing. "I love looking at this. It's so fascinating to see our little part of the world captured all in one shot like this."

"Wow," Brent says. "This is impressive." He runs his hand over Gessend. I wonder if he misses it. I've never really asked, partially because I kind of forget and partially because I'm afraid he'll say yes.

"Is one of these Maris Island?" Zane says, pointing to a cluster of tiny islands."

I point to one specifically in the middle. "Yes, this one."

"It isn't labeled."

"This map hasn't been updated in decades. Obviously we'll have to make that change."

"So, these are all provinces of Trilland?" Zane asks, pointing to several land masses.

I nod, and point to the northwest. "These, too."

"Ah, yes, the disputed territories," Alex says.

When Zane raises an eyebrow, I point to Riagala on the map. "Riagala believes that those territories should be theirs. They've been threatening war over it for a long time."

"They're the reason Captain Wilson's got the navy so beefed up?"

I nod. "He's worried about a surprise attack."

"We would warn you if we knew that anything was going to happen," Alex says.

"I tried to tell him that, but you know how he can be. He doesn't trust anyone but himself. He's happier putting a bunch of fleets practically on top of Eterand so that he can watch Riagala instead of trusting our allies."

"I certainly don't blame him for wanting to protect you," says Alex, "but we've got your back."

"I know you do."

"You know, I've had an idea for a while, but it wasn't fully formed, and I didn't want to suggest it unless I thought it would be helpful. You reminded me of it just now. I think I'll go ahead and suggest it and see what you think."

"Go ahead."

"What if Eterand and Trilland merged navies?"

"What?" Brent says.

"Think about it. Eterand has no imminent threats right now, so our naval forces are somewhat useless. You need your naval forces active, but you also need to spend a whole lot less money on the navy. If you partnered with our navy, then you could significantly reduce your operations to only what is necessary to work jointly with ours."

"I'm not sure that's a good idea," Brent says.

"Why not?" Alex says. "It seems like a win-win. Besides, I'm not saying you dump your entire navy in favor of Eterand's. I'm talking specifically about the northern waters. You obviously don't need fleets around Eterand, and you can maximize your defense against Riagala by utilizing ours. I think it would put Captain Wilson's mind at ease."

"I'm not sure it would," Zane says. "He's made it pretty clear he doesn't trust anyone but himself and his own men."

I say, "Zane's right. Uncle Lawrence would never go for that. But it's not a terrible idea."

"You're not actually considering this, are you?" Brent says. "Lorraine, this is a serious threat to Trilland's sovereignty."

I audibly scoff. "It's hardly dangerous. Eterand is our ally. If we can't trust our ally, then who can we trust?"

"I'm not sure the people of Trilland are going to be willing to hand over their security to someone else, even someone they respect. After everything that's happened, they only trust you and Parliament, and you can't blame them."

"What does this mean for the rest of Trilland's waters?" Zane says. "Are Eterand's fleets going to occupy all the waters? What about Maris Island and the provinces?"

"Calm down, men," Alex says. "I'm not invading, I promise. I'm just trying to offer a solution that might help Lorraine with the problems she's having with Trilland. What are allies for, right?"

"It's certainly an idea worth considering," I say, and I don't have to look at Zane and Brent to know they're not happy with me. "We'd have to hammer out the details of course, but at least short-term, it might be a solution."

"Can I talk to you for a minute?" Zane says, pulling me into another room.

I'm vaguely aware we're in the oceanography display room, but my eyes glaze over when I glance at all of the sea creatures and fossils on display as I wait for Zane to close the door behind him.

"That wasn't obvious at all," I say. "Alex knows we're talking about him."

"I don't care what Alex thinks. I can't believe you're actually making deals like that with this guy."

"First of all, I haven't decided anything, and second of all, he's not some random guy. He's the heir to the throne of our closest ally."

Zane rolls his eyes. "Yeah, I've heard. That doesn't make it a good idea for Trilland."

"It seems like a good idea. It would fix a lot of problems. I don't see anything wrong with giving the idea a chance."

"You can't just hand over your kingdom to someone else right after you rescue it from a tyrant."

"Utilizing another country's military is hardly handing anything over. If anyone were to threaten Trilland, Eterand would step up and help as is. What's wrong with expanding that agreement?"

"What's wrong with the agreement as is? You have no idea what this guy's motives are. He could be planning something bigger."

I scoff. "He's not some nefarious villain like Cassandra. I've known him forever. I trust him."

"You don't know anything about him or what he wants."

"No, *you* don't know anything about him or what he wants. Ever since he got here, you've been making all kinds of judgments about him, and you don't even know him. He's an old friend, his parents are my godparents, and he's trying just as hard as I am to be worthy of our fathers' legacies. He's trying so hard to be helpful, and you and Brent just keep taking swipes at him. I haven't even told him about my amnesia at your request even though I feel like I'm lying to him. You owe him a chance."

"I don't owe him anything. As you said, I don't even know him, but I know that I don't like what I see. I don't trust him, and just because I haven't known him for twenty years doesn't make that less valid. It's a bad idea to get involved with him."

"I'm already involved with him, Zane. We're allies."

Zane leans back and raises his eyebrows. "So, that's how it is?"

I close my eyes and take a deep breath. "Don't read something into that. My point is that we're not talking about starting a new alliance with someone which is always risky. This relationship between our countries already exists."

"What makes you think that's enough explanation for all of Trilland when you hand over its national security to someone else?"

"What makes you think it isn't? You haven't been here that long. You don't know how the people of Trilland would react to this."

"That's right, I forgot." Zane practically shouts, and I'm pretty sure Alex and Brent can probably hear us by now. "Then, by all means, talk to Alex since he knows Trilland so well. It's not like Brent and I are the ones who have been here since you got back, and he couldn't be bothered to show up until now."

Zane walks through the other door and out of the museum, leaving me standing in the middle of a non-operational room in the museum wondering whether I should go after him, go back to Alex and Brent, or leave all together. Every option sounds like the right one and the wrong one all at the same time, but even though I know Alex will ask a lot of questions if I go back, I also know he will ask more questions than I want to answer if I don't go back, so I force my feet to carry me back into the international room.

"Everything okay?" Alex asks.

I nod. "Yes, everything is fine."

"Where is Zane?" Brent asks, but I know him well enough to know that he knows the answer.

"He had to go home. He'll meet up with us later." I'm pretty sure that's a lie because I'm pretty sure he's going to avoid Alex entirely if he can help it, but I don't know what else to say.

"Perhaps we should follow his lead," Alex says. It strikes me as odd that Alex seems entirely unfazed by everything, but then, maybe he's just being polite. "We could all use some rest before our busy days tomorrow."

We follow Alex out of the museum just as we followed him in, but one significant person short, more questions than answers, and a whole heap of emotions that I am not ready to process.

~~~

Later that night, when I'm sure that everyone, especially Zane and Alex, are asleep, I slip across the palace to Jane's room and knock as quietly as I can, but it takes a few knocks before she answers.

"If you're knocking this late, you better be offering ice cream," she says, rubbing her eyes grumpily.
~~~

I shake my head. "I need to talk if that's okay."

Jane's arm drops to her side, and she squints at me. "Is everything okay?" I shake my head again. "Maybe you need ice cream more than I do."

"I don't think this is something ice cream can fix."

"You've obviously never tried it with toppings."

Jane drags me down to the kitchen and assembles my ice cream for me, piling on way more chocolate syrup and sprinkles than I would put on myself, but when she pulls out the can of whipped cream, I don't limit the amount she puts on. After she assembles her own bowl of frozen stomachache, she sits down and shoves a spoon in each of our bowls.

"Okay, what happened?"

I sigh. "Alex happened."

"Yeah, Brent kind of alluded to something. He didn't want to share details without your permission, and I didn't want to pry."

"Brent doesn't need my permission to talk to his girlfriend."

"He just wasn't sure who you wanted to know about everything."

I laugh. "Please. Of all people, you are the one I worry about the least. Feel free to pry details about me from him."

"How about I just pry them from you?"

So, I lay everything out on the table. I tell her about Zane's increasing anger toward Alex, how Alex keeps asking about my lost year, about Alex's latest naval proposal, Uncle Lawrence's anger, and about Brent and Zane's opposition to it that led to the infamous museum confrontation.

"I just don't think it's a bad idea, you know?" I continue about Alex's proposal. "It's at least worth considering. But Zane and Brent just immediately shot it down. I don't know why Brent shot it down, but Zane obviously did because he hates Alex. I tried to explain that

I know Alex, and I know he wouldn't do anything to harm Trilland, but he just got jealous and angry. I didn't really get a chance to talk to Brent yet."

"Have you told anyone else about Alex's idea? Captain Wilson, maybe, or Secretary Johnson?"

I shake my head. "This just happened tonight. Haven't had a chance to tell anyone about it yet other than you. Besides, Uncle Lawrence and I still haven't really spoken." That last part hurts the most. I knew he would be angry at my suggestion to cut back on the navy, and we've both been so busy since then that it might be nothing, but I haven't seen him in days, and I miss him.

"All Brent really said about it is that he worried about Trilland's sovereignty under a deal like that. He was afraid that it might cause people to perceive you as weak and inept when they really need to see you as in charge and taking action."

"But this is taking action."

"I know that," she says. "And Brent does, too. But it's his job to worry about how you're perceived by everyone, and that's what he's concerned about."

"Yeah, I guess that makes sense."

"And Zane? Is it just jealousy?"

"He said something about the possibility of Alex wanting to expand this later, like he was afraid that Alex would eventually station fleets all around Trilland, including Maris Island. I guess he's worried about that, too. I don't think Alex wants to do that, but even if he does, he can't just unilaterally decide to do that without my permission."

"The whole promise behind the annexation was that the island would be unchanged. I'm sure he's just worried about that."

"He should trust me."

"I agree." When I don't say anything, Jane adds, "What do you think of Alex's plan independent of Brent and Zane now that you've had some time to think about it?"

"Honestly, I haven't thought about it as much as I want to because I've been so worried about Zane, but I still think it might be a good option. I'd have to lay out hypothetical budgets and hash out the details with Alex, but I think there's potential."

"And do you think Parliament will feel the same way?"

I shrug. "Do they like anything I suggest?"

"If you're gearing up for a battle with Parliament over this, you need to be sure you think it's the right thing."

"I know. That's why I want to figure out all of the details first." I study Jane for a moment. "Do you think it's a bad idea, too?"

"It's not really my area of expertise. I just work here."

"Don't do that. You're brilliant, you're my best friend, and I want your opinion."

Jane takes a deep breath in but doesn't release it right away and twists the side of her mouth. "I'm not as ready to throw the idea out the window as the boys are, but I do have my reservations. I think there's room to maybe split some cost with them, but allowing their navy to dominate the northern waters completely does make me a little nervous. I trust you more than I trust him."

"Why does everyone say that?"

"It's nothing against Alex," she says. "It's in favor of you. I believe in you and your ability to be queen, and so do a lot of other people. Alex doesn't mean to us what you do. Plus, I think a lot of people are upset that he didn't come around to help while you were gone."

"Yeah, Brent mentioned something like that. So, they wanted Alex to intervene and usurp our sovereignty then, but if he does it now, he's the bad guy?"

"There's a big difference between those two periods of time, and that difference is you. No one would have complained if he threatened Cassandra's power and authority. The last thing anyone wants is for him or anyone else to threaten yours."

I shovel in a few more spoonfuls of ice cream and avoid eye contact with Jane. I know she's right—really, I do. Sometimes, I think maybe the Cartwrights should have stepped in and removed Cassandra. Would it really matter that it was a violation of Trilland's sovereignty? Cassandra threw that out the window when she tried to have me killed.

"Just be careful," she says. "That's all any of us are saying."

"There's more than just that. If I'm going to work that closely with Alex, I have to tell him."

"About—"

"Yes."

"Are you su—"

"I'm pretty sure, yeah."

Jane sighs. "Look, I'm not going to tell you that telling Alex is the right decision or the wrong one. I think that's a decision you have to make for yourself. Just be sure of your decision and the reason you're doing it before you do it. Don't tell him because you feel guilty he doesn't know, and don't hide it because you're afraid of what might happen if he knew. Ultimately, that's your decision, and anyone who cares about you will respect that."

I'd like to believe that, but somehow, I feel that if I do tell Alex the truth, Zane and Brent won't respect it. But do I need to tell Alex more, or do I need the favor of Zane and Brent more? And does that decision say something about me that I won't like?

Chapter 13

It's drizzling outside, but honestly, I like the feeling of the rain right now. It's concrete. I like when things feel clear and obvious to understand. There are lots of clouds, which means it's raining. I'm sitting outside in the rain, which means I'm getting wet. Getting wet means my hair will be frizzy tomorrow and I'll have to do laundry. I can still picture my parents dancing in front of the center fountain which makes my heart ache with loss. Simple cause and effect. Not always pleasant but simple. I wish everything could be this simple. If things were simple, I could save the oceanography department, I could downsize the military without offending Uncle Lawrence, I could master this job for which I'm so woefully unprepared, I could make the people of Trilland trust me, I could fix my relationship with Brent, and I could finally explain to Zane just how much he means to me.

But things aren't simple, so the best I can hope for is the simplicity of sitting in the light rain in my parents' garden. One of the things I've always liked about this garden is the way rain sounds here. The pathways are mostly sand with the occasional sand glass or pebble, so the sound of the rain is just a little bit muted. I used to find it relaxing because it was soft and covered the sound of the waves outside and helped me fall asleep. Now I like it because it sounds a little like the rain sounded on Maris Island—just a little muted and soft.

The sand starts crunching with the sound of footsteps, and when I look over, Alex waves at me, so I wave back. Even though he pries into my life, it's been good to reconnect, but he's got to stop interrupting my midnight garden walks.

"I feel like I'm starting to come across as a stalker," Alex says with a chuckle. "I didn't mean to interrupt your solitude."

"That's all right," I say, even though it's not. "Couldn't sleep?"

He shakes his head. "Too many thoughts."

"About?"

A heavy sigh escapes his lips seemingly against his will as he sits next to me. "I can't help but feel trepidation over becoming king. My father is such a good king, so how can I possibly live up to him?"

"I couldn't agree more. I have the same fear. My father used to tell me that I shouldn't try to live up to him, that I should live up to me. I've tried to trust that advice, but it's hard."

He nods in a way that speaks to me so much more than any words could have. The pressure to rule an entire country is immense, and people who do not have that kind of pressure just don't understand.

"I think you've got an advantage over me though," he says, avoiding eye contact.

"What do you mean?"

"Your father was a fantastic king. One of the best. But he died many years ago. Parliament basically sustained the country until Cassandra took over. I think people are going to be more inclined to compare you to Cassandra and not to your father."

"I don't think that's the case."

He nods again, except this time I don't feel that I understand. "You're the hero right now. You come in after Cassandra ruined everything and try to fix it. Even if you fail, people know you're trying to help. If I fail, I'm ruining my father's legacy."

I put my hand on his shoulder. "I don't think you could ruin his legacy. You'll be a good king." He doesn't say anything, so I continue, voicing fears I've rarely let myself verbalize. "If anything, my absence has made me more concerned about being a good queen. People held out hope that I would return for so long that their expectations of me and what I'll do for them are so high. It would be so easy for me to let them down. Sometimes, I wonder if I'm the best thing for Trilland."

Alex moves his hand on top of mine and gives it a squeeze. "There is no way that you're not the best thing for Trilland. I've been walking around town. People look so happy. It's just how I remembered it from when we were kids. Trilland always seemed so carefree and happy to me. Eterand has always been a little more uptight."

I laugh. "More professional, I'd say, which makes sense since its primary resource is technology. Trilland is basically a glorified fishing town. It's so much like—"

"So much like what?" Alex says when I don't continue. "Tell me."

"So much like Maris Island. I guess that's why I was fairly comfortable there. It felt familiar in a lot of ways."

"It did?"

"Yeah. I mean, it's a fishing town, too, and the beaches look pretty similar to here, but it was the people that really felt like Trilland. One of my closest friends on the island is so much like Jane, and Zane's mother reminds me so much of Annette and Lady Vivian."

"And let's not forget the man himself," Alex says with a smirk, and when I raise one eyebrow, he adds, "Zane."

"Zane didn't remind me of anyone from Trilland, actually. He's unique. He's so unlike anyone I've ever known."

Alex's lips form a tense smile. "I can tell you really love him. The way you look at him—I used to wish you'd look at me like that."

My face burns red, and I pull back my hand. "Alex, you know I care about you. I always have. You and your parents have always been family to me."

He chuckles. "I guess I can't blame you for not being interested in someone who was like your brother."

"There was a time when I thought we could be more, when I wanted us to be more, but it never really made sense. We're best as friends."

He nods, but the way he avoids eye contact tells me he doesn't agree. "What I really miss is how close we were as kids. We used to spend so much time together."

"Because we were avoiding training from our fathers."

He smiles. "Maybe, but we used to be so close. We would tell each other everything. Do you remember the pink parlor room?"

A hazy memory comes back to me of a gaudy pink room. My mother had attempted to redecorate one of the smaller parlor rooms without Lady Vivian's help. She wanted it to be a muted salmon color, but the entire thing ended up being bubblegum pink—the carpet, walls, curtains, sofas, everything. She was so mortified that she wouldn't let anyone in there until Lady Vivian returned from her vacation. Alex and I used to sneak in there and play and talk because we knew our parents would never think to look for us there. I don't think either of our parents ever found out.

"How could I forget?" I say, though the sentence itself haunts me. It seems impossible now that I could have ever forgotten the pink parlor room, but I did. For a year, I didn't remember the heart-to-hearts we had there, that first kiss we shared just to see what it was like, the laugh-until-your-sides-hurt conversations we used to have, and suddenly there's an ache in my chest. "I miss that, too."

That feeling returns, stronger than ever. That feeling that I have to tell Alex everything about Cassandra and Maris Island and my memory. Every time I talk to him, I feel that tremendous weight like I'm lying to him every time I don't explain it.

"Lorraine?"

"Yes?"

"What happened last year? Why didn't you come back?"

I know Zane and Brent don't want to me to tell him, and I listened because I haven't seen them agree or even speak since everything happened except about this, but I can't help but feel like they're wrong. They don't know Alex. They think it will be dangerous for me to tell him, like if he knows he'll suddenly attack Trilland or expose me or something, but Alex would never do that.

"I know you, Lorraine. I know there's something you're not telling me. Please tell me."

I take a deep breath, and then another, before finally exhaling. He deserves to know. If the pink parlor room still existed, we'd go there now to talk, but it's late, and the garden's empty, so I speak.

"When Cassandra tried to have me killed, one of the sailors hit me in the head. The crew thought he killed me, and Uncle Lawrence convinced them they had, but they had just knocked me unconscious. Uncle Lawrence put me on a lifeboat headed for a small chain of islands he knew existed, and he told me to stay safe and that we would find each other and get back to Trilland. But when I got to the is-lands—to Maris Island—I couldn't remember anything. The blow to my head was pretty bad, and I couldn't remember anything at all."

Alex grips the edge of the bench, yet his hand shakes just a little. "What? Nothing? Nothing at all?"

I shake my head. "I didn't know who I was, where I was supposed to be, or what had happened. I couldn't even remember my name. That's actually how Maris Island got its name. Zane picked the name for me so that I wouldn't feel so alone."

"I—I can't even believe it."

"That's why I didn't come back right away. It took me nearly a year to get my memory back. It didn't fully come back until Brent and I got to Trilland—the day before Cassandra gave the press conference saying I was an impostor."

"You didn't remember anything until then?"

"I remembered pieces but not everything." I turn around to face the palace and point to the family portrait hanging on the wall in the main hall. "When I saw that picture, everything came back. Well, at least I think everything."

"What do you mean?"

Now it's my hand that trembles. "I can't shake the feeling that it's not all there."

"Is something missing?"

I shrug. "I don't know. I don't feel like there is, but how would I know? If I don't remember it, how am I supposed to know I don't remember? I just keep worrying that there might be gaps, and I can't do anything about it. Every time someone mentions something from the past that I don't remember, I panic. Like the other day when you mentioned that my father talked yours out of disbanding the navy. I don't remember that at all."

"Well, we were kids. It probably didn't matter that much to you. If it had been my father talking to yours, you might have remembered."

"Logically, I know that makes sense, but I can't help but wonder. I'm just so afraid that there's something that didn't come back, and if everyone finds out, what would that mean for Trilland? Would they ever trust me again? Would I even be able to do my job?"

"Have you told anyone about this?"

"The members of this household know as well as Zane, Brent, and Maris Island."

"No, I mean, have you told anyone about this fear?"

I shake my head. "I mentioned it briefly to Jane and Zane once, but I don't want to worry anyone." I do notice that I feel lighter having told Alex, and it's not just because Alex knows now but because I really haven't voiced that fear before. Somehow, it feels less threatening now that it was said out loud. It's like when you're a child and you have a nightmare that seems so frightening at the time, but when you try to describe it to your parents, it doesn't sound nearly as bad as it felt. Telling Alex makes me feel a little less afraid. "I do feel better telling you."

"I'm glad you told me."

"I'm so sorry I didn't tell you sooner. We were really selective about who we told."

Alex laughs. "You told an entire island."

I roll my eyes. "They already kind of knew. They knew me as Maris before they ever knew Lorraine."

Alex furrows his eyebrows and shakes his head with a laugh. "It's weird to hear you refer to yourself as Maris."

"It was weird back then to hear Brent call me Lorraine."

"If my family had known—if *I* had known—I would have come to Trilland right away. I would have helped."

"I really appreciate that, and I wanted to tell you right away, but we tried to keep the circle of people who knew small and Trilland-based. Besides, Trilland needed their rightful ruler back, not a foreign involvement, however friendly it would have been. They needed to learn to trust again."

"You sounded like your father just now." He smiles. "Do you think you'll ever tell all of Trilland?"

"If it were ever in Trilland's best interest to know, of course. But right now, I think it's better if they don't know."

"But if they knew, wouldn't they understand better why it took you so long to come back? In Eterand, we were all wondering why you would take so long. It isn't like you."

"Maybe, but they would also trust me less."

"Won't they trust you less when they find out you've been keeping something from them all this time?"

I shift a little on the bench, suddenly feeling uncomfortable with how close Alex and are sitting to each other. "I have faith in the people of Trilland that they would trust that I did what I thought was best."

Alex shakes his head. "I can't believe you were out there for a year with no memory of anything. If only somebody had known and could come find you."

"Uncle Lawrence knew. He sent Brent to find me, and he did."

"I guess, selfishly, I know I would have come after you. I wish Uncle Lawrence had found a way to contact me."

I shrug. "He knew Brent could do it. He wouldn't have sent Brent if he thought even for a minute that Brent wouldn't be able to find me." I don't think I've ever thought about that or said it out loud, but it's true. Uncle Lawrence wouldn't have trusted Brent with something so important to him if he doubted him. That must be why he was so angry at Brent when he found out about my amnesia. Hearing Alex criticize his decision to send Brent makes me weirdly defensive of Brent. Why am I so intent on defending the person who caused so many problems? Does this mean I have finally forgiven him? Does it mean I always had? "Besides, it might have been a little startling to scared little Maris if a prince had shown up with a whole processional. Brent was just a regular guy."

"I guess that makes sense. But you didn't know him before that. You knew me. You might have remembered me."

"There's no guarantee that I would have." It sounds harsher than I intended, but he and I both know it's true.

Alex's silence speaks more than words could right now. When Alex is quiet, it's because you've said something true that he doesn't want to be true. The best thing I can do right now is nothing.

"I should really get some sleep," I say. "I've got a long day tomorrow."

"I should sleep as well." We both stand, and he takes my hands in his again. "Thank you for telling me. I'm glad we can be like we used to."

He drops my hands, and we go our separate ways, and while I'm glad I finally told him, I find that the uneasy feeling in my stomach has not gone away but rather changed.

Chapter 14

"Maris, what is wrong with you?" Zane's feet which were previously propped up on the table of the parlor room in a pose of ultimate relaxation now slam to the floor as he sits up. "I thought we agreed you wouldn't tell Alex anything."

"Uh, no, you and Brent agreed on that. I never did."

"You have no idea what he'll do with that information."

"I know more than you do. I've known him my whole life. He would never do anything that would hurt me or Trilland."

"Don't be too sure."

"Zane is right," Brent says quietly. Then, more firmly: "He might have good intentions, but he might slip up or think he's helping by telling others. He doesn't know Trilland's current state well enough to know how best to protect it. That's your job, not his."

"Then you have to trust me when I say that I trust him. I didn't do this to upset you or because I ignored your opinion or feelings. I really believe that this was the right thing to do. It changes nothing in my friendship with him or my relationship with you."

"I don't trust him as far as I can throw him," Zane says. "I've known plenty of guys like that. He just wormed his way back into your life, knew you were hiding something, and convinced you to tell him.

I glare at Zane. "He didn't do anything. I chose to tell him. We used to tell each other everything. Eterand is our oldest ally. His parents are basically family. It felt wrong not to tell them."

Brent says, "I could've understood if you wanted to tell King Norman, but Alex is not yet ready to be king. He is not your ally right now, Lorraine. His father is."

"And I will tell his father and his mother when they arrive for the summit, but that isn't the kind of information you share over the phone." I heave out a sigh. "You know, I wasn't really asking for your permission before, and I'm not asking for your forgiveness now. I'm only telling you because I want to be honest with you, and should Alex mention it, I don't want you to be caught off-guard. But I have wanted to tell Alex for some time now, and I have given it serious thought, and I feel that he can be trusted. This was my decision to make, and I made it."

They both stay silent for a quite a while, avoiding eye contact with each other and with me. I don't like talking to them like that. It makes me feel like some overbearing monarch, but they have to learn to respect my decisions. This problem with them goes all the way back to Maris Island. Neither one of them trusts me to make my own decisions. If I'm going to be successful at this job for which I've prepared my whole life, then I'm going to have to take charge more often.

I feel like saying more, especially to Zane, but I don't know what to say that won't be an apology for speaking my mind.

Brent stands up calmly but rather abruptly.

"If you'll excuse me, I have to see to some details for the summit. Do you need anything else before I go?"

"No, I'm fine." Then: "Thank you for your help with that."

"My pleasure. Really."

Brent walks out, gently closing the door behind him. Oddly, the air feels somewhat heavier without Brent here. Brent's gesture felt like a peace offering—whether it was or not—and I appreciate the gesture, but Zane is still huddled in his chair with his arms folded. In a way, it's been easier to solve my issues with Brent. I don't know if it's this gentle personality of his or the fact that I don't love him the way I love Zane, but when Zane and I have conflict, I find it much harder to resolve.

Before I can form any sentences in my head, some kind of peaceful gesture, Alex throws the door open to the parlor.

"Still working on the budget?" he says.

"Uh, yeah, I can't seem to reconcile anything."

Alex says, "Why don't you let me take a look at it?"

I gesture at the papers strewn on the floor. "You can try, but all you're going to see is what I already know. It's hopeless without change, and Parliament doesn't hate anything more than change."

Zane looks furious that I'm even allowing Alex to be in the room right now, much less participate in the budget conversation, but I think I've made my feelings clear, and he doesn't challenge Alex's presence.

"Where's most of the money going?" he says as he flips through papers.

"Military. I talked Uncle Lawrence into backing off on the ships near Eterand and on the coast where Maris Island is, but I couldn't get him to pull out of those coasts entirely, and he just keeps amping up the numbers near Riagala. I can't get him to back down."

"He just wants to protect you," Zane says, but there's a bite in his tone. It's been this way for a few days now, but it's worse now that he knows I told Alex.

"I know that, but it's killing our budget."

"Oh, I wouldn't worry about it," Alex says. "Some of his fleets won't be necessary now, so he'll be able to pull back without feeling like he's jeopardizing you."

I sit up straighter and look Alex in the eye. "What do you mean by that?"

Alex raises an eyebrow. "Some of Eterand's fleets have already arrived, and the others will get there tomorrow. He'll be able to pull back now. You'll see, it will help a lot of your problems."

Zane bolts out of his chair. "What?"

I hold my hand out to stop Zane. "What do you mean your fleets have arrived?"

"The ones we talked about the other day at the museum. I made the call that night since you were so worried about it. Eterand is happy to offer our help to you."

"Where?" Zane says.

"Where what?"

He grits his teeth and clenches his fists, and I wonder if I would stop him if he tried to punch Alex right now. "Where are the fleets?"

"I posted a few on Riagala's coast, but mostly they're around Eterand and Trilland's mutual coast and the provinces."

"*All* of the provinces?"

"Yes, why?"

"Maris Island?"

"Of course."

Zane doesn't even look at me as he bolts out of the room. I can't even begin to figure out what I'm going to say to Alex, but I have to follow Zane first, so I turn to Alex and say, "Don't go anywhere. We need to talk," and then take off down the hallway after Zane.

I have to call his name a few times before he stops, but when he does, part of me wishes that he had kept going because the anger in his eyes is unsettling.

"How could you let him do that?"

"I didn't let him do anything."

"I was there, Maris, I heard him tell you his idiotic plan."

"But I didn't accept. I didn't know he was going to do this."

Zane throws his arms up in frustration. "I told you he would. I told you. I knew he'd run wild with anything you gave him. You let him think he has a say in what Trilland does, and now he's completely taking advantage of it."

"Look, I'm not happy about this either, but you have to give me a chance to deal with it."

"You should have dealt with it by putting him in his place."

"He's not the enemy, Zane. I'm not going to shut him out completely. I have to work with him."

"He completely overstepped."

"And I'll address it."

He throws his arms again, but with less commitment this time. "Maris Island."

"I know."

"You let him invade Maris Island."

"I didn't let him do anything. I already said that."

"You promised them and you promised me that nothing would change over there without their consent. You promised us that you would be the only person involved in the island."

"I am."

"You're not. Now Alex is all over us. He's going to ruin everything about our island."

"What is this 'us' thing? You're mad at me, so now it's us vs. them, and you're one of them?"

"I've always been one of them, Maris. I'll always be one of them. Did you really think that just because I came here with you that I stopped being one of them?"

"I thought that you understood that Trilland and Maris Island were one now. I thought you understood that I'm on your side."

"I did, too, but apparently, you're on Alex's side."

"You've been jealous of Alex from the moment he got here."

"I have reason to be."

"Do you? Or is this just what you do? You did the same thing with Brent. You can't just go into a jealous rage every time another guy is around."

"Is that what you think this is?" Zane gestures around him. "You can't even fathom the possibility that I might see something in Alex that you don't see?"

I huff and feel tears stinging my eyes, and even though I've cried a million times in front of Zane, I refuse to let him be the reason I cry in front of him now. "You don't understand how hard all of this is for me. I'm trying to do everything right for everyone, and obviously, it's not going well. I need you to be patient with me."

"I've been nothing but patient with you. Everything I've done since I came to Trilland has been for you. You don't see that?"

"Coming to Trilland was your decision, not mine."

"That doesn't mean I didn't do it for you."

I huff again and clench my fists. "All I'm asking for is a little understanding."

"I've been understanding every time you've had to work late because I know that what you're doing is important. I was understanding when Alex came into town, I was understanding when you asked me to be nicer to him, and I was understanding when you said you wanted to tell him about your amnesia and when he first proposed his invasion."

"Uh, you yelled at me for those last two things."

"Because I got mad, and I think I have a right to be mad. But I backed off, and I tried to help, and I tried not to cause problems with Alex, but he's the one causing all of the problems here, not me."

"However misguided he might be, he's trying to help."

"Oh, but I'm not?"

"I didn't say that."

He gestures widely around him. "We're standing in a hallway arguing about it."

"I didn't follow you to argue with you. I followed you because I knew you were upset, and I care about you."

Zane drops his arms, and for the first time, I see some of the anger cool into sadness. "I don't want to be standing in a hallway arguing with you."

"Me neither."

"I want to help, but it seems like everything I do just makes it worse."

"That's not true."

"I'm worried about you."

"I'm not the amnesiac girl from the island anymore. I appreciate your concern, but I can take care of myself now."

He takes a step backward. "Look, maybe I should move my trip to the island up a few days."

I involuntarily take a step back as well, widening the physical gap between us as well as the emotional one. "What?"

He shrugs. "I was already planning to go to help my mom out and take some nets to Tito. Maybe it's good timing. We can both get some space."

"Zane—"

He forces something that resembles a smile. "It's okay. I'll come see you before I head out tomorrow."

And with that, Zane walks away, and I feel the last semblance of security I had go with him.

Chapter 15

"If I expand the fleets into the northwest territory, then Trilland can cut back its forces almost entirely," Alex says. "That should significantly reduce your military expenditures which means you can funnel more to your science departments. It's a win-win."

"Uh-huh," I say, though I've kind of been in and out of this conversation. Really, it's more like a sales pitch. Alex has been talking for a while, trying to sell me on his idea, but all I can think about is the fact that Zane left this morning. He said goodbye just like he promised, but he felt so distant that I wondered if it would have been better if he hadn't. Of course I know from experience that that is worse, but everything everyone has said to me today has come through a filter of *Zane isn't here because you let him down. Again.*

"Once Trilland's economy stabilizes, Eterand can pull back, and you can reinstate your own forces or decide that you don't need them depending on what happens between then and now. Really, I think Riagala is the biggest concern. If they don't put up a fight against Eterand, they won't challenge you either, I don't think."

"Sure."

"But if you're worried about it, we can put in the terms of our alliance that I can send fleets at will so that if Riagala does something, there will be an immediate response regardless of the status of your military at the time."

"Mm-hmm."

"Lorraine, is everything all right?"

"Yeah, why?"

"Because you haven't really been listening to a word I've said."

A sigh slips past my lips before I can stop it. "Maybe today isn't the day for us to talk about this."

Alex sits down next to me and props his arm up on the back of the couch. "Why, what's wrong?"

I hesitate because maybe I shouldn't tell Alex what happened with Zane, but it's only a split-second, and I just let it out. "Zane left this morning. He's taking a trip back to Maris Island to help out his mom. We had kind of a fight before he left, and I just feel weird without him here."

"Oh."

"I'm just in a funk. It's hard to focus on anything right now. It's not your fault."

"Oh good, because I was afraid I was boring you." He laughs, and I let myself laugh, too. "And I was worried about the other day. We haven't had a chance to talk since then."

"We did talk."

He shrugs. "Yeah, I guess so, but everything got so blown out of proportion. I wasn't trying to usurp your authority."

"I know."

"I'm just trying to help. I think this will really benefit Trilland."

"Look, your logic is good, and I appreciate what you're trying to do, but—"

"But you're not sure about it."

I shake my head. "No, I'm not."

I think I see Alex's lip twitch just for a moment—the kind of twitch someone does when they're annoyed but trying not to show it—but it disappears quickly, and he presses his lips into a small smile. "You've got to trust me, Lorraine. I really think I can help make things better here."

"Maybe you can, but I want to be able to talk about it."

"Isn't that what we're doing?"

I shake my head. "It feels more like a sales pitch right now, honestly. Like you're just telling me something I'm not a part of."

"Well, it was the same when you told me about your amnesia, right? Nothing wrong with that."

I twist my mouth. "That's kind of different."

"I can't imagine why you wouldn't want to tell Trilland about that," he says, and I shrug. "I just think Trilland might want to know. Eterand, too."

My eyes click up to his. "Why would Eterand want to know?"

"Because we care about you," he says, but I feel like that's not the real answer. "Besides, maybe the terms of this alliance could look different if they knew. You know, it could be more understanding of Trilland's situation."

I slump down in my chair. "I can't talk about this right now."

"Why don't you read this over and think about it?" He hands me his proposal which is uncomfortably thick. What else is in here? "We can talk later when you're feeling better."

I nod, take the papers with me, and walk out of the parlor without any sense of my legs being part of my body. Alex and I already had it out over his moving fleets into Trilland's waters without telling me. He apologized, but he didn't move the fleets, and I don't feel better about it. Somehow, we started negotiating terms, and this stack of papers is way bigger than a simple military agreement. I'm not sure Alex heard me at all when I said I wanted to work these details out together. Maybe Zane was right.

And now Zane isn't even here. I can't show him the proposal, ask for his thoughts, even just hug him. He's at home on Maris Island. Maybe that's where he belongs. Maybe I never should have let him follow me here. Or did I ask him to follow me? I'm not even sure anymore. I am sure that I never really listened to him about a lot of things, and without him here to ask, there's really only one other person who gets it.

I head upstairs toward Brent's suite and force myself to knock on his door. I don't normally come to Brent's suite. In fact, I think I've only done it a handful of times. Normally, we meet elsewhere in the palace, or he comes to me. When Brent answers the door, the look on his face says that he's thinking about how unusual this is, too.

"Lorraine. What are you doing here? Do you need something?"

I shake my head. "Are you busy? I just want to ask you something."

"Is it about the meeting notes, from Parliament? Because I've asked like three times for those to be sent over, but they never—"

"No, it's more of a personal question."

Brent rubs the back of his neck. "Uh, sure. Come on in."

I step into the small living room of the suite and immediately spot Jane sitting on the couch watching TV. She smiles when she sees me, but I think I turn several shades of red.

"Oh no, I'm not interrupting something, am I?"

Brent laughs. "No, no, we're just watching TV."

"Is everything okay?" Jane asks, and I shake my head.

Brent sits down next to Jane, places a hand on her leg, and I sit on the couch across from them. It makes my heart ache from missing Zane to see Brent and Jane together.

I can't remember now who used to stay in this suite when I was a child, but I feel certain that my mother decorated it because of how beautiful it is. I have a completely inappropriate urge to laugh when I think about how Brent's house was so haphazardly styled with mismatched pieces. Brent has clearly tried to make the room more masculine, but there's only so much he can do.

"Brent, can I ask you something about Gessend?"

"Sure."

"Do you miss it?"

He hesitates just for a moment, then says, "Sometimes. It's kind of a weird thing to explain. Like, I don't want to move back there, but I get homesick, yeah."

"Why don't you want to move back if you miss it?"

"Gessend will always be special to me, and I'll probably always miss it, but everything I want in life is here on the mainland. I have career opportunities here I could only dream of in Gessend. I had friends there, but here, everyone feels more like family."

"Really?"

Brent smiles. "You know, I remember the first time I ever saw you in person. We were probably about five or six years old. You came with your parents to visit Gessend. Gessend was struggling economically back then, and your dad promised to fix everything. I didn't totally understand everything, of course, but I knew how stressed out my parents were back then. Your dad gave them hope. I remember thinking that your parents looked like angels. After that, every time any member of the Everhart family came to visit, I would make sure I was there to see them. It was only a couple of times, but I remember them. I always thought you were the luckiest kid in the world because you lived on the mainland where everything was happy and good, and one day you would be the angel that little kids would see and know that things would get better because of you. I always wished I could make a difference like that. I know it's not exactly the same, but being here and working for you, I feel like I'm making a difference."

I smile. "You are."

"That's why I volunteered when Captain Wilson needed someone to look for you. I knew firsthand how important you were to Trilland. I can't imagine being anywhere else now. I'm doing what I always wanted right here." He takes Jane's hand and gives it a squeeze. "Plus, I found my ideal girl right here."

"Aww," Jane says.

"Ugh, stop, you guys are sickening," I say.

"Where's this coming from?" Brent says. "Do you miss Maris Island?"

I shrug. "Yeah, a little, but I'm actually thinking about Zane."

"Zane?"

"He left for the island this morning," Jane says to Brent. "He's taking a trip to help out his mother."

"I thought he was going next month," Brent says.

"He was," I say. "He was kind of homesick, so I suggested the trip, but he decided to go early. Something happened."

I explain what happened with Alex the other day after Brent left. I tell them about my fight with Zane, my subsequent argument with Alex, and how Zane left this morning with a goodbye and without a kiss. "I'm afraid he thinks he made a mistake coming to Trilland."

"Oh, I don't think that," Brent says.

"Why?"

"Lorraine, anyone can see he's crazy about you."

"But is that really enough? I've driven him away again. I didn't really listen to him or to you about Alex, and I didn't pay attention when he tried to tell me that he felt out of place here. He said something about feeling like he makes everything worse. I'm worried that he wants to go back to Maris Island permanently."

"I doubt that," says Jane. "I think he knew what he was getting into when he came here."

"Yeah," Brent says, "I mean, I know it's been kind of an adjustment for him—for both of us, really. We've talked about it before."

"You have?" It was one thing to think that Zane and Brent had become polite with each other or even that they had bonded over their mutual distrust of Alex, but this? Talking about being homesick is decidedly in friend territory. Maybe they've been closer for longer than I thought.

He nods. "We were kind of the only ones who understood each other's situation. It's been hard, but we both agree we made the right decision. I think it'll just take some time for him to figure out what he wants." As weird as it is to hear Brent talk about such an intimate conversation he had with Zane, I find it somewhat reassuring, and I'm not even sure why.

"He was just so mad when Alex posted ships near Maris Island. I can't blame him, but maybe he'll always consider that home, not Trilland. I wonder if anything will make him feel like he belongs in Trilland."

"Just give him time. He'll figure it out."

"I hope you're right."

Chapter 16

I don't often use my office because it doesn't feel like it's mine. At best, I can picture my father sitting in this chair, writing on these papers, shuffling pens on this desk, and it feels wrong to sit here, like I'm a small child who doesn't have permission to use Daddy's tools. At worst, I think of all of the papers I read that Cassandra had left here, and I picture her making backroom deals with our enemies, wrecking the economy without a care, signing prison sentences for anyone who dared to speak the truth about her, and I get chills that seem to run through my very bones. I only sit at this desk when it's absolutely necessary: meeting one-on-one with a member of Parliament, taking official photos for the newspaper of the lost Princess Lorraine Everhart back at work for Trilland, or when the work I have to do simply requires a desk. Today is a desk-required work day.

Usually, I can work anywhere: the couch, my bed, the garden, the beach, my balcony, and so on, but occasionally, the work is too demanding for that. After the eruption at Parliament over the school idea and Alex's latest proposal that makes me uneasy and hopeful all at once, I can't afford to do work anywhere else today, so here I sit in my father's chair in the middle of Cassandra's chaos trying desperately to find a solution. Maybe the desk will be the secret weapon.

I have about a million budget sheets all over the desk along with proposals from Amelia, Dennis, and Alex, and I'm actually grateful when I hear a knock on the door.

"Come in."

The door opens slowly, and it makes my heart stop for just a moment. Since I've been back, I've had moments of fear. They're unpredictable, and sometimes they're set off by nothing, but they're unsettling all the same. Every once in a while, something totally innocuous like someone opening a door fills me the undeniable feeling that someone is trying to hurt me. Dr. Offen tells me it's normal, that it's just the trauma of the mutiny that has affected me, but I hope one day, I won't have to live in fear of being afraid.

Gratefully again, once the door opens, I see the least threatening person in the entire world: Uncle Lawrence.

"Hard at work?"

"Trying to be."

"I'm not interrupting anything important, am I?"

"You're never interrupting."

Uncle Lawrence sits down in the chair where foreign dignitaries usually sit, where I used to sit while my father taught me about government, where I sat for the first month of using this office after I returned because I felt like I could smell Cassandra's perfume on my father's chair, and it made me want to vomit. He looks small, weirdly, and I don't know that I've ever seen him like that.

"I'd like to talk to you about our conversation the other day," he says. "I'm not happy with how it ended."

We've barely spoken since I asked him to back down with the navy, and it isn't because he's been purposely avoiding me but rather because we've just been busy and haven't crossed paths, but even though I know the reason we haven't spoken is the latter, it still feels like the former. I've wanted to say so much, but words are elusive, and so I haven't.

"We never really talked about everything that happened," he says. "About the mutiny, I mean."

"We did."

He shakes his head. "I filled in the blanks that you didn't remember, but I never told you about what happened when you weren't around, and I think you have a right to know."

"Okay," I say, even though it's not. I'm not sure I want to hear about this.

"Before we left on that trip, I had reservations. I didn't tell you about them because I didn't want you to worry, but there had been murmurs around the docks of rebellion. I didn't take that as seriously as I should have, and I will regret that for the rest of my life."

"Uncle Lawrence—"

"Please let me finish. I knew they were going to mutiny long before they did, but I didn't know what to do or which crew members I could trust. I tried to use the storm as an excuse to go back, but I think they were afraid to go back to Cassandra without finishing the mission. After I helped you escape, they wanted to kill me immediately. They knew I would tell everyone what happened when we got back to Trilland. After they broke my leg, I convinced them that I was too grief-stricken and injured to care what they did and begged them to just leave me alone. They didn't originally leave me in Gessend. They chose a nearby island with no affiliation to Trilland, but those people helped me get to Gessend for medical care.

"I cried every night for eight months. I sent out random communications to nearby islands asking for you, but you never responded. I know why now, but I didn't then. I started to think you were dead, and I wallowed in my injury and sadness. But the people of Gessend loved to hear stories about you, so I told childhood stories almost every night at the local bar. People loved it. One of the people that was always there was Brent.

"Brent was riveted by every story. He was young the last time you visited Gessend, so I don't think he had clear memories of you. My stories were the best he could get. He, along with others, started to believe that you had survived. Deep down, I wanted to believe the same, but it hurt too much to hope and risk finding out you were dead. It would be like you died all over again. But Brent pushed me, and then I pushed him. We spent a few months surveying the nearby islands trying to figure out which one you would have most likely landed on. We sent a lot of communications which led to rumors in other provinces that you might be alive. We hoped you would respond, but you didn't.

"I knew I'd have to go after you, but I was still recovering, so Brent offered to go. I told him what to look for, I told him enough information about you that he would be able to help no matter what had happened to you, and I insisted that he had to find you no matter what. "I never could have imagined what had happened to you. I suppose I should have considered the possibility, but I didn't."

"No one could have expected what happened," I say, but the smallness of my voice surprises me.

"I could have done more to protect you, and I could have tried to find you sooner, but I didn't listen to my own instincts, and it cost you time and nearly cost you the throne."

"None of that is your fault."

He shrugs. "Maybe so, but I promised your father on his deathbed that I would take care of you and your mother. Later, when she died, I promised to take care of you again. I can't help but feel like I failed them. I'm unwilling to take that risk again."

I try to wipe away the tear on my cheek quickly enough that he won't notice it escaped, but somehow, I don't think I succeed. He scoots his chair a little closer to the desk and holds out his hands, so I quickly put mine in his, and he gives them a squeeze.

"My instincts as a sailor tell me to trust no one but myself, but my instincts as a person also tell me to trust my family. Sometimes, I get those mixed up. At the end of the day, I'm lucky to call this intelligent soon-to-be-queen my family, and I have to trust that you have instincts as well. I also have to trust that you are trying to do what's best for our country. So, if that means cutting back the navy, I have to trust you."

"I promise I'm not doing this because I haven't evaluated the risks."

"I know."

"I'm just trying to fix our hemorrhaging budget."

"I know that, too."

"I don't want you think I don't care."

He smiles. "I could never think such a thing."

We sit in silence for a few moments, and it's awkward but nice. I enjoy feeling the wall between us come shattering down. But there's another wall that he doesn't even know about.

"You know, I was going to try to find a solution to cutting back the navy without compromising the secure border you have set up, and I might have found it."

"You have?"

I nod. "I'm sure you know Eterand has stationed ships at certain spots around our border."

He shifts uncomfortably. "I noticed."

"Alex's idea. He offered Eterand's help so we could cut back for our budget."

"That's great," he says, but the shifting and fidgeting says otherwise.

"But it's not. I didn't authorize it."

His eyes widen. "What?"

"We had been talking about a possible agreement, and I was pretty excited about the idea. I thought it seemed like the perfect solution, but everyone reacted so badly."

"Everyone?"

"Zane, Brent, even Jane. They all thought it was a bad idea, but I really believed in it. But Alex went ahead and did it. I thought he and I were still discussing, that we would hash out a formal plan that would be signed. He thought we had a verbal agreement."

"Do you disagree with the plan now that it's in motion?"

"Do you?"

"You first."

I sigh. "No, but I'm upset he did it without me. But should that matter if we were going to do it anyway and the signing was just a formality?"

He huffs. "I can't say it doesn't make me nervous. Sure, it's something you wanted this time, but it's a bad precedent to set."

I slump back into the chair. "That's what I was afraid you would say."

"I'm not here to tell you what to do, but you have to decide if you're okay with him acting without written agreements. And if you're not, you need to talk to him immediately."

"Aside from that, does having Eterand's ships make you feel better?"

He smirks. "I'm learning to trust others, but I'd still rather have control."

"I'd rather you have control, too, but Eterand is a close second."

"Well, I think you need to figure out what you want and have an honest conversation with him. Don't let him tell you what's best for

Trilland or what decision you should make. That's your decision and yours alone."

<center>~~~</center>

I walk straight out of my office to the guest house where Alex is staying. Uncle Lawrence has given me the motivation and the courage to do this which means I have to do it now before I lose my nerve. Alex has to be pushed back. I know he means well, and he's just trying to help, but he's overstepping. I'm pretty sure he'll understand that. I haven't exactly been clear when I've tried to voice my concerns in the past, but if I'm clear now, I think he'll get it. He might not be happy about it, but I think he'll understand.

I practically march through the gardens up to the door and knock loudly enough to sound confident and urgent but not so loudly that I seem angry. Can a knock on a door sound angry?

"Hey there," Alex says with a smile when he opens the door. "To what do I owe the pleasure?"

"I'd like to talk to you about your new deal. May I come in?"

Alex gestures for me to enter and smirks. "Of course." He flops onto the couch, so I sit next to him. "So, what did you want to talk about?"

"Alex, you know I respect you and our friendship as well as our fathers' friendship."

He furrows his brow. "Yes, of course."

"Okay, good. I need you to know that before I continue."

"I mean, I kind of got the message when you told me what happened after the mutiny. You know, your amnesia."

"I remember."

He smirks. "You do?"

"Yeah, I do," I say and fold my arms. Zane, Brent, Jane, and I all joke about my memory all the time. Why do I feel like Alex shouldn't be allowed to?

"Are you second-guessing our new terms?"

"Yeah, kind of."

"I thought so. Why?"

"Alex, they're not really 'our' terms," I say. "That's the problem. It feels more like something you're running with, and I'm just along for the ride. I want this to be a partnership."

Alex props his arm up on the head of the couch. "I do, too. Just because I'm the one that came up with a lot of the ideas doesn't mean you're not involved. I thought this was what you wanted."

"A close partnership with Eterand, yes. Secure borders without crippling my already dying budget, yes. Those are the things I want, but I want to make these decisions together. I don't like feeling blind-sided which is kind of how it's been lately."

He sits back a little. "I wasn't trying to blindside you, I promise. Based on all of our conversations, I thought this was what you want-ed."

"Maybe I thought so, too, and maybe I was a little bit misleading, and for that, I'm sorry. But right now, I feel much clearer about what I want, and I think you and I can work this out as the heirs to our countries, don't you think?"

He nods. "That's really what I want. I want to have the close rela-tionship our fathers had. I felt like there was a wall between us, and ever since you told me what happened, I feel like it finally came down, like we can be us again."

"It was important to me that you knew everything that happened as my ally and my friend."

"It really does mean the world to me that you told me. I don't think I really expressed that the other day."

"You did."

"And I want this to work out between us."

"I do, too. I want us to be on the same page," I say, but when he leans just a little too close to me, I feel like maybe we're not on the same page, and the urge to lean away is strong.

"I'm so glad we finally worked this out."

Before I can answer, his lips are on mine, and for a moment, an image of us at thirteen flashes through my mind as I see what I wanted more than anything to happen happening right now. I wanted nothing more back then than to be with Alex and to kiss Alex for real, not just so we could say we did. But it's just a flash, and the second it disappears, all I see is Zane's face, and even though Alex's lips are pressed against mine, my lips have never felt so empty, so vacant, without Zane's.

I push Alex's shoulder back rather harshly, then a little more gently, and turn my face away from his.

"What, what's wrong?" he says.

"What? Why did you do that?"

"What do you mean why did I do that? I thought we were being clear."

"I did, too."

"I thought we were talking about the same thing."

"I did, too."

"You said you wanted us on the same page, that you wanted us to be close."

"*You* said you wanted us to be close."

"So? I thought you were agreeing with me."

"Why on earth would you think that?"

"Is it so unbelievable?"

I jump up off the couch and run my hands down the sides of my face. "Alex, I have a boyfriend." And all I can picture is Zane's face, that beautiful face that warned me this might happen, and I laughed into it.

"I didn't think it was that serious."

"What? I introduced him to you as my boyfriend, I told you we've been seeing each other for a year, I told you that he moved his entire life here for me, I told you what he meant to me. How could you think I wasn't serious about him?" Even as I say the words, I wonder if I can totally blame Alex. Have I really made it clear? Would Zane think I had made it clear to Alex?

He raises his voice. "Look, I know he's important to you, but it seemed like you two weren't really connecting. He did leave, and it seemed like you wanted to see where this could go."

"Whether or not Zane and I are having problems is none of your business. And even if we are, what right does that give you to kiss me like that?"

He stands up, and the fire in his eyes is fierce. "Was it really so terrible, so undesirable to kiss me? You act like it's the worst thing in the world."

"I have a boyfriend."

"Can't you admit you always liked me?"

"It doesn't matter what I ever felt for you. I am with Zane."

"But we go way back. We have a connection that he'll never have with you."

"And he has a connection with me that you'll never have."

"What, because he just happened to be there when you needed him?"

"No, because he happened to love me and take care of me when neither he nor I knew who I was. Where were you?"

"You were dead."

"And Trilland? Was Trilland dead? You could have helped. You could have done something, anything, but you didn't. And now you have the nerve to kiss me and act like somehow it's Zane's fault and that I should be thrilled to be kissed by you?"

"So you never once wanted to kiss me?"

I sigh and lower my voice to something barely above a whisper. "Maybe when we were children, too young to know who we were yet, I thought we were meant to be. But that was a long time ago, Alex. We're different. I'm different. I'm in love with Zane. I need you to respect that."

He sits down on the couch and avoids eye contact, instead fiddling with a loose thread on his pant leg. "Fine. I get it." It's so quiet that I almost don't hear it. Neither one of us says anything for a while, but after a period of awkward silence, he says, "So did you want to talk about the terms of the deal?"

I shake my head. "Maybe I should just go. We can talk about it tomorrow or the day after when your father gets here."

He shrugs lazily. "Okay."

I feel a strange need to say something more, but why should I? What could I say? So I walk out the door without saying anything else.

I told Zane not to worry about Alex. I told him that I trusted him. I told him that he should trust him. I argued with him when he distrusted Alex. I told him off whenever he voiced his concern or his hurt or his anger. I watched him leave and didn't fight for him to stay. I actually put somebody else ahead of Zane again and then was surprised when he reacted badly. I ignored Jane when she warned me not to hurt Zane. I can hardly blame him for needing space, but it still feels like a knife in the gut.

If I ever see him again, I don't think "sorry" will ever be enough.

Chapter 17

I hardly notice the walk back to the palace today. Nothing seems sure or stable anymore. I don't know if I should trust Alex, if I should expand this alliance, allow Eterand's involvement in Trilland. I don't know if risking our sovereignty is worth it. But then I see the struggles of the people of Trilland, and I feel like I should do something, anything at all that might help even a little bit. But then I think of Zane, how much he's tried to support me, how he's put up with my indecision and with Alex's presence, how upset he's been recently, and how I've completely blown him off in favor of my own problems. I think of the people at the town hall and how they begged me for help. I think of Parliament the day they practically screamed at me for involving Alex. I think of the school with the students who gave me hope and the senators who crushed that hope. I think of Maris Island and how they trusted me to protect their way of life and how Alex is now infringing on that as I allow it to happen. I think of how Brent and I were just starting to feel normal again until I made a decision he had cautiously warned against and he began distancing himself again. I think of how I blamed Uncle Lawrence for Trilland's problems when he was just trying to keep me safe the way he couldn't before. And between all of those thoughts and the supreme effort it takes not to burst into tears out on the streets, I almost don't notice Zane standing outside of the palace.

When I do see him, I can hardly believe my eyes. He hasn't been gone for more than about a week, and yet I feel like it's been months. I was afraid he would be gone much longer than this. He was so angry, and I thought he would decide to go back to the island. But here he is standing outside of the palace, one foot propped against the wall, the way he always looks when he comes back from visiting the island.

"There you are," he says when I get close enough to hear him. "You took forever. I've been waiting here for a while now."

I can't stop the tears this time, so I run straight into Zane's arms so hard that I scratch my knuckles on the wall when I reach around his waist. I cry hard and ugly into his chest, and when he holds me just tightly enough and rubs my back, I feel whole just for a moment. I let everything come out without holding back, and I don't know if I stand there crying on the palace steps for a few seconds or twenty minutes, but when I finally stop, my eyes feel swollen, my nose feels stuffed, but I feel so much better.

"Uh, is everything okay?" he says. "You seem upset."

I can't help but laugh. "I'm okay now. I'm so glad you're back."

"Yeah, sorry about that. It took longer than I thought it would."

"Longer? I was afraid you'd be gone for a while."

Zane looks legitimately confused. "Why would I be gone for a long time?"

"I thought you needed space, that you were mad and trying to get away from me." I hesitate but decide that I've already sobbed all over him, so I might as well say it. "I thought you were thinking of going back permanently."

Zane's eyes get wide. "Permanently? Maris, no. I mean, yeah, I was kind of mad, but I'm not going anywhere. I just had some stuff to do. I didn't mean to scare you. I love you, and I want to be wherever you are."

He kisses me gently, and a feeling of warmth rushes over me. All of my fears and problems about Trilland are still swirling around in my head, but now I feel a little less like they might kill me.

"Actually, I've got a surprise for you."

"You do? I thought you were going to help your mom with something."

Zane takes my hand and leads me inside. "Well, I did, but you've been so stressed out lately. I wanted to bring you something from the island. Something that I thought would make you feel better."

"And what is that?"

Zane opens the door to the dining room, and I see Harper sitting at the table drinking tea, and somewhere in my brain it registers that the tea cup is one of hers from home, and it's laughable that this stubborn woman insisted on bringing her own cups and probably her own tea to Trilland. She looks perfect, just exactly Harper-like, as if she were just teleported to this place right now. She's wearing one of her nicer dresses, but her hair is still in the same kind of messy half-up style. Before I can even process my excitement, Zane lets out a huff.

"Ma, you were supposed to watch her."

Harper shrugs. "She wanted ice cream." Zane sighs again.

"Who?"

As if I called them, Elise and Daisy walk in from the kitchen, each with a giant bowl of ice cream. It isn't lost on me that Elise is eating Jane's mint chocolate chip, as if I needed another comparison between the two. Daisy seems to have mixed several flavors together in what is sure to be a stomachache tonight. Elise squeals, sets her bowl down, and runs at me, throwing her arms around my neck.

"You're here," I stammer out. "You're all here."

"We are," Elise says. "Okay. You have awesome ice cream, this house is huge, your hair looks gorgeous, and the weather here is way better than on the island. Also, I met your chef, and we traded a few recipes."

I fall apart into fits of laughter because Elise is here and she's perfect. I can only imagine Chef James's reaction to Elise trying to critique his food and exchange recipes. The moment Elise lets go, Daisy replaces her. I'm startled by how far up her arms reach. She's nearly my height.

"You're so tall," I exclaim.

"Three inches this year," she says.

Zane adds, "Two and a half."

"*Three*."

"What are you all doing here?"

"Zane thought you needed a piece of home," Elise says. "Even though, I guess technically, this is home. That's still confusing to me."

"Don't let them fool you," Zane says. "I was only planning on bringing my mom, but Elise insisted on coming, and that little brat practically snuck onto the ship."

I face Zane. "You went back to get your mom? For me?"

He smiles and nods. "It seemed like you could use a talk with her."

I feel the tears start again even though I thought I had cried them all out already. Zane and Harper see it coming, so they quickly try to get Daisy out of the room.

"Daisy, why don't you and Elise go finish your ice cream in the kitchen?" Harper says.

"But we just got here," Daisy says.

"Zane," I say, "Why don't you find Jane and have her take them to my closet. I think Elise will love to see my dresses, and Daisy once threatened me with trying on my tiaras."

"You remembered," Daisy says with a smirk.

I shrug. "I do remember some things now, you know."

Elise and Daisy collect their ice cream bowls and head out, but I grab Zane's arm and give him a quick kiss.

"Thank you."

He smiles. "Anything for you."

Once they've left, I sit down next to Harper, and she wraps her arms around me and hugs me the way only a mother can. I cry again, not as dramatically this time, but it feels like a release once again. She scratches my back, and I catch a whiff of her tea and confirm that it is, in fact, her own blend from Tito's herbs.

"Trilland is beautiful," Harper says. "It isn't anything like I pictured."

"What did you picture?"

"I'm not sure. Something more extravagant, I guess." She takes a sip of tea. "So, what's going on?"

"What do you mean?"

"I mean, my son sailed across the sea to bring me to you because he thought you needed me. What's going on?"

And it all pours out of me. Everything about the budget and Parliament and Alex and Trilland and Maris Island and how I'm possibly failing everyone and how I don't know how to fix everything. I cry a few more times as I talk, but Harper never says anything. She only stops a couple of times to ask for clarification, but otherwise, she lets me talk freely and without interruption or judgment. It's nice to talk without anyone contributing what they think are helpful suggestions or opinions.

"I've known Alex my whole life, you know? His family and my family were best friends, and Eterand is our oldest ally, so it seems like a good idea, but I don't want to risk Trilland's independence for anyone, including the Cartwrights. And now it's impacting Maris Island."

"You have to decide what is right for Trilland and for you. You know your country best, better than anyone."

"That's just the thing: I don't. I lost a year, and I was so young before that. I'm not sure that I do know it best."

Harper sips her tea again. "Knowing a country isn't about how long you've lived there or how much experience you have. It's about how much you care about that country. Maris Island is my home not because I've lived there my whole life but because it's where I belong. I feel it in my heart. I feel it when I look out at the ocean where Zane fishes and where Daisy swims. I feel it in that community that is my family. Based on the way you talk about it, I can tell you feel that for Trilland. You have to tap into that to make your decision."

"Trilland is my home, but you make it sound so easy. I'm so afraid of failing these people again."

"You didn't fail them, Maris, Cassandra did."

"I'm afraid I might have failed them in another way."

"What do you mean?"

I twist my lip. "I've been considering telling Trilland."

"About what, dear? Your memory loss?"

I nod. "I feel like I'm lying to them. Brent and Zane both think it's a terrible idea. They protested enough as it is when I told Alex. But do you think that's the right decision?"

"Do you?"

"I asked you first."

Harper smiles that motherly smile that seems to communicate that she's trying to teach you something that you're not picking up on. "Dear, it doesn't matter what I think or what Brent, Alex, or even Zane thinks. They are not in charge of Trilland or in charge of your life. What matters is what you think is the right decision. You chose not to tell Trilland because you felt it was the right decision at the time, but you always said you would change that if you thought they should know. What you need to ask yourself is, is it time that they need to know? And don't worry about all those boys. Zane and Brent will respect whatever decision you make because they respect you. I don't know Alex, but if he is who you say he is, he'll respect it, too."

I slump back into my chair. "I'm just not sure about much of anything."

"Are you sure that you love Trilland and want the best for it?"

"Of course."

"Are you sure that you love my son?"

I can't stop myself from blushing. "Yes."

"And are you sure that you have no regrets about coming back here?"

"None."

"Then you are sure of the most important things. You just have to trust yourself."

"I wish you could have met my mother," I say. "I think you would have really liked her. You two are different, but there is something so similar."

Harper holds my hand in hers. "I wish I could have met her, too. But what's most important to me is that I met you."

Chapter 18

When I was a kid, I never liked days when foreign dignitaries arrived because there was always a lot of chaos and preparation. I always felt like it disrupted everything I liked about my sleepy little beach town. I hardly believed my eyes when I saw Alex a few weeks ago because there had been no fanfare, and it isn't like Alex to show up without a lot of show.

I still don't like the chaos now as I watch Eterand's ships pull into the docks from my balcony. Brent, Lady Vivian, Annette, and Jane have all come in here at least a dozen times each to ask questions I don't care about, and it looks like the entirety of the docks has been completely disrupted by the arrival. It isn't even that King Norman wants it this way—it's just the way it is.

I can't seem to decide how I feel about Norman's arrival. My stomach does flip-flops at the idea of having to look him in the eye and not tell him about the amnesia. It also churns at the idea of going behind Alex's back to tell Norman that I don't agree with his son's plans for the alliance restructuring. But I feel a kind of peace at seeing an old friend step off the plank onto the docks. He looks just like he always has; I swear, that man hasn't aged a single day since I was a child. Seeing him the way he's always been makes me think of my father, and that brings a smile to my face. I only wish his wife were joining him. Nothing and no one reminds me of my parents more than they do.

A knock at the door for the thousandth time this morning disrupts my reminiscing, and I can't help but let out a sigh. It's just going to be one of those days.

"Come in."

Lady Vivian steps in, Brent following closely behind. "He's here."

I nod. "I watched him from the window. Is everything ready?"

Lady Vivian smiles coyly. "Of course. Are you ready?"

"As I'll ever be. Is Alex downstairs already?" Lady Vivian and Brent exchange a strange look. "What is it?"

"He's not downstairs," Brent says.

"What do you mean?"

"He came over a little while ago, but he decided not to wait for his arrival. He said that he'll see him later."

"He's not greeting his father? That's awful, not to mention that it's going to look terrible to the press."

Brent shrugs, but his eyes betray pity. "I tried to convince him to stay, but he would not be persuaded."

I nod slowly. "Is Zane downstairs?"

"I didn't see him," Brent says. "I'm not sure where he is. I checked his room, but he wasn't there."

Another slow nod. I'm not sure I ever would have guessed that Brent would be the most reliable person in a situation like this, but here we are. I'm not sure what I would do without him here.

"Okay, it's now or never, I guess. Let's go."

The three of us walk down the steps as quickly as we can without looking undignified and take our respective places in the foyer. I stand on my own in the center, Brent and Lady Vivian to the right, the household staff to the right, and a painfully obvious gap beside me where Alex should be and an even more obvious gap where Zane should be. I face the staff and smile as pleasantly as I can, but I spot Harper next to Annette and smile for real.

"Harper, you're here for this?"

"Is that okay?" she says, as if it could ever be anything but absolutely wonderful to have her around. "Annette let me borrow a dress so that I wouldn't embarrass you."

I rush over to her and kiss her on the forehead. "You could never. I'm so, so happy to have you here. Daisy?"

"She's at the beach with Elise. I didn't think her screaming over a king and a prince would be a good image to present."

We both laugh, and I see that all of the staff members are holding back laughter as well. Daisy has certainly made quite an impression since she's been here.

"Am I too late?" I hear over the crowd, and when the staff part to let him through, I see Zane wearing a beige suit, and it looks like he actually brushed his hair. He's a little red and sweaty and out of breath presumably from rushing over here, but I don't even care. "Is this suit okay?" he says to me as soon as he reaches me. "I got it at the shop down the street, and I wanted to get black or navy, but I couldn't afford that, so I got this, and I thought it would be okay since this is a beach town, but now I'm second-guessing everything because you're wearing a beautiful dress, and I look stupid next to you—"

I grab his face and kiss him as passionately as I can without looking unprofessional, and he almost tries to keep babbling, but he stops pretty quickly. I notice that he smells like a pretty expensive cologne, and I start to wonder just how much money he spent on all of this just because he thinks he needs to compare to me or Alex or someone when he could have shown up straight from fishing, and I would have been ecstatic.

"So, this is okay?" he says, gesturing to his suit.

"Oh my word, Zane," Harper says with an eye roll.

"It's perfect," I say. "But you didn't have to spend your own money on this."

Zane smiles that perfect, uneven, quirky smile I fell in love with, and my heartbeat speeds up. "I know this is important to you."

"But you could have used the royal funds—"

"No." Zane shakes his head. "I needed to do this."

"King Norman Cartwright of Eterand entering," the guards shout, and everyone straightens up.

Zane steps to my side and looks around. "Where's Alex?"

"That's a whole other story."

The processional ahead of Norman is elaborate and, in my opinion, kind of ridiculous. My father always used to limit his processional because he thought it looked pompous. I didn't know what pompous meant as a kid, but I always knew he considered Norman, as good of friends as they were, to be a little pompous. I see what he meant now. I would be beet red by the time I got to any front door if I had this going in front of me.

Norman's frame enters the doorway, obscured by the sunshine behind him, and I somehow feel calmer than I did even five minutes ago. For all of the show and excess and chaos that comes with his arrival, I'll always see the man who came immediately after my father died and held the pieces together and refused to let anyone push my mother around or make condescending remarks about my young age, and I think of his wife who held my mother's hand as she cried and never said a word because she knew words were meaningless at that point and that my mother just needed a friend.

"Lorraine!" His booming voice is followed by outstretched arms, and I have to stop myself from actually running to him. "It's been too long."

I walk as quickly as I can in these unbelievably uncomfortable shoes and practically collapse into his arms, which probably doesn't make me look mature in all of the video footage, but I can't help but be happy right now, just for a moment.

"It has," I say. "What has it been, four years? Five?"

"Ugh, it can't have been that long, can it? Promise me that we'll never go that long without seeing each other again."

"Promise."

"You have to visit Eterand. My wife is dying to see you. She was so disappointed that she couldn't come along, but Eterand has an important charity benefit coming up, and she just didn't feel that she could leave with so much still to plan."

"I'd love to see Eterand. It's been years."

"A lot has changed."

"A lot has changed here, too."

He looks sad for just a moment—not sad, exactly, maybe sentimental. He scans the room quickly, probably hoping I won't notice his eyes glancing around the room with Alex nowhere to be found, so I pretend that I don't notice, but the expression on his face is comical when he spots Zane. His eyes widen, and he raises an eyebrow at me.

"Well, why don't you introduce me to those I don't already know."

I take his arm and walk him over to Zane first. "This is Zane Adler, my boyfriend."

"Well, it's very nice to meet you, Mr. Adler."

"You as well, Your Majesty." Zane's bowing has gotten much better. "And please, call me Zane."

"Are you from Trilland?"

"No, sir, I am from Maris Island."

"Ah, yes, the new province. How exciting."

"Yes, Zane and I met while I was there. He and his family were extremely kind, taking care of me while I was there and helping me get back to Trilland."

Norman nods slowly. "Well, I think all of Trilland and Eterand owe you a debt of gratitude, then. I can't imagine Trilland without Lorraine."

"It certainly wouldn't be the same, sir."

I lead him over to Harper. "And this is Zane's mother Harper. She's in town for a few days to visit. Zane's sister Daisy and my friend Elise are also here, but they are at the beach right now enjoying the beautiful day, so you'll have to meet them later."

Harper curtsies possibly the worst curtsy I've ever seen, and yet, I can tell that she's been practicing probably with Annette. The effort these two have gone to for me is truly touching.

"Your Majesty."

"A pleasure to meet you as well."

"And this is Brent Grayson," I say, gesturing for Brent to step forward, and he does. "Brent is my press secretary, but he is also the person Uncle Lawrence sent to find me. He's from Gessend."

"Your Majesty." Brent's bow is the best yet, of course.

"Ah, well, thank you, young man, for all you've done. We're very grateful."

"I'm just glad Lorraine was able to make it back."

Norman takes the liberty of greeting everyone else that he knows, kissing the hands of Annette and Jane and Lady Vivian. This is something I have loved about my father and Norman since I was a small child. Other foreign dignitaries often would not greet Annette or Jane and sometimes not even Lady Vivian because they considered them servants. My father and Norman never did that. They always understood that these people are family.

After he's made the rounds, Norman very gently takes me by the arm and pulls me aside, out of earshot of everyone else, especially the cameras.

"Do you know where my son is?"

I shake my head slowly, trying to convey some kind of remorse. "I told him what time you were arriving, but I haven't seen him since yesterday. Brent looked for him this morning but couldn't find him."

"Couldn't find him, or couldn't convince him to be here?" He knows Alex too well. When I don't say anything, he's got his answer. He nods, clears his throat, and puts his public face back on.

"Well, we have much to discuss, so let's get right to it. I'll just freshen up and meet you in half an hour. Is that all right?"

"Of course. I'll see you in the parlor room in the west wing."

"Is Alex staying in our usual quarters?"

"He is."

"Then I'll head over there." He takes my hands in his and kisses each one. "Lovely to see you again. I'm looking forward to talking with you."

And with that, the entire processional heads out through the gardens. I maintain a smile on my face, which isn't hard after seeing Norman, until the cameras click off and the press members start heading out, directed by Brent. The entire room breathes a sigh of relief that the entire thing is over now, and members of the household staff resume their usual duties. Lady Vivian briefs me on a couple of details for the press conference with the Cartwrights later this week and then leaves, and Brent practically pushes everyone else out the door. Honestly, that is what makes him the best press secretary ever: he always gets rid of the cameras as soon as they're turned off.

"He seems really nice," Zane says.

"He is."

"I'm glad I got a chance to meet him."

"I'm so glad you were here. I was afraid you weren't going to make it."

Zane's mouth twitches just a little. "Would you like to take a walk in the garden with me?"

I nod, he takes my hand, and we walk into the garden. The processional is nearly at the guest quarters by now, and everyone else is busying themselves preparing the house for Norman's return, so we have the garden mostly to ourselves other than few gardeners. We walk for a few minutes without saying anything, and even though it's a beautiful day, the air feels heavy. We haven't spoken much since our fight over Alex's invasion. He left right after that, and even since he's been back, we've only spoken a few times. It's been friendly, but the tension hasn't completely dissipated. I hate this feeling like we're not normal. I want everything between Zane and me to be like it was. Maybe that isn't possible anymore.

"We haven't really talked about my leaving since I got back."

"Sure, we did."

He shakes his head. "You told me that you were afraid that I was leaving, and I told you that I'm never leaving. But we didn't talk about why I left."

We turn a corner in the gardens to avoid some of the gardeners, but we don't stop walking. It feels nice to walk. Somehow walking makes difficult conversations easier to have. Something about the constant movement and the lack of eye contact makes it easier to be open.

"I feel really bad that I scared you like that," he says. "I didn't mean to, but I can't blame you for thinking that. After all, I'm the stupid idiot who didn't come to see you when you left for Trilland."

"Zane, we've talked about that. That's water under the bridge."

"But it's not. I can't stop kicking myself for that. It was so wrong."

I squeeze his hand. "You can't keep beating yourself up over that. It's over."

"But that's why you were afraid that I was leaving when I went to the island, isn't it?" My silence is his answer. "That's why I'm still bothered by it. I'm not going anywhere. I felt like you needed help, and I obviously wasn't helping, so I thought I would go get someone who would help. I didn't think about the fact that if I didn't tell you, you would think the worst. It's my own stupid fault for yelling at you."

"You were right not to trust Alex."

"I wasn't."

"You were. I didn't think Alex would do any of this. I guess I put too much into my memories of him when we were kids. I shouldn't have trusted him so much without finding out what kind of a king he was going to be. He isn't like his father."

"But it was your decision, and I shouldn't have made you feel bad about it. And I hate that I was jealous of him. Sometimes, I just feel so out of place here like I'm embarrassing you or like everyone thinks I'm not good enough to be with you. It just seems so obvious that a princess would be with a prince, and it seemed like he had a thing for you, but nothing happened, and I shouldn't have projected my own insecurities onto him."

I stop walking and force Zane to look at me. Somehow, I feel like I do need eye contact for this one. "Zane, you could never embarrass me. Honestly, sometimes I think I'm not good enough for you. You're so kind and strong, and you've done so much for me these past two years, and you've uprooted your entire life for me. I worry that you regret leaving everything behind. I know how much you love that island."

"I do love that island, but it's just a piece of land. Nothing can compare to the way that I love you."

I twist my mouth. "And you should know that you weren't totally projecting. Alex did try to make a move."

"What?" he shouts, and the gardeners risk a glance at us.

"Nothing happened. When I refused him, he got kind of mad, and that's when he started acting like this, skipping out on his duties. I guess I upset him."

"You didn't do anything. He's a jerk for pulling that just because you turned him down."

"The thing is a lot of people, including me for a period of time when we were young, thought that Alex and I would end up together. It seemed obvious since our parents were so close and Eterand and Trilland were such good allies. Politically, it made perfect sense. But I never loved him, not even for a day. And I don't think he loves me either. I didn't want to acknowledge any of that to you because I was afraid you'd get jealous or you'd be hurt if you knew, but maybe I just made you feel like your concerns didn't matter when nothing could be further from the truth."

Zane nods just slightly. His eyes look just a little red, and I know I've hit a nerve. Part of me still wonders if telling him about Alex's attempts was the right decision, but there's no going back now, and Zane isn't yelling or anything, so I guess it's okay.

"How did we let this get so messed up?" he says.

I shrug. "I had so much going on with Parliament and Alex and everything that I think I just took you for granted. In a weird way, when you left for the island, it reminded me of what I have with you."

Zane hugs me, and I feel that familiar safe feeling that I always feel when I'm in his arms. Sometimes, I think about what the past two years would have looked like without Zane. Would I have survived the mutiny? Would I have been able to handle the stress back in Trilland? I don't like dwelling on it because a world without Zane sounds miserable. It's then that I realize Zane and I can't be, will never be what we were, and maybe it's better this way. What we have now is beyond what I ever could have hoped we could have.

"What are you going to do about Alex?"

"Well, I can't go through with Alex's plan, that's for sure. And I don't think Norman is aware of anything Alex has done so far. My hunch is that's why Alex didn't show up today."

"Is he just missing?"

"Brent says he talked to him this morning and tried to convince him to come, but he refused. I haven't actually seen him myself since early yesterday."

"Are you going to tell King Norman about Alex's plan?"

I pick at the side of my finger a moment before answering. "It seems kind of sneaky to go behind Alex's back to his father and undermine his authority as prince, but I don't know what else to do."

"He's not king yet."

"And I'm not queen yet."

"That's different. There isn't a current ruler."

My heart starts beating quickly, and my skin feels cold. "I'm also worried he's going to tell Trilland."

"About—"

"Yes."

"What makes you say that?"

"He's been commenting on it ever since I told him. He keeps making remarks about how I should trust Trilland and how Eterand would want to know, too. I'm afraid he might say so at the press conference, especially if he catches wind that I'm backing out of the deal."

"Is he that devious?"

"I didn't think so, but people can be desperate when they think there's something at stake. He's desperate to prove to himself, his father, and his country that he's a capable and powerful king. If I back out of our deal, it makes him look immature. He doesn't want that."

"And blabbing someone else's secret doesn't make him look bad?"

I shake my head. "He wouldn't frame it that way."

Zane sighs. "So, what are you going to do?"

"I wish I knew. Your mom says that I do know what to do somewhere deep inside."

He laughs. "Yeah, she's like that."

"I do know that if anyone is going to tell Trilland about my memory, it's going to be me."

Zane's breath hitches, but he tries to hide it. "Will you tell them?"

"I know you and everyone else don't think it's a good idea, but maybe it's the right thing to do at this point. Maybe I finally need to be honest with everyone."

"It's your call. Whatever decision you make, I'll support it."

I look around the gardens, but it's still quiet—just the gardeners around. "I wish I knew where Alex was."

Zane snorts. "It's for the best. I might've punched him out for coming on to you."

I can't help but chuckle. "You didn't know he did that until now."

He squints. "I would have seen it on his face."

I look around the gardens again, but still no Alex. I wonder where he went after he talked to Brent. I wonder if he's in the guest quarters right now talking to his father. I wonder if he's going behind my back to Parliament. A small part of me wonders if he left Trilland entirely. I may not know what he's up to at this point, but I do know that I can't let him control me anymore.

~~~

The meeting with Norman is televised, unfortunately. I'd rather be able to talk to him freely about my concerns with Alex's deal, but
~~~

I can't trash Alex on TV. Luckily, Norman knows as well as I do that you can't talk freely in front of cameras, so his comments are pretty restrained as well. He gives me a few updates on how Eterand is doing, and I do the same with Trilland, we discuss the basics of our alliance terms, and then move on to the new alliance terms. During the discussions about Alex's deal, he keeps his questions simple and without complication.

"Have you discussed the specific terms with my son?"

"I have, but I'd like to meet with him again later today before the press conference tomorrow. I think we still have a few details to hammer out."

He nods. "I'll have a word with both of you after that. It's his deal to handle, but I'd like to be kept up-to-date."

"Of course."

"Captain," Norman says, turning to Uncle Lawrence, "I'd also like to speak with you later, if I could. I know you've made some changes to the naval structure since you returned, and I'd like to hear the logic behind it to determine if it's something Eterand should consider."

"I'd be happy to," he says.

"Lorraine, is there anything else that is pressing? If not, I'd like to take a break and sightsee Trilland a little bit. It's been so many years since I've been here."

"I have nothing else for now. Thank you for meeting."

I dismiss the cameras, the press, and everyone except for Norman, Lady Vivian, Brent, and Uncle Lawrence. Once everyone is gone, I take a deep breath and turn to face Norman again.

"Norman, if you wouldn't mind staying, there's something I need to tell you about what happened to me after the mutiny."

Everyone in the room except for Norman tenses up. They all know what I'm about to say. Uncle Lawrence and Brent give me a look that seems to communicate *are you sure?* But Lady Vivian's expression surprises me. She looks calm, almost happy that I'm about to tell him. She seems at peace about it. Maybe she thinks it's the right idea. Maybe I should have talked to her about this. She might've helped.

Norman smiles slightly, but he senses the tension in the room. He looks around, holding eye contact with Uncle Lawrence as if trying to read the topic of conversation in his eyes, and it seems he almost succeeds as Uncle Lawrence turns away from his gaze.

"Should I be concerned?" Norman says. "I know I'm getting older, but I can tell when everyone is nervous."

I shake my head. "There's nothing to be concerned about anymore, but I think you deserve to know what really happened, especially before we get any further into talks about our alliance going forward."

I tell him every little detail—more detail than I told Alex. I tell him about waking up in Ms. Flora's house, about my inability to answer Zane's and Harper's questions, moving in with Elise, the outfit I was wearing when I arrived that haunted me for nearly a year, Brent's arrival, the picture of myself that I thought would come to life and attack me, that awful day in Anden, and Brent's and my adventure running from Cassandra and crafting a plan to take her down. I let myself be a little more vulnerable than I have with anyone else that I've told this story to. I share all the little insecurities, the fears, the doubts that I never tell anyone that really only Zane and Jane have any understanding of. He tries to interrupt a few times, though it's clear he doesn't really know what to say, but I don't let him until everything stops tumbling out of me like word vomit, the poison that has been making me sick, and now that it's out, I feel just a little less contaminated.

Now that I'm done and need him to say something, of course, he doesn't. He just stares at me, twisting his mouth repeatedly, his mustache mimicking the movement of his lips. He sniffs a few times, and I can tell he's holding back tears. I hope he doesn't let them loose because if he cries, I know that I will and probably so will Uncle Lawrence and Lady Vivian, leaving Brent awkwardly by himself as the only one who can control his emotions.

"I hardly know what to say," he says. "I just have half-thoughts spinning in my head, and I don't know how to say any of them."

Uncle Lawrence nods slowly. "The same thing happened to me. I just sputtered random things at her until I thoroughly overwhelmed her when she told me."

Norman spins around in his chair. "You didn't know?" Uncle Lawrence shakes his head. "When did you find out what happened?"

"When she and Brent got to Gessend. I had no way of knowing that she was hurt. Brent got there and found out what had happened. I found out when Lorraine looked at me like a stranger when I threw my arms around her and cried tears of joy that she was alive."

I can't help but look at Brent, who looks pained and shifts in his seat. All was forgiven long ago, but I think Uncle Lawrence remained angry longer than I did about Brent's actions.

"I can't believe you didn't know sooner."

"It was an extremely complicated situation," I say.

Brent sighs ever so slightly and stares down at his hands which are folded in his lap. I wait for Brent to make eye contact with me. When he does, I raise my eyebrows, and he shakes his head just the slightest little bit, telling me not to defend him, or maybe not to expose him, but either way, it doesn't matter. He didn't decide to tell the king of Eterand his life story of the last two years; I did.

"Does my son know?"

I nod. "He knows me too well. He knew I wasn't being completely honest with him, and I just couldn't hide it anymore from people I consider family. I would have told you sooner, but it's not the kind of conversation you have over the phone or in a letter." I lock eyes with Brent again, and he offers the smallest, meekest smile. "I chose not to tell Trilland because I feared Cassandra would use it against me or because it would worry them, but I hope you understand why I did what I did."

Norman nods vigorously. "I completely understand. In my opinion, you did the right thing. But what does this mean going forward?"

I breathe in, then again, before finally breathing out. "I can't say that I know if telling Trilland now is the right decision. I wish I could. But I do know that I think Alex is going to tell them at the press conference tomorrow."

"What?" Norman stands up suddenly, throwing his chair back and startling everyone in the room. "He has no right. What makes you say that? Did he say he was going to do that?"

I shake my head. "Not directly, but he's said several things that give me the impression. I can't say it's anything more than a gut feeling, to be fair, but if the information is going to get out, it should be me that shares it, not him."

"If I may," Brent says quietly, "while I agree that it should be you, it shouldn't be you just to stop him. It should be because it's the right decision."

Norman says, "I can pull him from the press conference. You and I can do it instead."

I shake my head again. "That would irreparably damage his ethos as a future ruler, and I can't do that to him."

"But—"

"The pressure of living up to our fathers and proving ourselves is something that no one understands in this room except for me. Alex is not a villain. He is my friend and my ally, and I won't undermine his authority even if, in his misguided efforts, he is about to undermine mine."

"Well, maybe the three of us need to sit down to rewrite some of the language of the agreement."

"I didn't have a hand in that the first time," I say. "Alex wrote the whole thing."

Norman says, "Well, what do you want?"

"I have ideas."

"Write them down. You two should be equals here. I think you should write your own proposal to give to Alex after I approve it, of course."

"I have been working on something."

"Good."

"But that doesn't help us right now."

Norman sighs, rights his chair, and sits back down. "So, what do we do going forward?"

Chapter 19

The only thing I can ever think to do when I don't know what else to do is go down to the beach. I've done this my whole life. Any time something has gone wrong in my life or I haven't known what decision to make or I've failed at something, I've come down to the private beach behind the palace. This is where I came after my first flubbed speech, when I caught Alex kissing Princess Rhea, before my first meeting with Parliament, my first night back in the palace, the night Zane went back to the island, and just about every night for the past two weeks. I stand here at the edge of the beach just close enough for the water to graze my feet just barely and let the chill from the ocean wind whip my face just until it stings.

I feel better now that Norman knows everything that happened, but I'm still uncomfortable taking the stage with Alex tomorrow without talking to him first today. The last thing I want to do is shame him publicly by refusing the new agreement without telling him first, but how can I when he isn't around? His father is itching to work things out with me without Alex, and I'm trying to be respectful of Alex's budding leadership, but he isn't making it easy.

I could always delay it, I suppose. Just announce at the press conference that we're still hammering out the details. But Trilland is already furious at how long it's taking to see any real improvement. If I don't offer something tangible, everything will get worse.

And that doesn't even address what I'm going to do about Eterand's ships that are crawling everywhere. A lot of the provinces are extremely nervous about that, but I don't want to just command them away without explanation as to why they were there in the first place.

"Lorraine."

I turn around to see Alex staggering down the beach, stumbling over every slight mound of sand. So, he finally emerges.

"Lorraine, hey," he says a little too loudly. "How's it going?"

"Uh, fine. What are you doing?"

He spreads his arms out. "Just hanging. Enjoying Trilland's beautiful scapesea—seascape."

When he gets closer, the smell of Trilland's finest spirits weighs the air down tangibly. "Alex, are you drunk?"

He jerks his head back in drunk astonishment and makes that face that drunks always make when they are deeply insulted that you would accuse them of being drunk when they can't even walk straight. "Why would you say that? I've had a few drinks, but I can handle it."

"So, that's where you've been all morning? Off drinking somewhere instead of greeting your father when he arrived?"

"I see him all the time. He doesn't need me to greet him. Besides, I'm celebrating. You and me, we're closing the deal tomorrow."

"Yeah, about that, I need to talk to you about the deal. I've been looking for you since yesterday."

"Yeah, Brent rambled something like that."

"Right. This morning when he was going beyond his job description and desperately trying to convince you to do your duty. I know."

He furrows his eyebrows, and when I see him clench his fist, I know I've hit a nerve. "My duty is not to my father. I'm Prince of Eterand, not Prince of Norman Cartwright. I don't need your press secretary telling me what my job is."

"Well considering the fact that my *press secretary* is doing better at his job right now than you, I suggest you take some hints from him when he tries to help you out."

"Are you seriously mad at me for not showing up for my own father?"

"I'm mad that you didn't show up for me. You expect me to sign this deal with you, and I can't even trust you to show up for five minutes and do something simple? How can I trust you to protect Trilland's coast or even me? How can I put Trilland's independence on the line for you right now?"

He shifts his weight and stumbles. "I never asked you to put aside Trilland's independence."

"Your invasion of our provinces kind of did that for you."

"I didn't invade any provinces."

"Maris Island?"

He scoffs. "That hardly counts."

I fold my arms. "You're not the one who gets to decide what counts and what doesn't. It's my province, and I told you that I didn't want your ships hanging around, especially not before we sign the deal."

"Fine, I'll move them if it's that big a deal."

"It's not just about the ships, Alex. We still have a lot of issues to work out before tomorrow."

He squints. "You're not backing out are you?"

"How can I back out of something we haven't really discussed?"

He sighs hard and kicks the sand under his feet, causing him to wobble. "You know, I thought we were really getting somewhere. It seemed like the old days when we trusted each other. I told you how important this deal was for me and my image, and I thought you understood."

"I do understand, but—"

"When I heard you were back, I thought it would be so great to work with you as rulers, and now you're just tossing that out."

"I'm not tossing anything out. I'm saying that it's best for both of our countries if we consider everything carefully. When I was talking to your dad this morning, I said—"

"Wait." He holds up his hands. "You talked to my dad?"

"I'm the one that showed up to see him, yeah."

"About the deal?"

"Not in detail, but yes. I kind of assumed he already knew. He is still king, after all."

"So, that's how it's going to be?"

"What?"

"I told you I wanted to do this on my own and prove myself to my father, so you went behind my back and told him everything?"

I fold my hands and huff into them. "Alex, you weren't there. You didn't show up. You have no right to be mad at me now. I told him I wanted to deal with you, but nobody knew where you were."

"Why didn't you just send Brent to spy on me again?"

"He's got more important things to do than chase you down every time you decide you're too good to show up. I'm not going to waste his time on that anymore."

Alex turns around, and for a moment, I think I might have gone too far and that Alex is going to walk away, but he only turns away for a few moments before turning back around with a pointed finger.

"You know, it's a real jerk move to act like you trust me and beg me for my trust and then turn around and betray me like this. I didn't betray you, and walking out on the deal like this is not cool."

"I didn't say I was walking out on the deal."

"You might as well have."

"All I want is to have a real conversation with you about the details of this agreement without standing on the beach screaming at you while you're drunk. Is that really too much to ask?" He doesn't say anything, so I decide that I will. "Is this about the other day? Are you still upset about the kiss?"

He scoffs, but it sounds more like a drunken gargle. "Of course not. I'm upset that you don't respect me."

"If you want my respect, then do something to demand it."

"Just don't expect me to trust you if you don't trust me."

I take a step back. "What is that supposed to mean?"

"You know what I mean."

"Alex—"

"Just go have a talk with my father. It seems you two can just work everything out without me."

And this time, when Alex turns around, he really does walk away. He still stumbles, but it seems his rage propels his inebriated body at least in a somewhat straight direction. That nagging feeling in my stomach is back: that feeling like he just threatened me with exposing my amnesia. Once again, he didn't say so directly, but I can feel it in my very bones.

But I also feel another feeling, a sort of revelation that seems to move throughout my body like a calm warmth. Alex says I begged him for his trust, which I guess is kind of true. I knew I couldn't continue our friendship and partnership until I trusted him with everything. And as much as I care about the Cartwright family, I care so much more for Trilland. How can I not beg for their trust above all others? How can I not tell them and hope against hope that they accept it?

Chapter 20

I haven't seen Alex since yesterday when he smelled of liquor and sweat, when he was completely unrecognizable as the Alex Cartwright I've known and loved, the Alex who let me cry all over his shoulder when my mother died and never once brought up the fact that I was now the heir to Trilland but knew that my new orphan status was more important. The Alex I knew used to sneak out of the guest house in the middle of the night and meet me in the garden where we would say every fear we had out loud without worrying what our fathers would say if they could hear us. Alex, who was the only real friend I had that didn't have parents who worked for my parents. Alex, who not long ago, defended me when my own country's Parliament tried to tear me down. That Alex was not who I faced last night.

But it also is not the Alex who stands in front of me now. The Alex I see walking over to me in a pressed suit, painted smile, and easy swagger is the on-camera Alex, the I'm-the-prince-of-Eterand Alex, the Alex who's always just a little bit better than you. This is an Alex that always existed as a public persona, but this is not an Alex I was ever acquainted with.

"Good morning, Lorraine," he says in that voice he used with Zane when he first met him. That voice indicates distance, lack of familiarity, superiority. It is a voice that has never been directed at me. "How are you doing this morning? Are you adequately prepared for today?"

I bite the inside of my cheek until it bleeds. "Are you?"

A flicker, just for a moment, that shows annoyance, and I'm kind of glad that I'm the reason it flashed across his face. "Of course. I've been preparing my whole life for this."

Actually, *I've* been preparing my whole life for this, but whatever. I force a smile as fake as his. "After you, then."

Alex walks just to the right of the stage and waits for Brent's introduction. I don't walk over there, and I won't until I absolutely have to so that I don't have to be near that person that looks like Alex but feels completely unrecognizable.

Brent says, "Have you decided what you will do?"

I nod. "I think I have."

He looks at me like he understands, but he doesn't push it, and I'm glad. The truth is that I'm not sure I have decided. All that I know for sure is that I will know in the moment.

Brent introduces Alex, and he saunters on stage, thoroughly enjoying the applause he's getting. Alex's presence may not have been entirely peaceful and acceptable to Trilland, but Prince Alex Cartwright can still capture hearts when he wants to. He says a few words of adoration of Trilland and me, but Brent doesn't let him wax eloquently for long before introducing me.

I hardly pay attention to Brent's introduction of me because I've heard it so many times, and I stare at Brent's face instead of the camera flashes in the crowd just as my mother taught me to do to avoid getting dizzy. I let Alex kiss my hand for the sake of appearances, but out here in the lights, I can see that he has the slightest darkness under his eyes that he's tried to cover up with enough makeup to hide the remnants of a hangover but not enough that anyone is aware he's wearing concealer. We take our seats, and Brent sits in his usual place across the stage from us but in full view of me. I introduce the conference and let Alex do most of the talking. I want to see what he'll say, and I want to feel the moment to learn if I will say the words.

"Princess Lorraine and I have been talking quite a bit over the past few days about our plans moving forward. We both have a profound interest in renewing the alliance between our countries. However, things have changed. This is not the Eterand or the Trilland of our fathers. So much time has passed, so many events have transpired, that we can hardly renew the terms as is. It simply doesn't make sense."

"It would not benefit our countries as it once did," I add to soften his harsh-sounding words. "This alliance is based on friendship, but it is also based on mutual benefit. A change in terms is necessary to continue that mutual benefit."

"Yes, and Princess Lorraine and I, though we are old friends, have had a chance to reconnect since I arrived in Trilland. We've been able to discuss what has happened since we last saw each other so many years ago. We have a relationship of trust and openness that could only lead to a sound alliance. I must admit that once the relief I felt when I heard the news that Lorraine was alive and well faded, it gave way to concern. What if she were different, what if Cassandra had caused more damage than I knew, what if things could not be restored as I am now optimistic that they can be? These are the same fears that I know the people of Eterand felt, and I'm sure that you, the people of Trilland felt tenfold. But I can tell you with confidence that Lorraine is not only returned to us, but she is better prepared for this position and a better person for what she's experienced as a result of Cassandra's tyranny."

This is the moment: I can tell. He's about to say those words I've only voiced out loud a handful of times. No one else has ever said these words for me except for the day Zane told Brent when he first arrived on the island. It sounded weird when Zane said it then, and it will sound much worse if Alex says it now. I tried to make my peace with the fact that Alex might say this here today, but I couldn't. I tried to figure out how to prevent him from ever saying it, but I can't, and sitting here on this stage while Alex drones on and on about our new alliance agreement that I'm not going to accept and somehow I know that he knows I'm not accepting, I can feel the words hovering in his mouth. Zane and Brent knew this would happen, and however misguided their attitude toward me might have been, I now understand why they were so concerned. This information is out in the hands of a non-Trillandite who now has power over Trilland, and that's not okay with me. Alex is certainly no Cassandra, but Trilland has suffered for too long to have an outsider come in now and cause more turmoil, no matter how well-intentioned it might be. And suddenly, I know. If this is going to happen, it's going to be on my terms as the future queen of Trilland.

"Excuse me, Prince Alex," I say, and he smiles politely, but I see the frustration in his eyes that only those close to him would notice. "I'd like to add something if I may."

"Of course." He gestures toward the mic but doesn't look sure of what I'm doing.

"Prince Alex and I are here today to discuss the renewed alliance between Trilland and Eterand. Our fathers were best friends and confidants, and they were our heroes as I'm sure they were to many of you. They valued their political relationship in addition to their personal friendship, and that has proven beneficial to both countries. When Prince Alex came to Trilland a little while ago, we immediately began discussing renewing that partnership." I glance over at Alex, and he looks nervous, like I'm about to cancel the whole thing. "I still believe in this goal, and I think it would not only be foolish to cast aside

Eterand as an ally but dishonoring to the memories of our fathers, who were the most honorable kings, husbands, and fathers.

"But there is something that has been eating away at me as we discussed these plans, and that is the well-being of Trilland. Trilland suffered a year of Cassandra Wellington's tyrannical rule, and when I came back, I felt ill-equipped to fix all the damage she caused. I did my best, but those efforts meant a lot of change. I know that some of the change was welcomed and other change was met with hesitation or even hostility. It was never my intention to cause my people any distress, and for that, I am truly sorry. Please know that my heart is for Trilland, and everything I have done has been with you at the forefront of my mind."

I look off-stage and smile at King Norman, waving him up to the stage. "I would like to ask King Norman Cartwright of Eterand to come up to the stage as well as the current king and as my friend." He happily comes up, pats me on the shoulder, and takes a seat next to his son. Alex's entire body tenses up.

"I firmly believe in this alliance, but I do not want to threaten Trilland's independence. From talking to many of you, I know you were all concerned for Trilland's sovereignty during Cassandra's takeover. The last thing I want you to do is question that sovereignty now. As the future queen of Trilland, I believe in our country being independent, and I hope you will trust me as I work on policies that will enable that freedom with as little upheaval as possible. However, I feel that in order for me to ask that you trust me, I must be honest with you about something."

My hands are shaking in my lap, and I take a deep breath, feeling like that breath will either slow my heart rate or cause me to pass out. I look over and see Alex looking just a little disappointed and Norman smiling a confused smile. I clench my hands into fists in a futile attempt to stop the shaking and hope that Trilland doesn't hate me for this.

"When I first returned to Trilland, I explained the circumstances of Cassandra's attempt on my life. What I didn't explain was why I did not come back sooner. Many of you have asked why I waited until the last minute to return. The truth is I didn't wait until the last minute. There were circumstances beyond my control that prevented my return. I did not share those details back then because I did not want Cassandra to take advantage of it or for any of you to worry. I felt that Trilland had been through enough and didn't need to panic. I told myself that if it ever became important for you all to know the details of what happened that I would share them, and I feel it is important now prior to this merging."

One more deep breath, two more fist clenches. "When I was knocked out and Captain Wilson managed to get me safely to the island you all know now as Maris Island, I suffered a severe head injury. When I woke up, I had no memory of myself, my family, or Trilland. I had no idea who I was or where I was."

A collective gasp spreads through the crowd, much like when I told the household staff, except this is much more unsettling. The senators in the front row stare with what feels like a penetrating gaze, and I can't tell if they are angry or concerned. Whatever authority I was starting to gain might have just been undermined.

"I did not regain any memory until a few weeks before I returned. Pieces came back in conversations with Brent Grayson and Captain Wilson, but the entire memory returned the first day I returned to Trilland and confronted Cassandra." Another gasp. "Many of you sensed my insecurities, though you couldn't have known why, and there was a lot of concern about my well-being when I returned. Know that I appreciate your concern, and I heard your fears. I had many of my own fears as well. I worried that parts of my memory were still missing. I still worry about that. I worry that the lapsed time where Cassandra took advantage of me will have lasting or even permanent effects on Trilland. I worry that you, the people of Trilland, will not accept me now that you know the truth and that I did not tell you back then.

"What I do not fear, and what you should not fear, is that I will ever stop fighting for this country that I love so much. I chose to keep that information among a select few in Trilland's best interest, and I am telling you now in Trilland's best interest. I feel that you should have all the information before you consider Prince Alex's and my plan for restructuring the alliance. Please understand my feelings on the matter, and if we may, I'd like to postpone the summit until tomorrow when you all have time to process this news. King Norman?"

He leans into Alex's mic. "I agree."

We will meet here at the same time tomorrow. Thank you for coming today. I hope to see you all again tomorrow. And thank you for believing that I could be even a fraction of the ruler my father was."

I stand up to walk off the stage quickly, but applause breaks out very suddenly. I look up to see all of Trilland standing and clapping for me. My eyes well up and tears stream down my face faster than I can wipe them away. After everything that's happened, Trilland still cares for me.

Chapter 21

I let myself enjoy the applause just for a moment before walking off-stage holding Norman's arm. Alex follows behind us at a pace brisker than ours, and I know he's livid, but he's not stupid, so he knows better than to do anything but smile at the cameras until we're alone. Backstage, Brent, Lady Vivian, Zane, and Uncle Lawrence greet us. I accept hugs and congratulations from everyone, Zane kisses my hand, and I exhale more air than I thought my lungs were capable of holding. It's hard to believe I just did that, that I just told Trilland everything. It feels at once freeing and terrifying. I have concurrent images flashing through my mind of applause and Parliamentary grimaces, and I have no idea how everything is going to shake out. The not-knowing has terrified me for nearly a year, but now I find a strange kind of peace in it. I could control whether or not I told Trilland, but I cannot control how everyone will react, and in a time in my life where I am supposed to be in control of everything, it's nice to know that at least one thing is not my responsibility.

Once everyone except for Zane, Brent, Alex, and Norman has cleared out, Alex rips his jacket open so fiercely that I think he's going to pop a button.

"What just happened?"

"I didn't feel right keeping that from everyone and asking them to trust me. I'm sorry that I kind of commandeered our joint conference, but I feel very strongly that I had to say something before we went any further."

"Why didn't you tell me that you were going to do that?"

"I wasn't totally sure that I was going to," I say, and it's the truth. "I mean, I had mostly made up my mind last night, but I was still unsure about it until you started talking."

"Something I said made you do it?"

I rub the side of my arm. "Something you were about to say."

"What?"

"Were you going to tell Trilland?"

"Tell them what?"

"Alex."

He sighs. "No. Maybe, I don't know. I guess I thought about it, yeah."

Norman lets out a low, deep sigh that verges on a rumble. "Alexander, how could you?"

"That was not your information to share," I say. "I trusted you with that."

"I wasn't—if I had said it—I wasn't trying to expose you or anything. I just thought it was the right thing to do and that maybe you would chicken out of doing it."

"It's my right to chicken out. And besides, do you really think so little of me?"

"I think the world of you," he says, and somehow I believe him. Even after everything I've gone through with Alex these past few days, he's still that boy I grew up with, the only one who ever understood how hard it was to train to rule a country as a child.

"There's something else," I say. Brent hands me the stack of papers I wrote last night, and I hand them over to Alex. "I'd like to revise our agreement before we submit it to Trilland and Eterand for review. I've been working on pieces of this for some time, but I put this together last night. I want you to look over it and let me know what you think. I want this to be the best thing for both of our countries."

He looks at it but doesn't take it. "Are you sure you don't just want him to look at it?" He points at his father.

"I already have," Norman says.

"But I still want you to look at it," I say. "I tried to tell you the other day that I still wanted to work with you on this, but you blew me off." I hold the papers out further. "Please just take it and look it over."

He huffs and snatches the papers. "You completely embarrassed me today. This conference was a trainwreck when it didn't have to be."

"You're right," I say. "It didn't have to be."

Alex seems to be waiting for me to say something more, so when I don't, he practically stomps off. Nobody says anything for a moment—probably Brent and Zane are afraid to—and the tension in the room dissipates only after the door closes solidly behind Alex.

Finally, Zane says, "Well, I think he took that pretty well."

Brent suppresses a chuckle, and Norman sighs. "I'm so sorry about my son, Lorraine. I thought I had prepared him for this position better than that."

"You are a spectacular king. Definitely the second-best king I've ever known." Norman can't help but laugh. I continue, "It's extremely hard for him to try to live up to your legacy. He's just trying to win your approval and respect."

"His behavior these last few days certainly won't do that."

"Give him a chance. He just wants to make you proud."

Norman nods, and I think my point has sunken in at least a little bit. "Well, I think I'll let him cool off, and then I'll try to talk to him. I hope he reads your proposal and sees how fantastic it is."

"Me, too."

After Norman, followed closely by Lady Vivian, leaves, Brent, Zane, and I sit down, and something about this moment feels right. The last two years of my life have been plagued by so much tumultuous uncertainty. The memory loss, Brent's arrival, the conflict between Zane and Brent, Brent's betrayal, traveling the provinces, the unrest in Anden, getting arrested by Cassandra, finally getting my memory back, Zane coming back for me, the struggles with getting Parliament to take me seriously, all the proposals that went unsigned, Alex's arrival, all culminating in my telling Trilland everything. Summed up like that, it seems like it's been so much longer than two years, but in other ways, it feels like it happened in the blink of an eye. It's hard to believe everything that's happened, but this all began with the three of us here. Zane, the one who always protected me, Brent, the one who always believed in me, and Maris, the girl who never thought she'd be here right now.

Sometimes, I like to think about what my parents would say if they could see what my life has become. What would they think knowing that I survived an assassination attempt, lost my memory, nearly lost Trilland, and then came back to power and fought for what I believed in. I wish I knew what my mother would say or what my father would try to teach me. I wish I could know if they thought I had made the right decisions. Mostly, I wish I could hug them again, smell the scent of roses on my mother's neck, feel my father's beard tickle my face when he kisses my forehead.

But this moment, the peace I feel sitting across from Brent's easy smile with Zane's hand in mine, is worth everything that happened the past two years. It all brought me to here.

"So," Brent says, "how are you feeling? Any regrets?"

I shake my head. "None, surprisingly."

"I think you did the right thing."

"Me, too," Zane says.

"That means the world to me," I say. "I'm so grateful to have you both."

A knock on the door shatters this perfect moment, so I allow a small sigh to slip out before inviting Lady Vivian in.

"Lorraine, Parliament is asking for an emergency meeting. Do you agree to call it?"

"Yes. I'll be there as soon as I can."

Zane and Brent both stand. Zane says, "We'll see you back at the palace."

"Actually," Lady Vivian says, "you both should come with her. There's still a crowd outside. She might need the escort."

"Really?"

She nods. "Just get there as soon as you can."

She leaves, and Zane, Brent, and I exchange a confused look.

"Do you think this is good or bad?" Brent says.

I shrug. "I can't imagine it's too bad."

"Are you sure you want an escort?"

I nod. "Besides, I actually want you both there anyway. I think it's time you were a part of these conversations."

Outside, I find that Lady Vivian seriously undersold just how many people were still outside. It doesn't look like anybody has left at all. As soon as I'm visible, applause and cheering breaks out. People are happy to see me. It's still a little mind-blowing that they don't seem to be upset at all. I wave and smile, but we mostly just forge ahead through the short walk to the Parliament building. It's surprising how a two-minute walk can become a ten-minute walk when pushing through crowds, but I don't mind the delay. This is exactly where I want to be: in the heart of Trilland.

When we reach the building, we walk straight in without hesitation up to the door of the meeting room where I grab the arms of Zane and Brent.

"Listen, I don't know what they're going to say, but thank you both for being here."

"Whatever happens, we've got your back," Brent says, and Zane nods.

With a deep breath from each of us and an extra from me, we walk in and sit down.

~~~

The room feels tense but not as tense as it has in the past. The tension now feels more like a heavy anticipation rather than a judgmental weight. I don't know if that's a good sign, but I take it as one.

Brent takes his usual seat behind me and to my right, and Zane awkwardly squishes in next to him, but Senator Flint moves over to give him more room and encourages him to sit further up, and Zane reluctantly agrees. Alex isn't here, nor his father, and other than Zane, no one else in this room is unusual.

Secretary Johnson stands briefly, just to get the attention of the room, then sits again. Normally I start these meetings, but since I'm the one summoned, Secretary Johnson has the honors. He does give Zane a strange look but doesn't comment on it.

"Thank you everyone for coming to this last minute meeting. In light of Princess Lorraine's announcements at today's press conference, I felt that we had much to discuss. Before I move on to the business we need to discuss, I want to be personal for just a moment, if I may." He clears his throat and then locks eyes with me. "Lorraine, I've known you my whole life. Since you were a child sitting in your father's lap at these meetings, I have been watching you. I considered myself an expert on knowing you and what you're thinking or feeling,
~~~

but I have to confess that I may not be the expert I claim to be. I never suspected the real reason behind your extended absence, and that is a testimony to how well you handled everything. In fact, none of the senators here had any idea what was really going on. That is not a judgment but a simple statement of respect for how well you have carried yourself since your return."

"Thank you," I manage to say. I can hardly believe that no one suspected. I always kind of felt like everyone knew but just never said anything because they thought I was incompetent or because they thought they shouldn't speak out against an Everhart.

"With that being said, we are sorry that we never knew. We all feel that a lot of circumstances would have been different had we known what was going on."

"That's exactly why I was hesitant to say anything," I say. "I didn't want to be coddled. As it is, I felt that I had to establish myself as qualified, so I didn't want to hinder that further by revealing a weakness." This is probably the most honest Parliament and I have ever been with each other. A year ago, or even last month, I never could have imagined admitting to a weakness in front of everyone.

"What happened to you is not a weakness," Secretary Johnson says with kindness in his eyes. "It is the result of a horrible crime committed against you. It never should have been the case." He pauses a moment, adjusting his glasses. "While we understand why you chose to keep this information personal, going forward, we would like to request to be included in any information that affects Trilland."

I nod. "Agreed."

He softens his voice. "We'd also like to discuss your previous amnesia, if we may." I nod hesitantly. "Could we know some of the details?"

A small sigh escapes my lips that I didn't mean to allow. It's a story I've told several times now. I'm tired of telling it, of reliving it.

When I talk about it, I can feel the haze that used to consume my brain coming back. I always fear that the haze might take over again. But I tell the story again, of waking up in Ms. Flora's of Harper and Zane's questions, of Brent's arrival, of how the memories came back too slowly, then too quickly. Everyone listens intently, and when I finish, the haze recedes again, and I sigh again, this time out of relief.

"And you've seen Dr. Offen? Has he checked everything out?"

"Yes, I saw him as soon as Cassandra was ousted."

He smiles. "Good. I'm glad to know you're all right. I think we all are." Everyone nods vigorously.

"I don't think any of us can pretend to know what that was like," Senator Greene says. "I can't imagine the challenge of not knowing anything and then having to deal with the magnitude of everything that Brent told you. It must have been truly frightening."

"It was." This is the most vulnerable moment we've ever shared together. We're always just government, just coworkers in a way, never just humans. This is refreshing.

"You've handled it well. Your return to Trilland was well-done, but in light of this, it's truly impressive."

"Thank you."

"However," Johnson says, "we have to discuss the decision to inform Trilland of what happened. That should have been a decision that was discussed here in this room."

"I appreciate the concern, and with all due respect, it was personal to me and my decision to say or not say. It was not a rash action. I've been thinking about it casually since I returned and seriously for a few months."

"I don't think we're necessarily saying you were wrong," Emerson says, "just that we think it should have been a conversation."

"If we're being honest here, then I have to say that I had not committed to saying anything until today. I had seriously considered it and was pretty sure that I would go through with it, but the final decision happened on that stage just now. I couldn't in good conscience ask Trilland to trust me if I didn't trust them, and I was afraid I'd lose my nerve if I postponed it."

"You realize this will create a firestorm," Johnson says. "News will spread fast to our allies and our enemies. They may already know, and if they don't, they will by tomorrow. The reactions will not all be as favorable as they were today."

I press my lips together. "I know. I am prepared for those reactions."

Uncle Lawrence says, "Riagala is a particular concern for me. They will certainly perceive this as a weakness. This might be the opportunity they've been waiting for."

"We have defenses built up in their direction, and I think the alliance renewal will be solidified with Eterand by the time they try anything, so they will be on guard as well. I'm not particularly worried about how our allies will react. Norman and Alex have both responded well, and I think the others will, too."

"We must also anticipate the changes in foreign relations," Johnson says. "They may treat you differently in negotiations. They may see you as somehow faulty or incapable."

I wince at the words. It's an insecurity I've had myself, so I can hardly blame anyone else for sharing the same thought, but still, it's upsetting to hear.

"After speaking with her, I think anyone will see that she is often the most capable person in the room," Flint says.

I force myself to sit up a little straighter. "I can manage the doubts of our allies. Our navy can manage our enemies. I think Riagala is the only real physical threat. I imagine the others will engage in a war of words, trying to discredit me. None of our allies will fall for it."

Senator Emerson sighs. "The fallout from this will be big, even here. I can't say I'm entirely convinced that it was the right decision to expose this information. It may prove to be dangerous in ways we can't anticipate."

I look around the room and see that Senator Weston nods in agreement, and though Greene doesn't, it seems to me that she wants to. This is the moment I knew would happen if I decided to tell Trilland. I knew Parliament would reject the decision. If I were to be completely honest, they're a big part of the reason I chose not to tell them I was doing it. I knew they wouldn't approve.

But it's also the moment where I can prove myself, act like the responsible adult in the room, display all the training my father gave me, let the strength I've built up over the last two years shine.

"I understand the concerns, and believe me, I did not do this lightly. But as I said before, ultimately, this was my decision, and I did not do it for selfish reasons but purely because I think it is in Trilland's best interest. I am prepared for the fallout that will follow, and I will be open with you all moving forward as we address the issues I know will arise. This is the position I've been preparing for my whole life, and today is the day I've spent the last two years preparing for. I am confident in my actions, and I ask you all to respect them."

There is a pause in the room that is almost palpable. I know I have not won them over to my way of thinking yet, but I think I have won their respect, and right now, that is what matters.

I take a quick breath. "Is there anything else related to my memory that needs to be discussed? I'd rather address any other concerns or questions now rather than later." Many shake their heads, and no one seems to be suppressing any comments, so I gesture to Secretary Johnson. "Then I guess the floor is yours."

He smiles just slightly. "Okay then. On to other business. Since the vote has been delayed, we want to take advantage of the extra opportunity to go over everything. Where does Eterand stand on the delay? It seemed that perhaps there was a disconnect between King Norman and Prince Alex."

"There was a miscommunication between Alex and I, yes. Alex has been given a new proposal that Norman has already approved. Brent, do you still have copies?"

Before I can even finish the question, Brent pulls out several copies, just enough for all of the senators. It's like he knew what I was going to ask hours before I asked it. I hope he never quits.

"This was written entirely by me, and I think it will solve our problems, protect our sovereignty, and honor our alliance with Eterand. I regret that I did not get it to you all sooner, but in the spirit of honesty, I completed in only last night, and I did not feel good about continuing the press conference until you all had read and approved it and until Alex had approved it."

"With all due respect to the prince of Eterand," Senator Emerson says, "do we need his approval if King Norman has already signed off?"

"No, we don't need it, but it's important to me that we have it. He will be king in just a few years, and this agreement will affect his country. Also, I want to respect his position as the future king and include him on all negotiations. It is the right thing to do."

A few senators look like they don't agree, but no one challenges me on it, and I feel like that's a win for my professional authority. They start glancing through the pages, but the sheer size of it makes a few of them visibly nervous.

"You don't need to read my giant novel of policy right now," I say. "I don't want to torture you."

That elicits a few laughs, and some of the earlier tension dissipates.

"At first glance, I think it looks great," Flint says.

"Agreed," says Senator Emerson, and that one surprises me.

"One thing I'd like to highlight right now from the policy is the inclusion of new innovations to maximize our productivity and the possibility of technology trade with Eterand. I know this was previously a matter of contention, but I really do think that this can only help, and if you check my numbers, I think you'll agree. In addition to the calculations done by Amelia in her project, my policy includes that Eterand would front some of the costs associated with getting solar energy off the ground in Trilland. Solar power is already well-established there, and King Norman is very willing to help. In exchange, we would offer the data of some of our scientific research to help them get their program off the ground. This benefits both of our countries where we need it without compromising sovereignty for either nation." When I pause, I'm a little surprised to see several senators nodding in agreement. Finally, I did something right.

"When I first proposed solar power and everything associated with it, it was not because I was trying to make a statement but because I truly believe this will only benefit Trilland in multiple ways. I don't ask for you to approve it blindly, but I do ask that you seriously consider it, and if you still want to reject it with a reasonable argument, I will be more than willing to accept that and come up with something new."

Uncle Lawrence's smile looks like it might break his face, he's so proud. And I'm proud, too. I'm proud of how I handled that. I'm proud of my actions these last few days.

"We will consider it, and we can have a meeting tomorrow morning before it is released to the public," Johnson says. "Is it still the plan to release it?"

I nod. "I think Trilland deserves to know firsthand. Plus, I think it's only right for the people of Trilland to be included in a major decision after so long of being excluded."

"Agreed," Uncle Lawrence says, and several senators nod.

"8am work for everyone?" says Senator Johnson, and we all nod. "Then it's agreed."

"If I may," I say, "I'd like to discuss something else as well." I think back to what Secretary Johnson said about Shane Tisdale, my father's press secretary. I think about the empty chair next to me. I think about how my father commanded a room without raising his voice. "I asked Zane and Brent to come here with me today because I think they have merited a presence in these meetings."

"What do you mean?" Secretary Johnson says, and Zane and Brent look just about as confused as the other senators. I didn't tell them I was going to do this, and maybe I should have, but here we go.

I point at Brent first. "Brent is my press secretary and as such has been attending our meetings for some time now, and we may not have always been as welcoming and inclusive to him as we should have been. I'd like for that to change going forward. My father always included his press secretaries in the conversations that took place here, and I'd like Brent to do the same. As a lifelong resident of one of Trilland's provinces, and his, uh, unique position due to the role he played in my return, I think he has earned a spot in this room beyond sitting in the back of the room. I think he should be participating in our conversations since I already seek out his counsel regularly."

Everyone's eyes shift to Brent, and he squirms just a little under the weight of all the gazes. "I don't know if I'm qualified."

"You're extremely qualified," I say. "You are especially useful to our discussions related to the provinces. Everyone else here, excluding Zane, is from the mainland."

"I, for one, think it's a great idea," says Secretary Johnson. "Shane Tisdale was a great asset to this Parliament in King Arthur's day. I don't see why Brent can't do the same."

Uncle Lawrence shrugs. "I have no objections."

When no one says anything, Brent says, "Would I still be your press secretary?"

"I sure hope so," I say, and everyone laughs. "I think everyone in this room and possibly all of Trilland knows that I'd be completely lost without you."

Brent chuckles. "Then I accept. I'd be honored to advise the Parliament."

"On to Zane, then," I say. "Brent's presence in this room has been limited, but Zane has not even had that opportunity. I'd like for that to change as well."

"What do you mean?"

"Zane is an asset to us as the only person in all of Trilland who is originally from Maris Island. I know Maris Island's concerns are numerous and serious, and I have been taking on the bulk of managing it, which is a lot to handle when I need to manage so many other things. Ever since the annexation was completed, I've been thinking that we needed someone whose job it was to handle their affairs, but personally, I was afraid to pitch the idea because I wasn't sure how you all would feel about it. He's not me, but he knows Maris Island better than I ever could. He knows better than anyone in this room what the people of that island want. They need a representative. I think we should trust Zane to be Maris Island's ambassador."

Zane's eyes pop open as he stares at me, but otherwise, no one seems to react. In fact, there was more of a reaction to Brent. Is that because my suggestion about Brent was more contentious, or do they think Zane being an ambassador is so ridiculous that they don't even know where to begin with me? Or maybe, just maybe, it's as obvious to all of them as it is to me that Zane should be an ambassador.

After looking around the room, Secretary Johnson says, "Zane is in a very unique position. We've been discussing for some time how best to involve him in our country since it seems his residence here will be permanent given his closeness to you." I look over at Zane, and I'm glad to find him blushing as much as I am. They've been discussing Zane for some time?

Zane lets out what sounds like a laugh mixed with a confused lilt.

"I think Zane might be better at this than I am," I say. "If Zane wants it, I think it's the perfect position for him."

"There's nothing I'd want more," Zane says with a wide smile, that smile that first made me realized that I loved him. "I've actually been thinking that myself and wondering how best to propose it." Zane's been thinking that? For how long?

"For that to be official," Senator Emerson says, "the citizens of Maris Island would have to have a formal vote to approve him. Is there any reason to think Zane's nomination would be contested?"

"None whatsoever," I say, and Brent agrees.

"It's somewhat unprecedented," says Senator Weston.

Flint adds, "That doesn't make it bad. Princess Lorraine is right. She needs to devote her energy elsewhere. This seems like a good solution."

"I suppose it does make sense," Senator Greene says.

Uncle Lawrence says, "I'm not opposed."

Still looking a little surprised, Secretary Johnson says, "All right, pending a vote from Maris Island, Zane Adler will become ambassador. We'll get the paperwork you need to you at the close of this meeting. Brent?"

"I'm all over it," he says.

Zane whispers to me, "There's paperwork?" Zane's got an advantage in that he doesn't necessarily need to read all the information on Maris Island to understand it, but still.

"And one more thing regarding Zane," Johnson says. "It's my understanding that you have extensive knowledge of fishing, do you not?"

Zane smirks. "I'd like to think so."

"Trilland's fishermen tell me that you've been helping out a few days. They all tell me that the catch is significantly better when you're there or when they use your techniques. Trilland has always been a fishing town, but it seems we still have much to learn. If you don't mind, we'd like to beg for your help and ask that your service to our fishermen become an official, permanent role. "

I laugh. "I'd like to see you try to keep him away. You might as well have offered him a million dollars."

"I'd rather have the fishing than the million dollars, actually," Zane says.

"Should this proposal be approved, I imagine Zane would be instrumental in implementing the fishing reforms."

"About that, I've looked at those nets, and they're genius. That kid's got potential. We use something similar back on the island, and it works wonders. I took some with me to Maris Island, and my best mate Tito loves them. He says they work great."

"Excellent."

"I'm very happy about this new arrangement," I say. "I can't tell you what it means to me that Zane and Brent are included. In addition to Uncle Lawrence, I trust these two men with my life, and I've actually quite literally put my life in their hands."

"It seems we can't ignore Zane's significance anymore," Johnson says. "I imagine both he and Brent will be assets to Trilland."

Flint adds, "If Lorraine says they will be, then I feel confident having them in more active roles."

"All right then, it's settled," Secretary Johnson says. "Do you have anything else, Princess?"

I shake my head. "Do you, Secretary Johnson?"

He looks around the room, and everyone shakes their heads. "Then I think we're done here."

"I will see you all at 8am tomorrow," I say.

Everyone gets up, shuffling their papers like usual, but one by one, they come up to me to shake my hand, something only Secretary Johnson has ever done at these meetings, and Flint gives me a hug. They have never done this before. I can't help but feel like this is a direct result of my honesty. I'm finally taking control in the best way. I hoped this kind of thing would happen, and I vehemently argued with Zane and Brent that it would, but I don't know if I ever truly believed it myself. Things are finally going to change in Trilland.

Chapter 22

On Maris Island, I used to walk the beach at night whenever I was upset. It was quiet, peaceful, and the evening stars never asked me what I would do if my memory never came back, the moon never implied that no one cared enough to look for me. Even the waves that haunted me with their crashing and roaring never whispered stories about the girl with no name except for the fake one given to her by a boy who fell in love despite himself.

In Trilland, it's much harder to walk the beach at night. The townspeople live an active nightlife, so unlike the little island where everyone was in bed by nine. I've stayed close to the palace to avoid people as much as possible. If I'm being honest with myself, I was afraid of the questions I would get from Trillandites, and even the stars, moon, and waves seem so much more critical here.

But tonight, after dinner, I slipped out alone just like I used to and let my feet take me to the beach below my bedroom window. Except this time I don't walk the beach out of fear or worry. I walk the beach because it's calming. I still hear the waves at my window, but they don't threaten to break the glass and my resolve anymore. They don't sound like shipwrecks and mutinies and headaches anymore. Somehow, they seem welcoming now. They sound like home: like the background noise to my mother's voice reading me a bedtime story, the score to the music of my father's laugh, the tinkling of the necklaces hanging on my dresser when I open the window on a hot day. I'm no longer afraid of Cassandra or the holes in my memory that aren't there. Their vice grip on me has loosened and fallen to the ground, washed away by the waves.

I still stay close to the palace though just in case there are late night swimmers, fishermen, or lovers out on the sand. One group of older women spot me just as they are packing up their belongings and lifting sleeping grandchildren to their shoulders, but they don't do anything more than smile and wave. The smiles look genuine this time.

A young man waves at me from a distance, so I wave back, but he seems committed to walking my direction. I can't decide if I should go inside now to avoid being disturbed or wait to hear what he has to say, but when I make out Alex's blonde curls, I know I have to wait.

When he's close enough for me to make out his features in the moonlight, I see the Alex I was hoping to see: the one I've known since I was a child. It's a relief to see.

He says, "I looked for you in the garden, but when I couldn't find you, I thought I'd take a walk by the ocean. I guess I should have started here."

"The garden was a good guess. I was just feeling a little nostalgic for Maris Island. I used to walk by the ocean a lot there."

He nods slowly, glancing back and forth between me and the sand between his feet. "Are you homesick?"

I shake my head. "This is home."

"But so is that island, isn't it?" I nod. "I'm not sure I'll ever understand that."

"No one really does, but I don't need anyone to understand it. I just need everyone to accept it."

He nods then reaches for something in the messenger back that I hadn't noticed was slung across his shoulder. He pulls out a stack of papers littered with sticky notes and writing in the margins and holds it out to me. When I take it, I see that it's my proposal for the new alliance terms.

"This is brilliant," he says.

"Is it? This seems like a whole lot of notes for 'brilliant.'"

He laughs, cracking the grave expression on his face. "Most of those notes are my highlighting the best or most significant parts. I only made a couple of minor suggestions, if I'm even in a position to do that at this point."

"Of course you can make notes. It's your country involved, too. Why would you think that?"

"Because I've acted horribly for days. I'm ashamed of how I've treated you. You were all right about me."

"Who do you mean?"

"You, my father, Zane, Brent. You tried to tell me, but I didn't listen. I was just so determined to prove that I was a capable king, that I could do things on my own, that I completely shut you out of the process. And when you called me on it, I acted like a complete pig. I can hardly bear to think of the things I said to you and what I did. I guess I let the power go to my head. All I wanted was to make a difference, to be in charge for once, and all I did was prove to everyone that I'm not cut out to be king."

I tip Alex's jaw so that he looks at me. "Hey, just because you messed up doesn't mean you're not going to make a great king someday. Maybe it just means that you still need time and preparation. There's nothing wrong with that."

"It seems like you've got it together already. Why shouldn't I?"

I laugh. "Does it really seem like I've got it together? Trilland has a lot of problems that need to be fixed."

"That's not your doing."

"Maybe, but I'm not doing such a great job at fixing it. It only looks like I've got it together because I have to. There is no other option. Frankly, I wish I were in your position. I'd give anything for more time to learn from my father while he could still run the country so that if I messed up, it wouldn't be so catastrophic."

"I'm sorry," he says, "I didn't mean to make light of your situation."

"You don't need to be sorry for that, but you should recognize what you have. Trust me, your father isn't waiting for you to fail. He's trying to help you."

"I know. I know that now. He and I had a long talk today after the press conference."

"Really?"

He nods. "I apologized to him. I told him that I had read your proposal and made some notes. I asked him to approve them." He points at the stack of papers in my hand. "As king, he's approved everything there, so if you agree, it's all set to go. We've agreed that from now on until I officially become king, he and I will work jointly on all of Eterand's operations so that I can learn."

"I think that sounds like a great idea."

"And in addition to the apologies I owe Brent and Zane for the way I treated them, I owe you an apology most of all. I am so sorry that I tried to take over and usurp your authority even if I didn't mean to. I never should have done anything without talking to you, and I certainly shouldn't have tried to make it seem like it was your fault when we started disagreeing. I apologize for putting you in a compromising position and disrespecting your relationship with Zane and your right to your feelings. Most of all, I regret that I ever considered betraying your trust after you kindly chose to share a deep secret with what you thought was an old friend. Though there is no way to prove it, I want you to know that if you hadn't told Trilland about your amnesia, I wouldn't have. The fact that I even thought about it is bad enough."

"I believe you."

"I know things are different now, and maybe we can never be like we were, but I hope we can still be friends."

I put my arms around his neck, and he cautiously wraps one arm across my back. "We will always be friends, Alex. I hope you know that I want that."

He nods. "I do."

"It's all I ever really wanted from the moment you showed up a couple of weeks ago." I step back and hold up the stack of papers again. "I want this kind of collaboration. And thank you for what you said. It means the world to me."

"I meant it." After a moment of silence, he says, "If I may, have you decided what you will do about Trilland's budget?"

I nod. "I've spoken to Parliament. They've agreed to give my ideas a chance. Now that they know about my memory, they have a new respect for me, I guess. I'm going to announce it tomorrow along with the alliance terms now that you've approved them. Eterand's support of the solar power integration will make all the difference. That gave Parliament hope and confidence that maybe we have the ability to try out some new ideas. I think things are finally looking up."

"I think so, too."

We hug one more time, and a sharply cold ocean breeze reminds us that we should go inside. We start walking back toward the garden where he'll go left into the guest house and I'll go right into the palace, but tomorrow will feel different. Tomorrow, we will be allies.

Chapter 23

The walk to Parliament today feels different. I walk arm-in-arm with Zane who's never been allowed to participate before and is desperately trying to cram as much material into his head as he possibly can from that giant stack of paper he got yesterday despite my reassurances that Parliament won't expect him to have finished it already. Brent is with us, and this time he won't be in the back of the room as my press secretary. It seems the tension between us is finally gone. Now he's my press secretary, my personal assistant, my friend.

I don't feel an impending sense of doom that entering that conference room in the Parliament building will mean fighting and condescension and more wasted time for Trilland. It won't be easy, but starting today, we'll work together. Starting today, there are no more secrets, no more anger, no more distrust. For once, I feel at peace. I know there's still so much to work out, but I finally feel comfortable with my decisions and my situation. Somehow, I know it will work out.

I don't even avoid eye contact with the Trillandites this time because I'm not afraid anymore. Finally, they know everything, and I don't have to hide my face from them like I'm hiding my failures or my insecurities. Today, I smile at them, and they smile back, and Trilland finally feels like home again.

At Parliament, I put forth my proposal for the new alliance with Eterand, and with Alex and Norman in attendance, it is approved. Now it just has to be approved by Eterand's Parliament, the citizens of both of our countries, and it will be official: the first successful thing I've done of any importance since Cassandra's banishment. If it is approved—which I suspect that it will be—the economic effects should be pretty much immediate. Trilland will finally start to heal.

Jane, Elise, and Daisy meet Zane, Brent, and me outside of the Parliament building, and together we talk a long, leisurely walk around Trilland. I show Elise and Daisy the sights, Jane and I reminisce, Zane shares funny stories of fishing gone wrong, and Brent talks about Gessend. We stop frequently because every time we run into people, they want to talk to me, to hug me, to cry on my shoulder, and even to complain. Some are even awkward because they don't know how to talk about the amnesia even though they desperately want to. I welcome all of it. The wall between me and the rest of Trilland has finally been demolished, and I couldn't be happier.

Now, when I walk around Trilland, my hand in Zane's, I don't feel quite like bursting into tears, running straight home, or leaving altogether and returning to Maris Island. It isn't perfect, but now I walk straighter, my head held high, a smile on my face, a lightness in my step. I no longer feel like a failure. I no longer feel like a child impersonating her father. Instead, I feel my father on this island. I see him and my mother in every beautiful part of this island. I think they would be proud of who I've become.

Everything won't be fixed overnight, but things are getting better. Little by little, Trilland will pull itself out of the deep chasm Cassandra plunged it into. Little by little, I will let go of the imagined shadows in my mind.

As a child, I never could have imagined where I would end up a year ago. A year ago, I never could have imagined being here. Just a few months ago, I couldn't imagine things working out the way they have, and yet here I am.

Yesterday was stormy, and tomorrow will certainly have clouds of its own. But today it is sunny, and I intend to bask in the daylight.

Epilogue

Tomorrow is my coronation. After tomorrow, my mother is no longer considered the current queen even in death. Soon, I won't be the lost princess anymore. It's a thrilling kind of fear stepping into something so monumental; although, I've done it before.

I click the clasp of my mother's necklace behind my neck. This is the very necklace she wore the day she married my father and became queen of Trilland. It would feel wrong to have anything else on my neck.

"I hope you haven't messed up your hair already," Jane says. Jane and Elise walk in arm-in-arm, Elise wearing one of Jane's dresses, and even though she's at least four inches taller than Jane, Annette somehow managed to work some kind of magic.

"All I did was my makeup and put on a necklace," I huff and fold my arms. "How could I have possibly messed it up?"

Jane squints. "You have special abilities."

"So little faith in me."

Jane grabs the comb and Elise the hairspray, and like a well-oiled machine, they touch up the stray baby hairs that are already fighting back against the curled updo. I've never really liked my hair up, but today it looks regal.

"Nervous?" Elise says through a cloud of hairspray.

I shake my head. "The coronation isn't until tomorrow. It's just the queen's banquet tonight."

"And that doesn't make you nervous?"

I shake again. "It's like the rehearsal dinner to a wedding. Nothing's really happening tonight except eating, dancing, and speechmaking."

Jane snaps her fingers. "Speaking of rehearsal dinners, I need your help picking a dress."

I can't help but laugh. "Jane, you picked a wedding dress in under an hour, but you can't pick a rehearsal dress?"

"You dream about your wedding dress your whole life, but no one ever tells you to dream about the rehearsal dress. It's not like I've thought about it for twenty years like the wedding dress."

Jane has talked about nothing else since Brent proposed a couple of months ago. I'm so glad I've been able to be here to be a part of this occasion in Jane's life. She hasn't stopped smiling, and though I never say anything, I do catch her periodically staring at her ring.

"Are you going to wear white at the rehearsal?" Elise asks.

Jane scrunches her nose. "I don't think so. I want it to be different."

"We'll go to Angie's this weekend and take a look at what she has," I say. "Deal?"

"Deal. You're the best, Lorraine."

"That's a maid of honor's job," I say with a smile. "Has Brent written his vows yet?"

Jane scoffs. "I sure hope so. I've been telling him to do it for weeks. He says he's not a good writer."

"He literally writes thousands of words for me every day. Since Lady Vivian retired and he took over her responsibilities, I swear he never stops writing things for me."

"He says that's easy, those press releases and things, that writing with feelings is different."

I laugh. "Oh, whatever."

"What about you and Zane?" Elise says.

"What about me and Zane?"

"Have you talked about getting married?" The blood that rushes to my cheeks answers before I can say a word. "Spill."

"We've talked about it, but everything's been so busy with the coronation and establishing the new budget. We haven't really had a chance to hash out the details."

"The details?" Jane says with exasperation. "That's so unromantic sounding."

I shrug. "It'll happen when it happens. I'm not worried."

"That's a first," Elise says, and I give her arm a playful shove.

They finish my hair for the second time, and I step into the dress with their help. It's black with long sleeves and glitter in the bodice and a train. I wasn't thrilled about the train because I'm pretty sure that I'll be tripping on it all night, but Annette and Lady Vivian insisted that it was the right look. Looking in the mirror now, I can hardly disagree. Tomorrow, I'll wear the royal blue dress that Annette has spent months making and weighs more than I do, but tonight, the image is simple elegance, and I like how much I look like my mother in this dress.

Delicately, so that I don't mess up my hair, I affix the tiara that I will wear for the last time tonight. Tomorrow, I will wear my mother's tiara, the queen's tiara. It seems at once fitting and too big for my head. I wonder if that will ever change.

Jane opens the door to a knock, and there is Zane in a custom tux and a big smile. It's undeniable that Zane looks incredibly handsome in a tux, but I can't help but feel like he looks better in a ragged shirt that's stained in fish guts and cut-offs and bare feet. That's the real Zane.

"You look beautiful," he says. He kisses me, and Elise rebukes him for messing up my lipstick, but when he kisses my cheek, she laments my blush, so he sighs. "I'm going to kiss her, you know."

"You look great," I say, but then I run my hand through his hair to mess up the perfect styling just a little bit. "Now."

"Captain Wilson is going to kill you for doing that," he says, and I shrug. "Ready?"

It's customary for one of the parents to introduce the incoming royal, but for obvious reasons, Uncle Lawrence offered. That didn't stop Zane from walking me to the ballroom, though.

"Are you nervous?"

"Why does everyone keep asking me that? Elise asked the same thing."

"Well?"

I start to shake my head but then stop. "About tonight, no. About the coronation, still no. About being queen, yes."

"You'll be great. You basically already are queen."

"We'll see."

Zane kisses me on the cheek again, despite the obvious dissatisfaction from Elise and Jane, and flashes me a big smile. "See you out there."

Zane enters the ballroom with Elise on one arm and Jane on the other, and like clockwork, Uncle Lawrence comes around the corner and offers his arm to me. I take it, and even though I wish it were the thinner, frailer arm of my father, I'm grateful for the feeling of his strong arm right now.

"I won't get too mushy right now because I'll cry, and that'll look bad when we walk in, but I want you to know how proud of you I am. You have exceeded every high expectation I had for the woman you would become. I only wish your parents could see you now."

"Me, too. And thank you." I stretch my arms as far as they'll go so I can wrap my arms around his neck. "Ready?"

He nods to me, then to the guards at the door, and with a wink, Timothy opens the door and announces me. "Her Royal Highness, soon to be Queen, Princess Lorraine Alice Everhart."

Everyone applauds, and even though it's hard to see through the camera flashes, I feel comforted by the people in this room. Everyone here is a friend, even the media. Since things have improved, the media has softened on me just a little bit. Even Erin has let up.

I take my seat at the table in between Zane and Uncle Lawrence, and I couldn't be more thrilled with how Brent has arranged the people at our table. He sits next to Zane, and Secretary Johnson sits on the other side of Uncle Lawrence beside Lady Vivian. This is a comforting group of people.

"If I may," Secretary Johnson says as he stands, "I'd like to say a few words on behalf of Trilland before we begin." It's customary for the Secretary of State to do this at the king and queen's banquet, but usually, it's more toward the middle of the night. "I'll give a more formal speech later on tonight, but it was important to me to say a little something now.

"In the months since Princess Lorraine instituted our new national budget, we have seen Trilland begin to heal from Cassandra's poison. Fishing, our greatest industry, is thriving once again. Our oceanography department has been able to employ more citizens to help with their abundance of work. Our military is stable and efficient. Our students are eager to become active citizens. Even our renewed terms with our biggest ally Eterand has seen improvements for both of our countries. King Norman, Queen Florence, and Prince Alexander, we welcome you."

The Cartwright family stands and waves. I'm glad to see them all together. I'm really looking forward to my trip to Eterand next month.

Secretary Johnson continues. "We have less crime, less debt, less struggle than we did under Cassandra. The healing has certainly not happened overnight, and the growing pains along the way have been intense, but none of it would be possible without Princess Lorraine. I'm sure I speak for all of Trilland when I say that we are infinitely happy to have you back. I hate to think what would have become of you if Cassandra Wellington had gotten her way.

"I'd like to recognize a few guests here tonight from Maris Island, Trilland's newest province, that were responsible for Princess Lorraine's safety and return to Trilland. To Miss Elise Champlain, Mr. Tito Rodriguez, and Ms. Edna Flora, thank you for the roles you played in protecting her and helping her heal. To the Adler family, Zane, Harper, and Daisy, thank you for taking her in and welcoming her as family. To Brent Grayson, thank you for believing in Captain Wilson's faith and seeking our princess out."

I look around the room at everyone as Secretary Johnson names them and smile. Finally, both of my families, both my worlds, are in one room.

"And finally, to Princess Lorraine, thank you for fighting through unbelievable odds and coming back to us. None of us can truly understand the mental and physical strength it must have taken to recover your memory, return to Trilland, and remove Cassandra. It is a debt that Trilland will forever owe the Everhart family."

He starts to tear up, so he stops, and I have a strange realization that the only time I ever saw him cry was when my father passed away. It seems so odd to see him cry now not out of sadness.

"Tonight, we celebrate the woman who will become our queen tomorrow. I couldn't be more honored to be seated here with her tonight. Dinner is now served."

Because it will take a significant amount of time for all of the food to be passed out, I take the opportunity to take a walk around the room. I greet the media and promise a few statements later tonight, I thank Elise, Jane, and Annette for their help tonight, and I stop by the table of Maris Island's citizens for a special thank you. I give each of them a long hug as if it could somehow repay them for everything they've done.

"I'm so glad you all could be here tonight," I say.

"I always knew you'd turn out to be someone special," Ms. Flora says. "Those clothes you washed up in were just too fancy for a drifter. Unlike Brent."

"Hey," Brent says.

"She was always special," Tito says. "Could see it in her eyes."

"And you all thought I was ridiculous when I said she could be a princess," Daisy says with folded arms. "*I* was right."

I give her a hug and then Harper, who says, "I'm so proud. I'm always here if you need me."

"I'll always need you."

"Good," she says.

I stop by the Eterand table and give Florence a warm hug. "It's so good to see you again."

"You too, dear," she says. "I can't wait for you to come to Eterand next month."

"Me neither. I'm so excited to see it."

Norman says, "I'm afraid you'll hardly recognize it. It's changed a lot."

"As long as you all haven't, I'll be fine."

"We're always here for you, dear." Florence offers me a warm smile.

"Congratulations, Lorraine," Alex says. "You're going to be a wonderful queen."

"Thank you. And you'll be a wonderful king."

"If I can be half the king my father is, then I'll be lucky."

"I'm sure you will."

"Good to see you both as well." Alex shakes Brent's and Zane's hands. "I hope we can do some business talk later."

They both agree, and after greeting a few of the local business owners, we head back to our table. Our food is there by the time we get back, but no one at our table seems to be eating yet. I guess they were waiting for me though they don't have to do that. I encourage them to start as I sit down, but Zane remains standing.

"I'd like to say a few words before we really get going," he says. "I don't know if I'm technically allowed, but I've never really been a following protocol kind of guy, so I'm just kind of going for it here."

Everyone laughs except Zane, who turns to face me and beams.

"Two and a half years ago, a lifeboat drifted close to our island now known as Maris Island. I didn't expect the person inside to be a beautiful girl with no memory of who she was. When my mother insisted on taking her in, I didn't expect to find that I enjoyed her company. When a drifter showed up and claimed she was the lost heiress to a small country, I didn't expect it to be true. When she left to find herself, I didn't expect to miss her. And when I saw the boat leaving with her on it, I didn't expect to realize that I loved her."

The room sighs, and I can't stop the smile on my face from spreading.

"I was afraid when I followed her that I would find her changed, no longer the girl I loved. Instead, I found a more confident, strong, beautiful woman than the girl I had known on the island. I found a better version of the girl I loved. I became afraid she couldn't possibly love me, too.

"I stuck around here hoping to persuade her to love me as much as I love her. She insists she does, but I can't believe that it could compare with how I feel about her. I also struggled with finding my place here in Trilland. At times I felt that I knew her better than you all did, and at other times, I worried that I didn't know her at all. I wasn't sure what my purpose was here. I found it, and I'm thankful to all of you for that.

"Many of you don't know this, but when Lorraine was on the island without memory, I gave her a name. I felt it was awkward not to have something to call her. I gave her the name Maris, the name of my grandmother. She radiated the same kind of gentleness, peace, and kindness that my grandmother did. Embarrassingly, I still struggle to remember to call her Lorraine, so forgive me if I slip. I didn't know when I gave her the name then that she would become the most important person to me. I simply cannot imagine my life without her."

Zane takes my hand in his and gently urges me to stand. Then, he gets down on one knee, and opens a ring box. "Maris, will you do me the honor of marrying me?"

I find myself staring at the ring, my mother's ring, that beautiful gold band with a radiant cut diamond that my father had made just for her, and somewhere in the haze of elation, I find myself wondering whether Zane got it from Annette or Lady Vivian. I used to try that ring on when I was younger. It looked wrong on my twelve-year-old hand, and I certainly never thought I would wear it because I thought it would still be on my mother's hand. When Zane slips it onto my finger, I realize that it finally looks "right" on my hand, and the only thing my brain can manage to think and my mouth manage to say is "Yes."

My ears fill with the applause of everyone in the room as Zane stands up, cups my cheek and chin with his hands, and kisses me just perfectly. When we manage to let go of each other, Brent slaps Zane on the back with a big smile, and I see that Uncle Lawrence is bawling his eyes out. I search the room for Harper, and when I spot her, she folds her hands over her heart and smiles.

"Well, I guess Trilland is going to have a new prince consort," says Secretary Johnson to the cheerful laughter of the room.

Zane loops his arm around my waist and pulls me close to him. "Happy?"

My face breaks into a smile. "Are you kidding? This is the perfect day. I want to remember this day forever."

Zane flashes me an impish grin. "Are you sure you won't forget or something?"

I kiss him again. "Positive."

~~~
~~~

Acknowledgements

When I first wrote *The Waves at My Window*, I thought it was going to be a stand-alone novel. I had no plans for a sequel. However, the moment I finished the first draft, I had the idea for *The Shadows at My Door*. I ended up writing the first draft pretty quickly during a very busy year of my life when writing a story about a princess felt a lot easier than everything else.

After I finished the draft, it sat on the proverbial shelf for years because (1) I started a new job and new Master's program and had no time to look at this, (2) I focused my attention on a different book that I knew had real potential (hello *Thank You for Applying*), and (3) I didn't think it was worth working on because I didn't think I could sell a sequel.

But over the months that *Waves* has been out, I've seen so many readers respond to the story. It's one of my bestsellers at events, and I've had several readers message me asking for a sequel. They had no idea one already existed. I decided that maybe I should dust it off and revisit the world of Trilland, and I've so enjoyed that process.

Thank you to readers who take a chance on my books just from seeing me at an in-person event or because we share mutual friends who hype me up to you. Thank you to readers who fangirl over my books, rant about characters, jump up and down with excitement, and tell me how much they love my books. You're a dream come true.

Thank you to my friends and family who consistently show up at book events, share my social media posts, and buy my books. It means more than you know. Thank you to Kayla Tirrell for being a phenomenal writing partner and friend. Thank you to Morgan Brownlee, Laina Strickland, Kristen Christensen, and Kelly Layne for being the best fan club of my books.

Thank you to my parents Brian and Sylvia and my sister Ashley for supporting all my wild book ideas. More to come, always.

About the author

When she's not writing books for YA readers, she's teaching them AP and DE English. Kristen Grafton is a Florida native with an MFA in Popular Fiction & Publishing and an MA in English Rhetoric. She was a triple major in college. She has an unhealthy obsession with her cats and Taylor Swift.

To learn more about Kristen Grafton, follow her on Instagram @kmgrafton1 and visit www.kristen mgrafton.com.

Also by Kristen Grafton

Young Adult

Adult Sweet Romance

TEN YEARS
FROM NOW
KRISTEN GRAFTON

Deck
the Shops
KRISTEN GRAFTON

www.ingramcontent.com/pod-product-compliance
Lightning Source LLC
Chambersburg PA
CBHW051317130726
47987CB00004B/1836